KU-707-482

The Garbage King

"Elizabeth Laird was born in New Zealand and moved to England when she was three. She has travelled to many parts of the world, and spent many years in Africa, the Middle East and India. The Garbage King was inspired by her experiences among the street children of Addis Ababa in Ethiopia.

Elizabeth has written many books for children. Her most recent book, Jake's Tower, was shortlisted for the Carnegie Medal and the Guardian Children's Fiction Prize."

the Garbage King

ELIZABETH LAIRD

ABERDEENSHIRE LIBRARIES

ABS 2015917

Heinemann
Inspiring generations

Heinemann is an imprint of Pearson
Education Limited, a company incorporated in England and Wales,
having its registered office at Edinburg Gate, Harlow, Essex,
CM20 2JE.Registered company number: 872828

Heinemann is the registered trademark of Pearson Education Limited

© Elizabeth Laird, 2003
The moral right of the author has been asserted.
First published in Great Britain by Macmillan Children's Books, 2003
First published in the New Windmills Series in 2004

6

British Library Cataloguing in Publication Data is available
from the British Library on request.

ISBN: 978 0 435130 54 1

Copyright notice
All rights reserved. No part of this publication may be reproduced in any form
or by any means (including photocopying or storing it in any medium by
electronic means and whether or not transiently or incidentally to some
other use of this publication) without the written permission of the
copyright owner, except in accordance with the provisions of the Copyright,
Designs and Patents Act 1988 or under the terms of a licence issued by the
Copyright Licensing Agency, 90 Tottenham Court Road, London W1T 4LP.
Applications for the copyright owner's written permission should
be addressed to the publisher.

Cover photo: Images of Africa
Cover design by Forepoint
Typeset by ✒ Tek-Art, Croydon, Surrey

Printed and bound in China (CTPS/06)

YA

AB2205917

Elizabeth Laird first travelled to Ethiopia in 1967, when the last Emperor, Haile Selassie, was still on the throne, and the dark days of war and famine were yet to come. She lived and worked in Addis Ababa, the capital city, for two years and travelled all over the country, on the tops of lorries, on buses, on horseback and on foot. She made many friends: farmers and their families, soldiers, students, teachers, street children and even princesses.

During the next three decades, Ethiopians suffered all the horrors of a long civil war and a devastating famine. But when peace came at last, Elizabeth went back. She revisited some of the places she had known and tried to find old friends. Some had fled the country, others had died, but she found several, including two happy and successful men who had begged from her when they were children on the streets. They showed her that sad stories can have happy endings.

Since then, Elizabeth Laird has often returned to Ethiopia, travelling from one end of the country to the other. She has made friends with many more people, among them a group of street children who live rough in Addis Ababa. They told her about their lives, showed her their 'pitch', introduced her to their dog and talked to her about their hopes and fears.

Glossary

Shamma – a thick white cotton shawl, used by men and women as an extra coat or blanket
Amharic – the national language of Ethiopia
Injera – a kind of flat pancake that Ethiopian people eat at every meal instead of bread
Ato – Mr
Tej – an alcoholic drink made with honey
Godana – a person who lives on the street; a beggar

*For the street children
of Addis Ababa*

Chapter 1

There was no light in the shack, none at all, except when the moon was shining. Mamo could see chinks of it then, through the gaps in the corrugated-iron roof.

But the moon wasn't out tonight. Mamo shivered, pulled the ragged blanket over his head and huddled against his sister's warm body. Tiggist had been facing away from him, but she turned over to lie on her back, the bare straw mattress rustling as she moved. He knew she was awake. He knew her eyes were open, and that she was staring up into the pitch-darkness.

'What are we going to do?' he said.

'I don't know.'

It was a week since their mother had died. Mamo hadn't felt much about it. Ma had been either sick or drunk for as long as he could remember, and he'd kept out of her way if he could, scared of her sudden, violent rages.

Tiggist was the person he loved. Years ago, when he was little, she'd staggered around with him on her hip, though she was hardly more than a toddler herself. She'd always looked out for him, saw that he was fed, picked him up when he fell over and screeched at anyone who threatened to hurt him.

'You're not going off, Tiggist, are you?' he said, his stomach suddenly contracting. 'You're not going to leave me?'

'I don't know,' she said again.

A black hole seemed to open up in front of Mamo. He wanted to push her, to force her to make promises, but there was a note in his sister's voice that he'd never heard before. It shrivelled him up. His skin was prickling all over.

'The rent's due next week,' she said. 'It's fifty birr. How are we going to find fifty birr?'

Fifty birr! Mamo had never seen so much money in his life.

'What'll they do,' he said, 'if we can't pay?'

'What do you think? They'll throw us out.'

'Where'll we go?'

'Oh, shut up, Mamo. How do I know? Work it out for yourself.'

The sharpness in her voice shocked him and made him feel even worse. He didn't dare speak again.

'I'll go to Mrs Faridah tomorrow,' Tiggist said at last. 'She got me to deliver stuff to her customers last week. She might give me a job. I could sleep in her shop.'

Mamo swallowed, and moved abruptly away from her.

'I wouldn't go without you, though.'

He could hear the uncertainty in her voice, and his fear turned to fury. He rolled right away from her, taking the blanket with him, and clenched his fists.

'Well, what do you want me to do?' She sounded angry herself. 'Work in a bar? Paint my face up and do it with the customers round the back? What else is there?'

He hadn't thought about it. He'd assumed they'd go on like before, that somehow Tiggist would do what their mother had done, rustle up the money for the rent each month, and scrape together enough every day for something to eat.

'I'll work,' he muttered. 'I'll get a shoe-shine kit.'

She snorted.

'Who's going to pay for a shoe-shine kit? And how will you get a pitch? You know how those boys fight over them. You wouldn't stand a chance.'

He stuffed his fingers into his ears. He couldn't bear to hear any more. Tiggist pulled at the blanket and he rolled back towards her so that it covered them both again. The old straw in the bare mattress beneath them rustled as they moved.

'If we're not careful,' Tiggist said, in a voice that was barely more than a whisper, 'we'll end up on the streets.'

The sun had come up at last, bringing warmth after the cold night, and the smoke from thousands of breakfast fires, all over Addis Ababa, spiralled up into the bright morning air. Mamo pulled at the piece of sharp-edged corrugated iron which formed the door of the shack. It creaked open, and he stepped outside into the narrow lane, blinking in the bright light.

He stood uncertainly, watching people hurrying off to their day's work. He ignored the crowds of chattering school children in their bright blue uniforms, who carried piles of crumpled books under their arms. He'd only gone to school for a couple of years, and he'd left for good ages ago when he was eight years old. There'd been no money since then to pay the fees. He'd long since forgotten the letters he'd begun to learn there.

He was more interested in the adults. There must be someone, among the clerks in their cotton-drill suits, the motherly women off to market, and the young secretaries and shop-girls with their bright knitted sweaters – among all these people there had to be someone who might help him, who would know what to do.

Tiggist had been gone at least half an hour by now. She'd washed her face and hands, tidied her hair and tried to scrub some of the stains out of her old skirt. Then she'd gone off to see Mrs Faridah. He could tell, watching the stiffness in her back as she walked quickly away from him down the stony lane, that she was tense with nerves.

Usually, Mamo went down to the street corner in the morning. He knew some of the boys that hung around there. They spent the long hours commenting on passers-by, or playing games on a chipped old game board, or begging off anyone well-dressed who walked past. Sometimes he went the other way, to the music shop. He'd sit on the wall outside, drinking in the melodies that poured out through the open door, singing along with them under his breath. Today, though, he felt too anxious to go anywhere.

He realised suddenly that he was hungry, and went inside. Tiggist had left some bread wrapped up in a plastic bag on the only shelf in the shack. He reached up for it, then poured himself some water from the jar in the corner. He sat down on the little stool beside the dead ashes in the hearth, which was in the middle of the earth floor, and began to eat.

The light streaming in through the doorway was suddenly blocked out. Mamo looked up, and saw the silhouette of a man. It was impossible to make out his face against the glare outside, but Mamo knew at once that he was a stranger.

'Hello,' the man said, stooping under the low lintel and stepping inside. 'Are you Mamo?'

His voice was high and light, almost jaunty.

Mamo nodded cautiously.

'Where's your father?' the man said.

Mamo could see him properly now. He was wearing a suit jacket over a green-and-brown striped shirt, and his shoes were made of leather and were well shined. When he lifted his hand, a big watch on a loose bracelet strap slid up his wrist.

'My father?' Mamo repeated, puzzled. 'He's dead, I think. In the army. Years ago.'

The man smiled. His face was thin, and his lips were twisted by a faint scar that ran down his cheek. His eyes were darting around the inside of the shack.

'Who are you, anyway?' Mamo said. He was beginning to feel uncomfortable.

The man turned his smile on him again, and it broadened.

'I'm your uncle. Don't you know me? Your mother's brother, Merga. Didn't she tell you about me?'

'No. She never said.'

Merga had crossed the floor with two strides and was running his eye along the shelf.

'Where did she keep her things?'

'What things? She didn't have any things.'

Merga bent down and lifted a corner of the mattress.

'Don't get cheeky with me.' His voice was hardening. 'Her radio. Money. Gold jewellery. Anything. Don't tell me this is all she had. One mattress. One stool. One blanket. A water jar. A couple of pans and spoons and glasses.'

'I told you,' said Mamo, backing towards the door. 'She didn't have anything. Nothing.'

'Who's going to pay me back, then?' Merga straightened up and stared down at Mamo.

'Pay you back? What for?'

'The money I lent her.'

'What money?'

'Last month. She came and begged 100 birr off me.'

His eyes had shifted sideways.

He's lying, thought Mamo, and took another sideways step towards the door.

Merga's hand shot out and caught his wrist. He smiled again, and the hardness left his voice. It was soft again. Affectionate, almost.

'Look,' he said, 'it's all right about the money. You're only a kid. I don't expect you to pay it back. I didn't come about that, anyway. I want to help you, see? I'm your uncle. I want to see you right. What are you planning to do? Now that she's gone?'

Mamo breathed deeply with relief, and felt his shoulders relax. He'd been wrong to be suspicious. This man was family. A relative. Someone he could trust.

'I don't know,' he said. 'Get a shoe-shine kit, maybe.'

Merga laughed and shook his head.

'Polishing shoes? Na – you can do better than that. I'll get you a job. A proper one. Decent food and nice people. What do you think about that?'

Mamo's heart, which had weighed heavily inside him since he'd woken up that morning, suddenly felt lighter inside his chest. This was like a miracle! He'd been looking hopelessly at the passers-by only half an hour ago, dreaming of a chance like this, and it had walked right in through the door.

'You mean it? You really can? Get me a job? Where? What would I have to do?'

'You'll see,' Merga said. 'Come on. I'll take you there now.'

Quickly, worried in case this heaven-sent stranger should change his mind, Mamo reached into the corner behind the water jar and pulled out his shoes. They were nearly too small for him, and he didn't bother to wear them most of the time, but they'd make a good impression, maybe, on his new employer.

He put them on, tied the laces, and stood up.

Merga was looking at him critically.

'How old are you? Ten? Eleven?'

'I don't know. Thirteen, I think.'

'Bit small for your age, aren't you?'

Mamo tried to straighten his back.

'I'm strong,' he said anxiously. 'I can carry a good load.'

'All right. Come on.' Merga took a last look round and shook his head. 'What a dump.'

Mamo's heart was beating fast with excitement as he followed Merga outside. He pulled the door shut on its protesting hinges and fixed the padlock. Merga was already setting off up the narrow lane when Mrs Hannah came out of the little house next door.

'Are you all right, Mamo?' she said kindly, hitching the baby, who was tied to her back, further up towards her shoulders.

'Yes, my uncle's come,' Mamo said proudly. 'He's got me a job. We're going to see about it now.'

'Your uncle?' Mrs Hannah looked at Merga with surprise. 'That's good. I hope it works out. Come and tell me about it tonight. I'll have some supper for you both if you like.'

'Mamo!' Merga had walked on, and was calling back sharply.

'Tell Tiggist if she gets back before I do!' cried Mamo, and he ran after Merga, up the lane.

'Who was that?' Merga said, when at last he'd caught him up.

'Our neighbour, Mrs Hannah. She's really kind. She—' began Mamo.

'And Tiggist, who's she?'

Mamo's eyes widened.

'My sister. Didn't you know?'

'Of course. I'd forgotten.' Merga looked pleased. 'How old is she?'

'Older than me. Sixteen, maybe.'

'Where is she?'

'She went to look for a job this morning. At the grocery store. Mrs Faridah—'

'That'll do. Stop chattering.'

Mamo had been feeling more and more expansive, his feet, pinched as they were in his old shoes, skipping lightly over the stones. Questions were boiling up inside him, but he kept them to himself.

Rosy dreams were flowering in his mind. Perhaps he'd be working in a pastry shop, one with a brightly painted front, and he'd wear a little bow tie, and serve customers with those luscious cakes and steaming cups of coffee he so loved to smell as he passed their open doors. Or

7

perhaps it would be in one of those furniture-making places, and he'd learn to make beds and chairs like the ones displayed on the pavement. More likely, he told himself, trying to be sensible, he'd be a porter in the market. Well, he could manage that. He was strong, whatever his uncle thought of his size.

It wasn't long before he was away from the familiar streets and lanes where he'd always lived, and a little shoot of anxiety began to sprout in his chest. How would he find his way home? He began to look carefully around for landmarks, noticing big buildings, colourful signs in shop windows and brightly flowering shrubs hanging over fences.

'Is it far?' he said at last, looking timidly up at Merga.

A bus roared past at that moment, belching out clouds of black exhaust, and Merga didn't appear to hear him. Instead, he grabbed Mamo by the arm and propelled him across the road. To his surprise, Mamo found himself in the crowded, noisy bus station.

Perhaps I'll work in the office, taking the ticket money, he thought, his excitement rising again. Or maybe we're going right through here to the garage over there, and I'll be the boy that does the petrol pumps.

He followed Merga through the ever-thickening crowd, dodging between groups of long-distance passengers and their bulging bundles, trying not to bump into peanut sellers and ticket touts.

It happened so quickly that Mamo had no time to react. One moment he was squeezing past a big red-and-gold bus, half deafened by the throbbing of the engine, and the next moment he felt Merga's hand close like a vice on his collar, and he was being thrust up the steps into the bus, and pushed down the crowded aisle to a couple of seats at the very back.

Merga pushed him down into the seat by the window and sat down beside him. Mamo turned a shocked face towards him. He couldn't understand what was happening. He was only aware of a frightening cold feeling that was growing in the pit of his stomach.

'Where are we going?' he said. 'This isn't an Addis bus. It goes out to the country. Where are you taking me? I want to get out. I've got to get back to Tiggist.'

But Merga's grip was tighter than ever. He was holding Mamo down in his seat. Now he thrust his face right into Mamo's, and Mamo smelled for the first time stale alcohol and a waft of old tobacco.

'Want to make a fuss?' he hissed. 'If you do, I'll tie your hands and feet. I'll say you're a runaway. You'll shut up if you know what's good for you. You said you wanted a job, and that's what you're going to get. You ought to be damn grateful, you snivelling little beggar.'

The throb of the engine changed suddenly to a deafening roar. The conductor slammed the door shut, and it began to move, turning quickly out of the bus station on to the main road out of Addis Ababa, away from everything and everyone that Mamo had ever known.

In another part of Addis Ababa, just off the magnificent avenue, blazing with flowering trees, that sweeps down the hill past the president's palace, another boy was sitting on the edge of a swimming pool in the grounds of a big hotel, dangling his legs in the water.

All around, children were playing and splashing noisily. A boy from his school, lithe and handsome, ran up behind him, leaped high into the air, his slim brown legs working like scissors, and landed in the water with a gigantic splash, swamping the boy and the other bobbing heads nearby. He surfaced and shook the water out of his eyes.

'Dani! Dani!' he chanted, looking mockingly at the boy. 'Fat boy! Can't swim!'

Dani hunched his plump shoulders and stared down at the pool. The sun, sparkling on the water, shot out almost painful sparks of light. He looked sideways. There was a shallower pool nearby. Meseret, his little sister, was strutting through it. She was wearing a pink bathing costume, and a pair of waterwings clung to her arms like giant puffed sleeves. Her hair, tightly plaited all over her head, was decorated with orange bobbles.

'Look, Mama!' she called out to the woman lying motionless nearby on a lounger under a striped umbrella. 'I'm a crocodile!'

Dani looked over his shoulder at his mother. She had raised her hand and was waving it slowly at Meseret. Then she tucked it back under the shawl that was wrapped round her shoulders. She must be the only person beside this crowded pool to feel cold on such a hot day.

Zeni, the maid, had been sitting next to her on an upright chair. She got up quickly and went to the edge of the paddling pool.

'Don't disturb Mama, darling,' she said to Meseret. 'She's resting.' Then she looked over towards Dani.

'Are you going to sit there all day?' she called out loudly. 'Why don't you go in?'

Dani's face felt hot with shame. Reluctantly, he shifted his bottom closer to the edge, then forced himself to slide over the side into the water. He sank immediately and kicked out wildly. Mercifully, his feet hit the bottom of the pool at once and he righted himself. The water wasn't very deep. It only came halfway up his shoulders. He began to move his arms, pretending to swim, while keeping one foot on the bottom.

He reached the far side of the pool and hauled himself out again. Then he took up his old position, sitting on the edge with his legs in the water. At least he was on the opposite side from Meseret and Zeni now. There were fewer children on this side too.

Several European women were lying out in the sun, grilling their pink oiled skin, their straw coloured hair looking brittle and stiff. Beyond them, in the shade of a tree, sat two Ethiopian women, talking with their heads together.

Dani let his mind wander away into a daydream. The sounds of the pool, the splashes, the squeals of children, the occasional trilling of a mobile phone, the bursts of laughter from the adults lounging around the pool enclosure, and the murmur of waiters circulating among them, faded away.

He was standing in front of a burning building. Flames were shooting out of the windows, and smoke was billowing up into the sky. His father was calling out, 'They're in there! Meseret and your mother! They'll burn to death!'

He was dashing into the building, fighting his way through the heat and smoke, braving instant death. His mother and sister were cowering in a corner.

'Come with me,' he said. 'You'll be all right.'

He was picking Meseret up now, and pulling his mother by the hand. As they emerged, choking, into the open air, his father ran forward.

'Dani! You've saved them!' he was crying. Then, as Dani sank in a dead faint at his father's feet, he heard him murmur, 'I'm sorry, son. I've misjudged you. That was the bravest thing I ever saw.'

His mother's name jerked him back to reality.

'Ruth,' he heard someone say.

He looked round. The two Ethiopian women were looking across the pool towards where his mother lay on her lounger, wrapped in her shawl. The pool had momentarily almost emptied itself, the noise had died down, and he could suddenly hear their conversation quite clearly.

'Yes, that's her. That's Ruth,' one of them was saying. 'Poor thing. Look at her. You can see from here how sick she is.'

'What is it? Cancer?' said the other one.

'No. Heart, someone told me. She needs an operation. She'd have to go to Europe or America for it.'

'But that would cost a fortune!'

'Oh, there's plenty of money. Paulos has done all right. I'm glad I'm not married to him, though.'

'I know. He scares me stiff. Those eyes! Every time I see him I feel I'm in court, up before the judge. He probably thinks poor little Ruth should pull herself together and stop malingering.'

'Oh, I don't know. My cousin's great friends with Ruth. She says he absolutely adores her, in his starchy sort of way. He'd take her off abroad tomorrow for treatment, only he's scared she won't survive the journey.'

'That bad? Sad, isn't it?'

'Yes, awful. Waiter! Over here! We ordered a club sandwich and a couple of Pepsis at least half an hour ago.'

The pool had filled up with children again, and Dani couldn't hear the women's voices any longer. He didn't want to, anyway. What did those stupid cows know about his mother? They'd only been gossiping. Women would say anything once they got going.

He looked over towards his mother's lounger. Zeni was bending over her, holding out a plateful of snacks. Without being able to hear, he knew she was coaxing his mother to eat.

Then he saw someone else. His father was walking in through the entrance to the enclosure, past the guard, who was standing to attention in his gold-braided uniform as if he was a soldier who had just seen a general. His father had spotted his mother at once, and was walking towards her, his firm tread radiating power. His tall, spare form was immaculately dressed in white tennis clothes, and he was carrying a heavy sports bag from which the handle of a racket was protruding.

Silently, Dani levered himself down into the water, and pretended to swim again, making purposeful movements with his arms. Out of the corner of his eye he could see that his father had reached his mother's lounger, and was standing still, looking down at her.

Dani reached their side of the pool. He could hear their conversation from here.

'Are you all right?'

'Yes. Fine.'

'What about your headache?'

'It's nearly better.'

'Did you eat something this morning?'

'Of course. I've been stuffing myself on all these snacks. And I walked all the way down to the pool without any help.'

She was trying to please him. It had taken two of the hotel staff, one on each side, to get her down the steps and through the hotel gardens.

'Good. Well done. Where's Dani?'

'In the pool. He's been swimming for hours. He must be worn out.'

Dani's heart glowed with gratitude. She always stood up for him. He looked away, and tried even harder to make it seem as if he was swimming. His father was frowning critically at him, he knew.

'Call that swimming?' He winced at the scorn in his father's voice. 'The boy's hopeless. I'd pay for a teacher only I know it would be a waste of money. Dani!' He had raised his voice. 'Come on out. It's time to go home. Zeni, get Meseret. We can't waste the whole day lounging around here.'

Dani floundered to the ladder at the side of the pool and climbed up it. He looked up briefly into his father's eyes, then looked down again. If he let his father read the fear and resentment in his face it would only make things worse. He picked up the towel and his bundle of clothes, lying on the grass under Zeni's chair, and moved off towards one of the changing rooms, a pretty booth made to look like a typical rural Ethiopian farmer's hut.

I hate him. I really do hate him, he muttered guiltily to himself, as he pulled on his T-shirt and shorts.

As he left the booth, he looked up at the sky. A fan-shaped cloud was blowing up across the vast expanse of blue sky, and a sudden sharp breeze was stirring the red hibiscus flowers in the hedges by the entrance to the pool. It almost looked as if it might rain.

Chapter 2

The bus, with Mamo and Merga on board, was two hours into its journey when the rain began. It came on with such fury and suddenness that the driver nearly skidded off the narrow ribbon of road into one of the fields of fresh green barley that stretched away into the distance.

The drops slashed against the window at the back of the bus where Mamo was squashed in beside Merga. He stared at it unseeingly. Like everything else that had happened today, it seemed unreal. Unbelievable. As if he was in the worst kind of dream.

While the bus had been weaving through the crowded outskirts of Addis Ababa, hooting its way through the dense traffic, Mamo had kept struggling, trying to get past Merga and force his way to the door. He had stormed and wept and even shouted out that he was being kidnapped, and pleaded with the passengers around to help him. But Merga had made a joke of it, telling everyone that Mamo was a runaway, and that he was taking him home to his father, to get the thrashing he deserved.

The whole bus had obviously believed him. Even if Mamo had been able to get past Merga, he'd have been stopped by a dozen others before he could possibly have reached the door.

He'd given up at last. He'd stared out of the window with a growing feeling of helpless desperation as the bus had ground up the steep mountain road above the city, leaving the familiar tangle of streets behind, to emerge at the top on to a vast high plateau stretching emptily away on all sides. He'd never been out in the countryside before. It terrified him.

He started going over everything in his mind, from the moment Merga's dark shape had appeared in the doorway. Was Merga really his uncle after all? His mother had never said anything about having a brother. She'd never mentioned any relatives at all. And if Merga was her brother, why had he asked about Mamo's father? Didn't he know that his father had disappeared, almost as soon as Mamo had been born? And why hadn't Merga ever heard of Tiggist? But then, on the other hand, if Merga wasn't his mother's brother, how did he know she had died? How did he know Mamo's name? Why had he come? If he'd been just a thief, looking for stuff to steal, why had he paid a fortune in bus fares to take the two of them all this way out of Addis Ababa? Maybe there was nothing to worry about. Perhaps it could turn out all right after all.

'Where are we?' he asked for the hundredth time. 'Where are we going? How much farther is it?'

'Stop your play-acting,' Merga said loudly, looking sideways at the man crammed into the seat on the opposite side to Mamo. 'You know where we're going. Home to your father, you little rascal.'

Mamo shivered. He hadn't been wrong. Merga wouldn't talk like that if he only wanted to help him.

The rain was long since over when at last they stopped. Mamo had no idea how many hours had passed. It had seemed like a lifetime. He followed Merga off the bus.

They were standing on a dusty patch of open ground in what seemed to be the middle of a little town. Single storey shops ran along the dirt road in both directions, but they soon petered out into open country.

Mamo's heart began to thump. Now, perhaps, was his chance to make a break for it. His eyes darted about, looking for a sign, a clue, for anything that might give him an idea.

16

A couple of trucks were pulled up on the far side of the road, facing back the way the bus had come. Maybe, if he managed to give Merga the slip, he could sneak under the tarpaulin into the back of one of them, and hitch a secret ride back to Addis Ababa. Or perhaps he could hide somewhere in the town – anywhere – and get on to the next bus home. He'd try to creep under one of the seats, so that the conductor wouldn't see him and throw him off for not being able to pay.

Not many other passengers had left the bus in this little place. A few had jumped off to run into the bar nearby, to grab a glass of tea or visit the toilet. The bus was sounding its horn now, trying to hurry them back on board. Perhaps, thought Mamo, he could pretend he needed the toilet too, and once inside the bar he could run through to the back, climb over the wall, and get away.

'I need to go in there, to the toilet,' he said to Merga, edging away from him towards the door of the bar.

Merga's hand shot out and caught his arm in a vicious grip above the shoulder.

'You can wait,' he said. 'I know what you're up to. What's your problem, anyway? I thought you wanted a job? Look at all the trouble I'm going to to get you one.'

The last passengers hurried back and climbed aboard. The conductor shut the door. The old engine coughed and wheezed as the bus lumbered off down the road. As Mamo watched it go, cold desolation swept over him. The bus was his last link with Addis Ababa, with Tiggist and home. Its chugging noise had begun to sound almost comforting. Now he was surrounded by a horrible eerie silence, like nothing he'd ever known before, used as he was to the constant din of the city.

Merga, still gripping his arm, was standing still, turning his head impatiently as he looked in turn in each direction. He seemed to be waiting for someone.

At last he gave a grunt, and set off at a fast pace down the road, dragging Mamo along with him. A middle-aged man was coming towards them. He was dressed like a farmer, with a heavy white *shamma* draped round his shoulders. He carried a thick stick, and his feet, below the ragged legs of his trousers, were bare.

Merga stopped when they reached him.

'Good day.'

'Good day.'

'How are you?'

'I'm well.'

'How is everything?'

'All is well, thank God.'

'Thank God.'

They exchanged the usual greetings quickly, without enthusiasm. The man spoke Amharic with a slow country accent, quite different from the fast city patter Mamo was used to.

'This is the boy, then?' the farmer said, looking critically at Mamo. 'Bit small, isn't he?'

Merga laughed.

'He's strong. Look at him! Fourteen last month.' He held up the arm he was still holding for the farmer to inspect.

'Hm.' The farmer frowned down at Mamo, but his eyes were not unkind. 'What work have you done before?'

'Oh, all kind of things,' Merga broke in quickly, before Mamo could say a word. 'Running errands, portering, helping out round the cattle market . . .'

'No, I—' objected Mamo, but Merga's fingers bit even deeper into his arm, and he subsided.

'All right.' The farmer jerked his head. 'It's a deal.'

He reached a hand under his voluminous *shamma*, looking for the pocket in his shirt. He pulled out a thin wad of notes and counted them into Merga's hand.

Mamo suddenly understood. Merga was selling him! He was being sold! He'd been snatched away from Addis

Ababa and Tiggist just so that this – this people thief could make some money!

For a moment, he was too shocked to react.

Merga was staring down incredulously at the money in his hand.

'What's this? We agreed on 150 birr!'

'130,' said the farmer.

'150!' Merga waved the notes derisively in the other man's face. 'And the bus fares. Two of us out to here, and my return.'

The farmer shrugged.

'It's all I've got. It'll have to do. Take him back if you don't like it.'

Mamo was suddenly warmed by a brief flame of hope flaring up inside him.

'A bargain's a bargain.' Merga was scowling now. 'Look at all the trouble I've gone to, coming out all this way . . .'

'All right.' The farmer smiled sourly. 'If you want the rest of the money you'll have to come and fetch it. From my house. It'll be a long walk in those fancy shoes.'

Merga hesitated. The farmer's grin widened. It seemed to flick Merga on the raw.

'Let's go then,' he said angrily. 'What are we waiting for?'

'You won't get another bus back to Addis tonight, if you come home with me,' the farmer said, looking uneasy now.

'You'll have to put me up then, won't you?' said Merga. 'I'll come home with you, get the money, and go back to Addis in the morning.'

The hope in Mamo's heart dwindled to nothing. There was to be no way out. This man was his new boss, his master. Working for him was to be his new life. He was going to be a farm boy, and live miles away from anywhere.

Merga's hand, which hadn't slackened its grip all this while, moved now from his arm up to his collar. Mamo felt it like a shackle on his neck. It would be impossible for him to break away.

All the terrible things he'd ever heard about the wild lands outside the city came flooding into his mind. Hyenas and jackals roamed about at night, people said. Everyone had to work from dawn to dusk. When the rains failed to come, the people starved.

A sob rose in his chest. He swallowed it down. He mustn't let himself give in yet. There might still be a chance to escape, if he kept his wits about him.

They were walking fast out of the little town now. Rolling countryside stretched out on all sides, frighteningly vast and empty, while above the sky seemed more huge and distant than it ever had at home. The track they were following was uneven and littered with large stones. Merga suddenly stumbled over one of these, and for a moment his grip on Mamo's collar slackened.

In an instant, Mamo had snatched his chance. He broke free and gathered himself to run, but before he had taken a single step, the farmer had thrust his stick between his legs, tripping him up. Mamo fell full length on the ground, grazing both his hands.

'Here, you hold him,' the farmer growled to Merga.

He reached under his *shamma* again and pulled out a length of rope. Quickly, he tied one end of it round Mamo's neck.

'Try running away again,' he said with dry humour, 'and you'll end up strangling yourself.'

The next couple of hours seemed to Mamo to last for ever. He was exhausted, famished and parched with thirst, and his feet were horribly pinched inside his old shoes. His throat was tight with misery, and his heart felt like lead inside his chest. His face burned with shame at the feel of the rope round his neck. He felt like a slave. An animal. A thing.

I've been sold, he kept thinking, the words running round and round in his head. Like a donkey, or a goat. That man sold me. He just put me up for sale and sold me. Like a sack of flour.

It was nearly dark when at last the farmer turned off the rough track they'd been following for the last hour. Mamo stumbled after him, up a narrow path between two fields. Thick cactus hedges, too high to see over, grew on each side of it.

The lane turned a sharp corner and suddenly, in front of them, was the entrance to a small compound. Two huts, their mud walls crumbling and their thatch thin and ragged with age, were clustered together inside a thick thorn and cactus fence. Three or four cows and a few sheep and goats turned their heads to look at the new arrivals, and a little boy with thin legs and a big round belly, naked except for a ragged shift that barely reached his belly button, let out a frightened wail at the sight of the strangers and bolted into the biggest of the huts.

A woman came out, wiping her hands on the long gathered skirt of her dress.

'Is this the boy, then?' she said to the farmer. 'What's his name?'

'Mamo,' said Merga, stepping forward. He and the farmer seemed to have buried their mutual resentment. They had been talking in a friendly enough manner for the last half hour of the journey.

The woman exchanged the usual greetings with Merga, but with little enthusiasm. She didn't seem surprised to see him, but threw her husband a look that seemed to say, 'I told you so'.

'Come in,' she said, leading the way into the hut.

Casually, as if he was unbridling a horse, the farmer untied the rope from Mamo's neck, and Mamo, whose spirits had lifted just a little at the thought that at least he might now get a drink and something to eat, followed the others inside.

Darkness had already fallen with African suddenness when Tiggist came hurrying home down the little lane.

On the one hand she was bursting with her news. On the other, she wasn't sure how Mamo was going to take it.

She undid the padlock and went inside. The shack was empty, but she wasn't surprised. Mamo would be somewhere around, with a neighbour, maybe, or hanging about outside the little shop by the main road, which sold CDs and cassettes. He liked sitting on the wall up there, listening to the music which blared out all day long from the makeshift loudspeakers.

She lit the lamp and set it on the rickety table, then took the bread Mrs Faridah had given her out of the plastic bag she'd been carrying. The bread would be stale and unsaleable by tomorrow, so it meant nothing to Mrs Faridah to let her take it, but it had been kind of her to add a few eggs as well. There'd be supper enough for both of them tonight.

She set about lighting the fire so she could cook the eggs, listening out for Mamo. Then she heard steps outside the shack.

'Mamo!' she called out. 'Come in. I've got so much to tell you.'

It was Mrs Hannah, though, who answered her.

'There you are, dear,' she said, stepping into the shack, her baby balanced on her hip. 'I came to see if you and Mamo wanted some supper. There's plenty for you both.'

Tiggist had been squatting by the fire, feeding it with sticks, but she stood up to hug Mrs Hannah.

'You've been so nice to us,' she said. 'I don't know what we'd have done.'

Mrs Hannah patted her shoulder.

'I know what it's like to lose your mother,' she said. 'Even when . . . You're a brave girl. I'd help you more if I could.'

Tiggist stepped back and beamed at her.

'I won't need anyone to help me now,' she said. 'Everything's going to be fine. I went to see Mrs Faridah today. She's given me a job! I'm going to work in her shop, run errands, help round the back, even serve customers when she's shown me how. She's going to get me a new dress tomorrow, and some shoes, and she says I can sleep in the storeroom.'

The baby had started to grizzle. Mrs Hannah gave him her knuckle to suck and beamed back at Tiggist.

'That's wonderful! Quite frankly, my dear, I was worried about you. I didn't see how you were going to manage. Let's hope your uncle finds something as good for Mamo.'

'My uncle?' Tiggist looked puzzled. 'What uncle?'

'He came round this morning. Said he'd got a job for Mamo. Mamo went off with him to see about it.'

'That's funny,' Tiggist said slowly. 'We haven't got any uncles. Not that I know about. We never knew anyone from my father's family. He came from up north. And Ma said both her brothers were killed in the war.'

'Perhaps it was a cousin then, or a friend even,' Mrs Hannah said comfortably. 'Mamo will tell us all about it when he comes back, if he ever does. You know what boys are like. They take off suddenly and never bother to let their families know they're all right.'

'Yes,' said Tiggist, her face clearing. 'It's a bit of a relief, to be honest. Mrs Faridah said she'd let him sleep in the shop with me till he got fixed up, but I could see she wasn't very keen. I can't believe it! Both of us getting a job in one day! I hope his is as nice as mine. I'm moving into the shop tomorrow. If Mamo doesn't get back till I've gone, will you tell him where I am?'

'You're giving this place up then?' said Mrs Hannah, looking round at the dingy walls and uneven mud floor.

'Oh yes,' said Tiggist happily. 'It's a horrible house anyway. I won't miss it at all. Except for you, of course. But I'll come and see you sometimes, when I can. It's going to be so lovely, working for Mrs Faridah! She's got the sweetest little baby (not as nice as yours, of course), and I'm going to look after her sometimes when

Mrs Faridah's busy. Can I really come to supper with you? I want to tell you everything – all about the shop, and my dress, and the place where I'm going to sleep.'

There was no light in the farmer's house except for the fire, which burned brightly in the middle of the floor. A boy was squatting in one corner, and sitting on the mud platform that ran right round the inside wall of the house was a girl, a little younger than Mamo. The boy was wearing a school uniform. They both turned and stared at him curiously, but did not smile.

The farmer's wife brought out a small stool for Merga and set it by the fire. No one spoke to Mamo. He stood awkwardly by the floor, not knowing what to do.

The farmer nodded at him.

'Get the cows inside,' he said.

'I don't know how,' muttered Mamo, embarrassed.

'Show him,' the farmer said to the boy.

The boy picked up his father's stick and pushed past Mamo. Mamo followed him outside The boy unlatched the door of the second, smaller hut. He went round behind the cows and waved the stick towards their rumps.

'Hedj! Get in!' he said, in a bored voice.

Mamo jumped back as the cows passed him, scared of their long horns. The boy stared at him disdainfully.

'Not scared of them, are you?'

Mamo didn't bother to answer.

The sheep and goats followed the cows automatically into the hut, in which a donkey was already standing, its head lowered as if it was asleep. Without another word, the boy latched the door and returned to the house. Mamo followed him.

Merga, the farmer and an old man were sitting around a large tray, sharing a flat *injera* pancake and some spicy stews set out on it. Almost faint with hunger, Mamo moved over to join them.

'What's up with you?' the farmer's wife said, frowning at him. 'You'll eat later, after me and the little ones.'

'Please,' said Mamo, 'can I have some water? I'm very thirsty.'

'The jar's in the corner,' the woman said, pointing to it with her chin.

Mamo drank from the horn cup by the water jar, then sat down in the shadows against the wall, put his arms round his knees and dropped his head down on them. Misery engulfed him. Loneliness washed over him. Tears trickled down his face, making two dark channels through the grey dust that coated it. He didn't sniff in case the sharp-eyed children saw him cry, but moved his head from side to side to wipe his nose and eyes on his knees.

Underneath the misery, anger was beginning to burn. He felt it warm his heart and stiffen his thoughts. He'd been cheated. Tricked. Stolen. But he wasn't going to give in to his fate. Somehow, one day, he'd get away from here. Then he'd find Merga and take his revenge.

The three men finished eating at last. His heart sinking, Mamo saw that there was almost nothing left on the tray. The woman took it across to the children, and shared the last morsels with them, then she went behind the screen that stretched across the far end of the round room and came out with four roasted corn cobs.

'Here you are,' she said, giving one to each of them, one to Mamo and keeping one for herself.

Mamo hadn't eaten anything since the bread he'd found at breakfast time. He fell on the corn ravenously. It barely touched his hunger. He waited, hoping for more, but nothing else appeared. The children seemed disappointed too, but they looked nervously towards their father and didn't dare complain.

Everyone was getting ready to sleep. They moved to the mud platforms at the edge of the hut and lay down on the cowskins that covered them. Mamo lay down too.

'All right,' the farmer said, looking down at him. 'Tonight you can stay in here, but from tomorrow you sleep with the cattle and guard them.' For a moment, the firelight caught a fleeting smile on his lean dark face that was almost understanding. 'Don't look so tragic. It's a hard life out here after the city, but you'll get used to it. If you're a good boy and work hard you'll find I'm a fair master. I'll only beat you for a proper reason.'

Mamo lay down, and silently turned his face to the wall.

Chapter 3

The worst thing about school, thought Dani, was the way people were impatient with you all the time. For some reason, he didn't know why, everyone always seemed to get exasperated.

'Daniel, you haven't forgotten your dictionary again?' Ato Markos would say, his thick eyebrows meeting in a frown above his long nose. 'How are you ever going to learn English when you keep leaving your books at home?'

He heard the same irritated note in the voice of the other boys.

'Are you crazy? Don't pick him,' they'd whisper, when a game of football was being planned. 'If he ever managed to kick a ball his foot would drop off with surprise.'

Even old Ibrahim, the taxi driver who picked him up from home to take him to school every morning, and collected him at the school gate every afternoon, had started to get at him. He spoke a funny sort of Amharic, with a thick accent from the south, but his meaning was perfectly clear.

'You should make the best of yourself,' he kept saying. 'Don't waste your opportunities. If I had the money to send my kids to school, I'd make them work till they came top of the class every time.'

Why is it, thought Dani, as he stared blindly out of the window of the taxi, that everyone wants something different from you? And when you try to do what you think they want, to keep them happy, it sort of slips out of reach, and goes wrong?

It had been like that today. He had really, really tried in his science class. The teacher was white, a young American, who usually smiled all the time, but his smile always seemed to slip when it rested on Dani.

'Are you following me here, big guy?' he'd said. 'This electron carries a negative charge – minus one. Have you got that?'

Dani had nodded, but he hadn't really got it at all. The trouble with English was that the words seemed to muddle themselves up when people, especially foreigners, spoke quickly. He thought he knew what they meant, then doubts crept in, and his mind sort of froze, and he ended up not being sure of anything. Not even the simplest sentence.

'OK,' the teacher had gone on. 'So if the electrons flow, forming the electric current, what happens then? Come on, Daniel. It's easy.'

The others had shuffled round in their seats impatiently, their hands shooting up into the air, desperate to give the answer. Dani's brain had seized into numbness. The answer ought to be there, bouncing confidently into his mind. He knew it really. He *knew* he knew it, but it had drifted away into uncertainty.

'Think about it, Daniel. Think,' the teacher kept saying.

Dani was thinking. It was no good. His head was filling up with a panicky fog, as insubstantial as cotton wool.

The teacher gave up and picked one of the others – clever Makonnen, the guy who'd jumped over Dani's head at the swimming pool – to give the answer. No one had looked at Dani again during the whole long lesson. It was as if he hadn't been there. As if, for all his bulk, he'd disappeared.

The only thing to do, Dani had discovered, when people started looking right through you, was to go away. You couldn't get up and walk out of the classroom, but you could go somewhere else in your head. You could just give yourself over to a story, one of the rich, exciting dramas that were always waiting there on the edge of your mind, ready to move in and take over.

It was like starting off a secret video and watching it with your inside eyes. You could take any part you like, be anyone you wanted. You could be handsome, strong, brave, clever and popular. Not irritating.

He'd got going on a good one this afternoon. It started off with a bank heist, like in a movie. He was in the National Bank with his father, when these gunmen burst in. Everyone froze. They were shouting, 'Get down on the floor! Don't move!' Only Dani had kept his head. He'd noticed the alarm bell, and had wriggled towards it, even though his father had pleaded with him, in frantic whispers, not to put his life at risk. He was just about to reach it, when . . .

'See those kids over there on the corner?' Ibrahim said. 'Those shoe-shine boys? Bet they wish they had your chances.'

A sigh gathered deep down in Dani's chest and gusted out through his mouth. That was the trouble with stuff in your head. It never lasted long enough. If someone broke in on your thoughts, they just blew away, like puffs of smoke, and you couldn't get them back again.

The taxi pulled up outside Dani's house and Ibrahim tooted his horn. The one-eyed guard, Negussie, opened the gates a crack, and put out his gnarled old face. He recognised the taxi, and swung the gates wide open. Ibrahim drove into the compound and pulled up. Dani opened the door and climbed out.

'Here,' Ibrahim called after him, as he went up the marble steps towards the ornate wrought-iron grill that covered the glass front door. 'You've forgotten half your books!'

And as he backed the taxi out through the gates again, Dani could hear his mocking laughter, and Negussie's heavy wheezing as he joined in.

***

Mamo woke to the sound of a grindstone turning. He lay in the pitch-dark listening.

Ma, he thought confusedly. Why is she up so early?

Then he woke properly and remembered everything. It wasn't his mother, grinding grain to make *injera*. She was dead, and he was miles and miles away from home, with people whose names he didn't even know. He was totally in their power.

His stomach turned over and he felt the blood drumming in his ears as he sat up.

The grinding stopped. A flicker of red light ran round the inside of the hut. The woman was blowing through a hollow stick on to the embers of last night's fire, and feeding them with a few dry leaves to make the flames sprout up.

Merga and the farmer, who had been sleeping on the mud platform against the far wall of the hut, stirred, stretched and stood up. They had been wrapped in old grey *shammas*, and they shook them off. The children slept on.

The farmer opened the door of the hut which creaked back on its leather hinges, and a draught of cold air hit Mamo, making him shiver all over. Through the open door, he could see the dark outline of the far horizon as the sky above turned grey. Dawn was coming.

I'm all alone, he told himself, his mind feeling weak with fright. There's no one to help me here.

'Come on, you,' the farmer said, looking across at him and jerking his head towards the door. 'Get the cows out.'

Mamo got up and stumbled outside. The farmer pointed to a ragged stack of hay in the corner of the compound.

'Give them some of that. Don't pull the pile about, mind.'

Mamo was walking across to the haystack when he was almost knocked flat by a thumping blow across his shoulders.

30

'When I say go, you run,' growled the farmer, lowering his stick.

He turned and went back inside. Mamo fumbled with the catch on the door of the stable hut.There was light enough to see by now, for the sky was growing paler minute by minute as dawn broke, but his eyes were half blinded with tears.

He got the door open at last, and the cows came out into the open, shaking their lowered heads. They followed Mamo across to the hay pile and he pulled a little of it off and spread it out for them on the ground. They began to lip it over, snuffling down their noses, ignoring Mamo who started away whenever one came too close to him.

Merga came out of the hut, yawned, stretched and walked outside into the lane. In the empty stillness, Mamo could hear him cough and grunt as he urinated against the thorn hedge.

When he came back, he looked over and caught Mamo's eye. An uneasy smile, almost apologetic, edged on to his face.

'You'll be all right,' he said. 'They're strict, but they're not bad people. You'll learn to work. It's better than loafing around in Addis. You'll thank me in the end. You'll see.'

Hatred simmered inside Mamo.

'Ma wasn't your sister,' he said. 'You're not my uncle.'

Merga's smile broadened and turned into a leer.

'I was a lot more than a brother to her. Me and half the other men in Addis.'

The hatred roared up through Mamo's head like water gushing into a fountain. He wanted to launch himself at Merga, to hit and kick, to hurt him any way he could, but Merga had seen the look in his eyes and retreated into the hut, leaving Mamo to stand helplessly by the cows, crushing handfuls of hay in his tightly clenched fists.

The sun was over the horizon when the boy and girl came outside, with the toddler staggering after them. The girl came up to Mamo, and without raising her eyes to his face put some *injera* and a beaker of water into his hands. He drank down the water and bolted the food at once.

The boy was watching him disgustedly.

'You don't even eat like a Christian. You don't pray first. Anyway, that was for your lunch too.'

The girl was calling to the sheep and goats. She led them, bleating, out of the compound, and he could hear their feet tapping against the stones as they trotted after her to graze.

The farmer and Merga came out and walked across the compound together to the entrance. Merga didn't look at Mamo again. He hurried through the formal farewells, to which the farmer responded with the barest politeness, then disappeared down the lane, out of sight.

In spite of his loathing, Mamo wanted to run after him, to beg, plead, threaten, anything, as long as the man would take him home. He held himself back. It wouldn't do any good. It would only make things worse.

'Tesfaye,' the farmer said to the boy, whose name Mamo now heard for the first time. 'Show him what to do. Take the cattle down to the river with him.'

'I'll be late for school, Father,' Tesfaye said. 'I'll get a beating.'

The farmer raised his hand.

'Are you arguing with me?'

'No, Father. Yes, Father,' Tesfaye said, turning away, resentment stiffening his shoulders.

He ran inside and came out a moment later with a pile of books under his arm and a stick in his hand. He began to round up the cows, tapping their rumps with the stick. Slowly, one after the other, they lumbered out of the compound with the two boys walking after them.

'Who's your father?' Tesfaye asked suddenly. 'Why has he sent you away from home?'

'He's dead,' said Mamo.

'Where did he come from?'

'Up north. He was a soldier.'

'Where in the north?'

'I don't know. He died when I was small.'

'Where's your mother?'

'Dead.'

'That man said she was a—'

'He doesn't know anything about me,' Mamo interrupted furiously. 'He doesn't know anything.'

They walked on in silence.

'You don't know much, either, do you?' said Tesfaye. 'You don't know about your parents. You don't know about cows. I bet you don't even know where you are.'

'What do you mean? I know more than you do, country boy.'

'How many years were you in school?'

Mamo hesitated.

'Nearly two, but . . .'

'You didn't even finish second grade? Bet you can't read.'

'I can,' lied Mamo.

'What's twelve times seven?'

Mamo felt hot red blood rise in his face and his fists tightened.

Tesfaye laughed.

'You get back at me, you get cheeky with me, and my father'll have the hide off your back.'

'Like your teacher's going to have your hide today when you're late for school,' Mamo retorted swiftly.

Tesfaye bit his lip and scowled.

They reached the bottom of the lane without speaking. The cows didn't need directing. They turned left automatically and followed the well-worn path that led down the hill towards the river. One paused and turned her head to nibble at a lush plant growing out of the bank. Tesfaye shouted and drove her on with a thwack on her rump.

'That plant's poisonous,' he said. 'You'd better watch it, city boy. If you let the cows eat that stuff they'll die, and my father will kill you. I mean it. He will kill you. Stone dead.'

They had come out now on to a slope above the stream. Twenty or thirty cows were already there, grazing slowly over grass that had been cropped so close it resembled green velvet. Two herd boys stood together talking, propping themselves up on their long sticks and watching curiously as Mamo and Tesfaye approached.

'Go with them,' Tesfaye said. 'They'll show you the grazing lands. Bring the cows home tonight in one piece if you want to stay alive.'

He threw the stick at Mamo, who caught it in mid-air, then he turned round and began to run, his bare feet kicking up the soft red dust of the path as he went.

The two herd boys stood still and stared at Mamo. He stared back at them. They looked younger than him. One was about nine or ten, and the other could only have been six or seven. They wore old *shammas*, grey now rather than white, wrapped round themselves like cloaks, and their knee joints looked large in their thin legs. They watched unsmilingly as Mamo's cows walked between theirs to reach the edge of the stream.

'Are you from up there?' the bigger one said at last, jerking his chin up towards the farmer's homestead.

'I suppose so,' Mamo said reluctantly. 'I'm supposed to be working for them. I'm from Addis. I don't know about farms and cows and stuff.'

The two boys exchanged excited looks.

'From Addis Ababa?' the big one said.

'Have you ever seen a TV?' said the little one.

They looked friendly and curious.

34

'Course I have,' said Mamo. 'Loads of times.'

Suddenly the smell of the bar where his mother had worked was in his nostrils, the cigarette smoke and beer and disinfectant. He'd been able to watch a whole five minutes of TV sometimes, before she'd shooed him away from the door.

'Have you ever been in a car?' the tall one said.

'No, but I've been in a bus. You go so fast everything outside looks like a kind of blur.'

He was expanding a little in the warmth of their interest.

'Tesfaye's father's an old terror,' the older boy said. 'You'll have to watch out the cows don't get scratched or anything. He beats Tesfaye for nothing.'

'My father's an old terror too,' said the little one.

The other snorted.

'Your father? He's the softest man in Ethiopia. He's already given you two calves of your own.'

'Yes, look, can you see them?' the little boy said proudly. 'That one at the back, he's mine, and the white one flicking her tail. Aren't they beautiful?'

The boys turned to scrutinise the cattle, focusing carefully through narrowed eyes. The big boy suddenly leaped forward, waving his arms. He ran down to the stream and tapped his stick on the flank of a black cow who was heading away from the others upstream towards a deeper pool of water.

'She's one of yours,' the little boy said. 'You'd better get down there and keep an eye on her. She's always getting into trouble, that one is. There's deep mud in that bit of the stream. She could sink right in and get stuck.'

'I can't look after her. I don't know what to do,' said Mamo frankly, dropping his superior city air.

The little boy smiled up at him.

'I'll show you. I'm a really good herd boy, my father says. I'm going to be a farmer like him when I grow up and have a huge herd. I'm going to be really rich.'

As the morning wore on, Mamo began to feel a little better. The two boys, Hailu (the older one) and Yohannes (the little one), were friendly. They bombarded Mamo with questions about city life. Had he ever seen a real game of football? Had he been in an aeroplane? Weren't there thieves everywhere in Addis Ababa?

('People thieves, they're the worst,' Mamo answered sourly to that one.)

In return for his answers, they looked after his cattle and showed him what to do. They taught him the cows' individual foibles – how this one liked to stray and that one always followed the others. They pointed out the dangers – the slippery banks where the cows could fall and break their legs, the various poisonous plants and the thorn bushes where they could tear their hides.

They showed Mamo the fruit of the prickly pear, ripening on the cactus hedges that surrounded the fields, and taught him how to get at the sweet insides without pricking his fingers on the spines.

When midday came, and the sun was burning down, they sat under a tree on a hillock while the cows grazed quietly along the verges of the lane.

'Tell us about the TV again,' Yohannes said. 'What's it like, really?'

Mamo stifled a yawn.

They're nice, but it'll be like this, on and on, for ever and ever, he thought. If I don't get away from here, I'll go mad.

'Hey look!' Hailu jumped to his feet. 'That old one of yours is getting into our field!'

Mamo scrambled after him. He waved his stick clumsily round the cow's head. She lumbered on, pushing further through the gap in the hedge which led into the field in which fresh green crops were growing. Hailu shoved him out of the way, and with a few deft taps of his stick drove the cow out into the lane again.

'That's our best field,' he said, frowning critically at Mamo. 'You mustn't let them get in there. We're going to get a bumper crop off it this year, my father says. I ploughed this end of it myself. It was the first time I'd tried. It's really difficult. You have to be really strong.'

There was pride in his voice.

They belong here, Mamo thought. They love this land. I'm just a servant to them.

Depression settled on him. He looked round with disgust. Fields and little homesteads stretched across the rolling plain to a fringe of blue mountains far away. It could be a desert as far as he was concerned, or a prison, even. There was nothing for him here.

Hailu and Yohannes sensed his mood. They stopped chivvying him with questions. They began a complicated game of their own, which they had obviously played many times before, and hardly spoke to him for the rest of the afternoon.

Mamo's heart sank even further as the time came to drive the cattle home. The other two would go off in different directions from the drinking place by the stream. He would have to manage the last part himself. And once back at the homestead, he would be face to face again with his stern, frightening master and the hostility of his son.

'I like you better than Tesfaye,' little Yohannes said, as their ways parted. 'He bullies us sometimes.'

Mamo's heart lifted a little.

'I like you,' he said.

'Be careful when you get to that turn in the lane, going up to your place,' warned Hailu. 'The old black one always tries to go off there.'

'Thanks,' nodded Mamo.

'See you tomorrow.'

'Yes, tomorrow.'

I needn't have worried about this bit, he thought, as the cows ambled up the last steep bit of the path towards the homestead. They seem to know the way by themselves, but he followed Hailu's advice and was ready with his stick at the bend to head off the black cow.

When he reached the entrance to the compound he looked up and saw the farmer standing there, his arms crossed, silently watching him. He waited till all the cows had come in and inspected them minutely, one by one, from head to tail, without saying a word.

'Get them into the stable,' he said curtly, and turned back into the house.

Ato Paulos, Dani's father, came home late. The guard, old Negussie, had been on the lookout by the double gates, ready to run out of his little shelter to open them a full hour before he heard the beep of the car in the road outside.

Dani had been leaning over his books in a corner of the sitting room, half-heartedly reading and rereading a piece about rainfall and evaporation in his geography textbook. The words slipped in and out of his mind without leaving any impression, while every word of the story which Zeni was telling Meseret on the verandah outside brought a vivid picture to life in his head.

Her voice stopped abruptly as Ato Paulos's footsteps crunched across the gravel towards the steps.

'Good evening, sir,' she said nervously.

'Baba!' cried Meseret, and Dani could see her in his mind's eye hurling herself forward and wrapping her arms round his knee.

She's the only person in the world who's not afraid of him, he thought enviously.

Ato Palos walked into the hallway. Dani bent his head again over his book. He could feel his father's eyes like twin lasers on the back of his neck, and he sat still, praying that he would go away.

After a moment, he heard him move on down the corridor and open the door of the main bedroom where his wife had been resting all afternoon. He heard her murmur something, but couldn't quite make out the words. His father's answering voice, though, was loud and clear.

'I know I'm late. I'm sorry. Trouble with the suppliers again. No one's prepared to take responsibility. If I want anything done I have to see to it myself, down to the smallest detail. It almost makes me wish I was back in the army. If these young chaps were under my command I'd make them hop like fleas.'

Ruth spoke again, too quietly for Dani to hear, but he heard his father say, 'No, get them to dish up in half an hour. I'll change first.' His voice softened. 'How are you? Did you sleep this afternoon?'

He had moved into the bathroom, and Ruth raised her voice to reach him.

'A little. I'm all right.' She coughed nervously. 'A letter's come for you.'

'Oh? Who from?'

'Dani's headmaster.'

Dani's heart gave one painful thudding kick, then settled into a fast beat that made him breathless.

'Wants to put the fees up again, I suppose.'

There was the sound of running water, then the tap was turned off. Ruth spoke again, her voice more nervous than ever.

'No, it's not about money. Promise you won't be too angry.'

Dani's hands were sweating. He balled his fists and dropped his forehead down on to them. He heard his father march back into the bedroom, and there was a long moment of silence.

He's reading the letter, he thought.

Then he heard a scrunching noise, and he knew that Ato Paulos was screwing the letter up and hurling it away from him.

'Failure, all the way down the line. Test results disappointing. Participation in class minimal. Poor prediction for end of year exams. What am I going to do with him, eh? What?'

His mother's voice was inaudible again. Dani stood up, taking care not to let his chair scrape on the floorboards, and stole across to the door.

'No,' his father was saying, and Dani could hear that he was trying to keep his anger on a tight rein so as not to upset his wife. 'You must face facts, my dear. The modern world's not like the old days, when your father got your brother a job in a government department because he was who he was. You're nothing now without qualifications. It's a skills-based economy. If Dani doesn't make something of himself, no one else can do it for him. You *know* that, Ruth.'

'Yes, but . . .' Ruth began.

'My God,' Ato Paulos swept on. 'When I think how I had to work to get where I am!' Dani knew now what was coming, almost word for word. 'No rich parents around to spoil me. No lazing around beside swimming pools. I didn't know the feeling of a pair of shoes on my feet till I was twelve years old. Sheer hard grind, and scholarships which I earned for myself all the way. The Military Academy doesn't take fools, I can tell you. Do you know how many boys competed for a single place in those days?'

'He's good at some things,' Ruth said, and Dani imagined her laying her hand on her husband's arm. Hot tears of gratitude stung the insides of his eyelids. 'His writing is excellent, Ato Mesfin says, and—'

'Writing! Stories!' Ato Paulos was clearly finding it harder and harder to hold his temper in check. 'You leave this to me. I'm going to sort things out with him right now. No, Ruth, you are not to get up. I won't have you distressed over this. Daniel can't hide behind you any longer. He's got to face up to reality.'

The blood seemed to rush to Dani's head, and for a couple of seconds he felt almost faint. He thought for a wild moment of hiding under one of the armchairs that stood with perfect neatness around the walls of the sitting room, but knew that he'd be discovered at once, and dragged out ignominiously.

Instead, he scurried back to the table, and was sitting there with his eyes down unseeingly on the page of his book when his father strode into the room and shut the door with a click behind him.

Dani forced himself to turn and look at him.

'Do you know what your headmaster has to say about you?' Ato Paulos began, his voice grating with the fury he had been suppressing.

'No, Father,' whispered Dani.

'Failure to work. Failure to pass tests. Failure to participate in class.' Ato Paulos ticked each item off his fingers. 'And I'll add some more. Physical slovenliness. Lack of application in sport. Laziness. Childishness. Inconsiderateness. Upsetting your mother.'

Dani sat with his eyes down, staring miserably at the dark brown border that ran round the edge of the pale brown rug.

'What have you got to say for yourself?'

Ato Paulos crossed the room and stood over his trembling son. Dani tried not to cower away from him.

'Nothing, Father. I've done my best. I . . .'

'Do you realise what I'm saying? Do you understand how serious all this is?'

'Yes, Father.'

'I suppose you think that because I've worked hard all my life, come up from nowhere, and made a decent living, you can sit back and sponge off me for the rest of your life, like some pampered little playboy.'

'Honestly, Father, I don't—'

'I'm giving you an ultimatum, Daniel.' Dani could sense that his father's hands were itching with the desire to slap him. He concentrated on sitting as still as possible so as not to set anything off. 'You're going to pass your end-of-year exams with flying colours, do you hear? If you don't . . .' Dani gulped and shut his eyes. He would be threatened now with the beating of a lifetime. 'If you don't,' Ato Paulos went on, 'I'll send you down to Jigjiga to my old Somali batman. If anyone can make a man of you, Feisal can. He faced a lion when he was your age with nothing but a spear in his hand.'

Dani's head jerked up. He was staring at his father, appalled. This was the last thing in the world he had expected. He remembered Feisal only too well. Feisal had lived in the servants' quarters behind the house for years after Ato Paulos had left the army, and had run the compound with military precision. If a ball had strayed on to a flower bed, violent reprisals followed. If one of the flowerpots that flanked the steps up to the front door was accidentally chipped, Feisal's scolding practically blistered the paint on the compound's big metal gates. Ruth had begged her husband again and again to get rid of Feisal, and he had at last reluctantly agreed, sending him off home to Jigjiga with a handsome sum to buy a small house for his retirement. A few beatings at home would be nothing compared to a sentence with Feisal.

'I'll work, I'll pass, Father, I promise,' he said faintly.

Ato Paulos, aware that his threat had hit the mark, nodded with satisfaction.

'And don't go whining to your mother, do you hear? It's high time you learned to leave her alone and face up to things like a man. She's a sick woman. You don't realise how serious it is. The least worry is bad for her.'

He turned sharply on his heel and went out of the room.

'Baba!' Dani heard Meseret shout delightedly, and Ato Paulos's voice changed at once as he bent down and swung her up into his arms.

'There, my little jewel. Come and sit beside your baba while he eats his supper.'

Chapter 4

Mamo lost count of the passing days. Each one was like the last, and the next, and the next. Every morning he was woken by the snuffling and trampling of cows in the round barn, where he slept on the floor near the door. Then he devoured the little bit of food the girl brought him, before he drove the animals down to the river.

He wasn't scared of the cows any more, and he managed them nearly as well as Hailu or Yohannes. The difference was that the other boys loved their beasts. They called them by name – Black Sides, Broken Horn, Wild One – and fussed over every small stumble or scratch. Mamo tolerated his little herd and occasionally even took pleasure in their quiet lowing and their gusts of sweet-smelling breath, but he feared and loathed their owner, the farmer, his master.

Nothing Mamo did was ever right in the man's eyes. Mamo always came home too late or too early. He didn't latch the door properly. He forked down too little hay from the stack, or too much. On Saturdays, when he loaded the donkey with sacks of grain for the farmer to take to market, the load slipped because it was too loose, or it chafed the donkey's back because it was too tight. Mamo cowered every time the man came near him, dreading the vicious thump of the stick on his back.

He didn't understand, either, why Tesfaye seemed to hate him so much. The boy would come back breathless after his long run home from school every day, and lean against the wall of the house, watching Mamo at his evening chore of sweeping out the barn.

44

'Muck sticks to muck,' he'd say. 'Don't you dare come near me. There's shit in your hair and shit in your armpits and shit between your toes.'

Only one thing would shut Tesfaye up. His father's curt growl from inside the house would make him stiffen, and he'd throw one more malevolent glance at Mamo before hurrying obediently inside.

The worst thing was that Mamo was always hungry. He thought of food all the time, from the moment he woke up in the morning till the moment he went to sleep at night.

For the first week or two, the farmer's wife had seemed to resent feeding him at all. She had given him the barest scraps left on the dish when everyone else had eaten, and an occasional length of sugar cane or a corn cob to chew on.

One day, when she had put only a tiny handful of food into his cupped palms, his eyes had filled with tears. He felt them splash down his cheeks as he looked up at her.

She had stared down at him for a brief moment, and he had seen a flicker of pity in her eyes. She had lifted some of the food from the small amount reserved for herself and given it to him.

'Perhaps next year, if God is good and the harvest is better, there'll be more for all of us,' she had murmured, then she'd leaned down to quieten the toddler, who was crying on the floor.

It was a bit better after that. She saw to it that Mamo had just enough to keep body and soul together, though it never filled his belly, and it was never as much as she gave to Tesfaye, who was ravenously hungry every night after his five-mile run to school in the morning and five-mile run home every afternoon, and who frowned jealously at every scrap of food that made its way into Mamo's mouth.

The herd boys Hailu and Yohannes, though their mothers sent them out every morning with something to eat for the middle of the day, were endlessly hungry too.

They were always on the lookout for ripe prickly pears, and when the chickpeas were nearly ready for harvest in the fields, they would surreptitiously help themselves to a few plants at a time, stripping off the crunchy green peas and eating them raw, one at a time, relishing their sharp bitter flavour.

'What a dump the countryside is. Everyone's always hungry here,' Mamo said one day, furiously flinging away a prickly pear that had turned out to be rotten inside.

'It's not always like this,' Hailu said defensively. He'd started to get annoyed when Mamo criticised country life. 'The rains failed last year, that's all. It'll be OK next year.'

Little Yohannes never seemed to notice these moments of tension.

'Let's play that game again,' he'd say sunnily. 'You know, riding motorbikes like you showed us, Mamo. Like what they do in Addis.'

Mamo couldn't help liking Yohannes. He couldn't help smiling back into his cheerful round face, or laughing at his voice. Yohannes had a lisp at the moment, since his two top front teeth had fallen out, and the new ones had only just started growing through.

Some of the time, Mamo didn't mind joining in with Yohannes's childish games, for which there was plenty of time as the cattle grazed along the banks of the stream, but he got bored with them long before Yohannes did.

He had retreated into himself one day, as he often did, and moved away from the other two to perch on a stone and look out across the endless patchwork of little fields, while black depression settled on his heart and loneliness ate into every corner of his mind.

No one in the whole world cares about me, he thought. No one knows I'm here. Tiggist thinks I just walked out on her, I expect, and even if she knew what happened, how could she find me? She could never come here and rescue me. She probably wouldn't even bother to try. I bet she's having a great time at Mrs Faridah's shop, anyway. She's probably forgotten she ever had a brother at all.

A delighted shout made him look up.

'Here comes my father!' cried Yohannes, dancing up and down on the spot. 'Look, he's riding Silk Ears.'

Yohannes's father trotted up on his black mule. He reined it in when he saw the three boys.

'Hello, lads,' he called out cheerfully. 'Have you driven off any cattle thieves today?'

'Hundreds, Father,' said Yohannes. 'And a leopard. It was as big as Silk Ears.'

His father laughed, then he noticed Mamo.

'Who are you?'

'That's Mamo,' Yohannes said proudly. 'He's the one I told you about, from Addis. He knows about TV and football and soldiers and everything. I told you, Father. He's been in a bus.'

Mamo stood to attention, looking up warily at the man. He couldn't see a stick, but a whip might be concealed inside the man's brown coat. But Yohannes's father was smiling down at him, and his eyes were kind.

'A bit slow for you here, after life in Addis, I expect.'

'Yes, sir,' said Mamo stiffly.

'Missing your family, are you?'

Mamo's throat suddenly felt tight. He jerked his head in a kind of nod.

The man hesitated.

'It's been a bad year. Hard for everyone. Not enough to go round. But God is good. Next year, maybe . . .'

Something was growing inside Mamo, a feeling that was too big for him to bear. It welled up and burst out in words that he couldn't control.

'Please, I can't bear it. I can't stay here. I want to go home. To Addis. Please help me. He'll beat me to death one day, I know he will. Let me go with you. Show me the way home.'

Yohannes's father said nothing for a moment, while the mule's long glossy tail twitched back and forth across its rump. Mamo stood stock still. He was almost faint with horror at what he'd said.

He'll go for me now, he thought. He'll tell the farmer and they'll kill me between them.

But Yohannes's father only bent down and put a gentle hand on Mamo's shoulder.

'It's not for me to interfere in a neighbour's household, however much . . . I can't do that. But don't despair, Mamo. Have faith in God. Don't despair.'

He dug his heels into Silk Ears' sides and the mule moved forward, breaking quickly into a trot.

'Father!' shouted Yohannes, running after him on his small hard bare feet. 'I want to show you my catapult. I made a catapult! Come back and see it, Father.'

But the man had ridden on, and the drumming of Silk Ears' hooves was already fading into the distance.

Tiggist had never been so happy in her life. She had a good place to sleep in, at the back of the shop in the storeroom, and every morning she rolled up her mat and blanket and put them neatly away behind an oil drum. She had some nice clothes now, too, a skirt, two blouses and a jumper that Mrs Faridah's sister had grown out of, and a blue dress with long sleeves. And then there were the shoes. They were nearly new, with pointed toes, and they made her look completely grown-up.

Best of all, was the tiny but growing store of worn birr notes, her wages, stowed away secretly in a tin, which she kept hidden in a high dark corner at the back of the storeroom.

She'd been nervous at first of the watchman, who slept outside against the door of the shop all night, wrapped in his ancient *shamma*. He'd given her some funny looks and come a bit too close to her once or twice. But Mrs

Faridah had seen him at it, and she'd let out such a screech, telling him to keep his dirty old hands to himself, that the watchman had got quite scared of losing his job.

He was all right after that, almost fatherly sometimes. Tiggist didn't mind him any more. She even stopped to chat with him occasionally.

She didn't mind the boy who served the fruit and vegetables out in the front of the shop, either. He was Mrs Faridah's nephew. One of his legs was shorter than the other, and his hip hurt him badly sometimes. He kept himself to himself and hobbled off home every night without usually saying a word to her.

She had to work hard. She was on the go from morning to night, sweeping out the shop and washing the floor, running errands, doing deliveries and looking after the baby. At first, Mrs Faridah kept a sharp eye on her. The last girl she'd had, she told Tiggist, had been secretly pinching stuff all the time, packets of sugar and biscuits and candles, all sorts of things, and passing them to her brother, who was always hanging around the front of the shop.

The word 'brother' made Tiggist think guiltily of Mamo. She'd gone back to see Mrs Hannah a couple of times, hoping she'd have heard something from Mamo, but he hadn't turned up again. Another family was living in their leaky old shack now. She'd left a message with the worn-out-looking mother, asking her to tell Mamo where she was if he came and asked. She didn't know what else to do.

She thought uneasily sometimes about the uncle Mrs Hannah had mentioned. He couldn't be a real uncle, she knew that, but Ma had had plenty of boyfriends at the bar, and some of them had stayed around for months.

Perhaps he was one of those, and he'd really liked Ma, and had really wanted to help Mamo. Perhaps he'd got him a wonderful job, and Mamo hadn't had any time off to come and tell her about it.

She tried not to think about the stories she'd heard, about children being taken off and sold as cheap labour. But even if that had happened to Mamo, what could she do about it? Where could she start to look for him?

She worried about him all the time at first, prayed every night and morning, and ran in to kiss the wall of the church of St Michael, pushing through the crowd of other supplicants there, whenever she went past the gates. But as the weeks passed, Mamo began to fade from her mind, and she became more and more engrossed in the world of the shop, the customers, and above all Yasmin, Mrs Faridah's baby.

'Come along, come along, my flower,' she'd say, bouncing the little girl up in her arms, loving the feel of the chubby little arms round her neck.

Yasmin loved her back, crowing with delight when Tiggist came near her, and crying when strangers took her out of Tiggist's arms.

Mrs Faridah watched approvingly.

'You've got quite a way with her,' she said once or twice, and Tiggist glowed with pleasure. Mrs Faridah didn't often dish out words of praise.

It was a while before Tiggist began to wonder about Mrs Faridah's husband, Mr Hamid, and it was the watchman who explained.

'Sick man, isn't he,' he said. 'Lost an eye in the northern campaign. It gets infected. He's down in Awassa where his family comes from. Left his missus to run things up here until he's well enough to take over again. He'll be back. Not that he bothers me. She's the one who runs the show. Always has been.'

Tiggist had put Mr Hamid out of her mind after that. In fact, she'd almost forgotten he'd existed. But one afternoon, the woman from the bigger shop next door, which had a telephone of its own, came running in, almost barging into the stands on which the fruit was displayed in front of the shop.

'Faridah! Come quickly!' she was calling out. 'There's a call for you from Awassa!'

Mrs Faridah had been serving a customer at the till, but she ran out at once, leaving Tiggist to take over. Tiggist had only been at the till once before, having her first lesson in how to manage it, and she was so intent on making sure that she was doing it right, ringing up the prices properly, and giving out the correct change, that she was hardly aware of the commotion in the street outside.

It was only when there was a lull between customers, and the little crowd around the till had melted away, that she could hear what people were saying.

'Don't worry, Faridah. He's a strong man. He'll pull through.'

'You must go right away. First thing in the morning. My cousin's got a taxi. He'll take you down to the bus station.'

'Can't your brother-in-law take over the shop for you? He did it before, when Yasmin was born.'

Tiggist had stood paralysed, her heart seeming to turn over in her chest.

If Mrs Faridah was going away, she might not need Tiggist any more. She'd take Yasmin with her, and at least half of Tiggist's job would have gone. Perhaps she'd get the sack. Perhaps she'd be thrown out, like the last girl was, the one who was caught stealing. She'd have nothing then. No one to turn to. Nowhere to go.

'Come on, are you asleep, or what? I said I wanted a bottle of oil. One of those big ones, on the shelf behind you.'

Her heart still fluttering. Tiggist fetched down the oil and took the money from the impatient man who was standing at the counter in front of her. She must be careful. She mustn't slip up now. If she gave the wrong change, and the till didn't add up this evening, she'd be for it.

Mrs Faridah came hurrying into the shop.

'Where's Yasmin?' she said distractedly to Tiggist.

'She's still asleep. She always—'

'You'll have to stay there and mind the till,' said Mrs Faridah. 'I can't — I've got to—'

People were pressing round her, trying to comfort her and giving her advice in loud, conflicting voices.

Out of the corner of her eye, Tiggist suddenly caught sight of a ragged boy, who had sneaked into the shop with the crowd, and was stuffing a packet of batteries up his filthy sweater.

'Thief!' she shrieked. 'Stop him!'

The boy, lithe as a cat, was out of the shop and away down the street, wriggling out of the grasp of the many hands that clutched at him.

The excitement seemed to shock Mrs Faridah into action.

'We'll have to close,' she said, 'till my brother-in-law gets here. Where's the watchman? Tiggist, tell him to put the shutters up. I'll go and pack. And Tiggist, go down to the bus station, and buy seats on the earliest bus out to Awassa tomorrow morning. Wait now, till I give you the money.'

'Seats?' said Tiggist. 'Won't Yasmin just sit on your knee?'

'One for me and one for you,' said Mrs Faridah. 'You'll have to come with me. I'm going to have to spend all my time nursing my husband, and his mother's too old and blind to manage Yasmin on her own. You don't mind, do you?'

Tiggist felt as if a huge flower had opened in her chest. She wasn't going to lose her job. She was needed. Mrs Faridah couldn't manage without her. And she was going in a bus, out of Addis Ababa, to exciting new places she'd never seen before.

'No, of course I don't mind,' she said. 'Do you want me to pack Yasmin's clothes? Can she wear her little yellow dress tomorrow? She looks gorgeous in that one.'

***

Something unexpected and wonderful had happened to Dani. His father had gone abroad. There had been days of turmoil at home. Zeni and his mother had fussed endlessly over Ato Paulos's clothes, and Ruth had spent hours making up little packages of Ethiopian treats for homesick relatives in London. Ato Paulos's temper had got shorter and shorter.

'Business worries,' Ruth had said soothingly to Dani. 'He's got so much on his mind. Nothing to do with you, darling.'

Ato Paulos had been gone for five weeks now, and Dani was happier than he had been for years. There were no interrogations to face every evening, no curt commands to pull himself together and stop daydreaming, no threats, no harsh remarks. He spent hours curled up at the end of his mother's bed, chatting and looking at old photographs with her. Then he'd go off to his room and draw elaborate pictures, and he'd take them to show her, and she'd tell him they were brilliant, and ask anxiously if he'd done his homework. He'd say yes, of course, and then he'd feel guilty, and sit down for a while in front of his pile of books.

The delightful thing was that time seemed to stretch endlessly ahead. There was the occasional phone call from his father in England. Business was going all right, but it was slow. Ato Paulos needed more time over there. He couldn't say when he'd be coming home, but it wouldn't be for a while yet.

I've got to get on with it, Dani told himself. I've got to learn all this boring stuff. I'll start properly tomorrow. It'll be easier then.

But the next day the words in his schoolbooks danced around as confusingly as ever. They bounced off his mind without going in. He would read the same sentence three times and nothing would stick. Then he'd look up and stare out of the window, allowing himself to be half mesmerised by the patterns of sunlight glancing through the stiff blue-green leaves of the eucalyptus tree outside.

Tomorrow, he thought again. I'll start with maths, then I'll do half an hour of geography, then I'll learn all that chemistry stuff off by heart.

He pushed the thought of the exams to the back of his mind. Now that his father wasn't there, the idea of Feisal, waiting like an ogre down in Jigjiga, seemed too fantastic and unreal to be true.

Father can't have meant it, he told himself. Mamma would stop him sending me there, anyway.

There was only one kind of homework that he tackled with enthusiasm. His Amharic teacher, Ato Mesfin, sometimes set essays and stories to write. Dani would spend hours on these. He'd write reams and reams, covering pages with large untidy Amharic letters. He'd read them to his mother before he took them into school, and she'd listen with admiring attention. Ato Mesfin was the only teacher who ever gave him a word of praise.

'Go on like this,' he'd say sometimes, 'and we'll make a writer of you.' Then he'd try to look stern. 'You won't get much further, though, if you don't improve your handwriting.'

The exams suddenly roared up out of the future as fast as an approaching train. One day, Dani was happily constructing another story for Ato Mesfin, and the next he had suddenly realised, with a jolt to his heart and a lurch to his stomach, that there were only ten days of revision time left. The thought settled down, after the first shock, into a block of painful anxiety, weighing on his mind and paralysing it. He sat for hours at his desk, but the books seemed more scarily remote than ever.

The first exam made him feel a little better. There were parts of it he could answer quite well. He did his best, bending his head over the paper, his tongue sticking out of the corner of his mouth. But the second exam was so awful, the questions so completely strange and incomprehensible, that he could do nothing but stare at them with horror. They seemed to jig about on the page, mocking him. He tried his best, writing down a few things that he thought he remembered, but he knew when the hours were up that he had failed miserably.

He was scared after that. The thought of Feisal began to loom large in his mind, no longer an ogre of fantasy, but a figure that was all too real.

Ato Paulos announced that he was coming home as suddenly as he had gone away. Dani heard his mother's voice, excited and happy, as she talked down the wires to London.

It's all right for her, Dani thought, feeling suddenly painfully distant from his mother. He loves her. She's not scared of him. Not really. She *wants* him to come home.

He hardly slept at all the night before his father's flight was due. He tossed and turned in bed, rehearsing over and over again what he would say when the results came out, the reasons he could give for the terrible marks he knew he'd have. He'd been desperately ill, at death's door. (No, not even his mother would back that one up.) His exam papers had got mixed up with another boy's. (Ato Paulos would wave that one aside with an infuriated frown.) The teachers had a down on him because they were jealous of his father's success. (That would be no good. Flattery disgusted Ato Paulos.)

It was a Sunday when his father arrived. Ruth had planned to meet him at the airport, but the doctor, who had come round the night before, had taken her blood pressure and told her firmly that she was to stay in bed.

Dani had calculated the time it would take for his father to get home from the airport. He planned to be surrounded by piles of books, mountains of books and sheets and sheets of handwritten pages when Ato Paulos came through the door. But the car was hooting outside the gates a full hour before he'd expected it, and Ato Paulos was striding up the steps and was in the house before Dani had time to hide the little soldiers he was playing with on his bed, and scramble over to his desk.

In fact, it didn't matter, anyway. Ato Paulos didn't even glance into Dani's room. He was hurrying along the corridor to his own bedroom in answer to Ruth's sharp cry of joy and welcome. And walking briskly behind him, a bag in her hand and a navy blue coat folded over her arm, was a white woman.

Astonished, Dani followed them down to his parents' room. His father was bending over his mother with a look of such unaccustomed tenderness on his face that it almost made Dani gasp.

'Ruth,' he was saying in English. 'This is Miss Watson. She's a nurse. She's going to take you to London on the morning flight tomorrow and look after you on the journey.' He lapsed back into Amharic. 'I've managed to fix up for you to see a heart surgeon, and he's taking you into the clinic straight away. He'll do the operation as soon as you're strong enough.' He coughed awkwardly. 'You're going to be all right. Everything's going to be all right. Where's Zeni? She's got to start getting your things together right away.'

Chapter 5

In spite of the desperate lack of food, and his constant gnawing hunger, Mamo was growing. He was hardly aware of it. He only knew that his voice was playing tricks on him, and that his hands and feet had become more clumsy.

He had lost count of the weeks and months that had passed since the man in the city clothes had brought him here. He had given up all thoughts of escaping.

The farmer, whose sudden rages were never far away, was becoming more tense as harvest time approached. A freak storm had wrecked the crops in a neighbouring district, and as his own fields began to ripen he lived in dread that the same thing would happen to him. The black cow, too, the awkward one who always got herself into trouble, was in calf, and the farmer inspected her suspiciously every evening, shooting angry glances at Mamo if he found so much as a burr sticking to her hide.

On Sundays, the stifling everyday routine changed a little. Tesfaye didn't go to school, and the family set off early in the morning, before it was light, to walk several miles to the nearest church, where the service started soon after dawn. For Mamo, this meant that he missed his breakfast, though the woman sometimes put a piece of sugar cane into his hand before hurrying after her family with the baby on her back.

The worst thing was that Tesfaye would run home ahead of the others, along the path by the stream. The sight of Mamo sitting together with Hailu and Yohannes always seemed to inflame him to a jealous rage.

'Where's your pride?' he'd say jeeringly to them. 'What do you want to talk to that dirty beggar for? Don't you know that you can catch diseases off people like that?'

Mamo usually looked out for Tesfaye on a Sunday, and moved away from the other two when he saw the boy's lithe figure appear on the hillside above the stream.

One bright Sunday morning, everyone had been in a better mood than usual. The farmer had actually smiled as Mamo had led the cows out of the hut.

'She'll calve any day now,' he'd grunted, feeling the black cow's swollen flanks. 'It'll be a big one by the look of it.' Then he'd gone to the gate and looked out over his few small fields. 'They'll be ready to harvest by the end of next week. Then you'll know what hard work really means.'

His tone had been almost friendly. It had lulled Mamo into a faint feeling of optimism.

Maybe Yohannes's father was right, he thought. Maybe things will be better when the harvest's in.

As he followed the cows down the worn path, he suddenly remembered one of the tunes he'd often heard blaring out from the music shop in Addis Ababa. He'd spent hours sitting on the wall near it, listening. He could even just remember the sounds of some of the words, or near enough, though he didn't have any idea of their meaning.

'We're the survivors. Yes! The black survivors . . .'

He was still crooning softly to himself when he joined the other boys.

'What's that song? What are you singing?' Yohannes said at once. 'Is it from Addis? Did you hear it on TV?'

Even Hailu looked interested, and asked him to sing it again.

The morning passed much more quickly than usual. Mamo discovered, once he tried to think about it, that he'd learned the tunes of six or seven songs, and could repeat a good many words. The three boys perched on the roots of a huge ancient tree, from which they could look down on the cattle, who were moving slowly upstream, seeking out the last few patches of greenery.

For the first time in months, Mamo felt almost happy. The music made him feel different, powerful somehow, and hopeful. In Addis, he'd only ever sung quietly, under his breath, afraid of drawing attention to himself, but here he could let his voice swoop and soar. It belled out into the vast silence of the countryside clear and true. He hadn't known he could sing like that. It felt good. He couldn't help responding to the whole-hearted admiration in Yohanne's eyes, and the respect in Hailu's.

He was so absorbed that he forgot to keep an eye on the shadows, which always shortened rapidly as the morning wore on. Normally, they gave him an idea of the time, so that he could be ready to slip away from the others the moment Tesfaye appeared. Today, he didn't give Tesfaye a single thought until a stone whizzed past his ear.

He jumped and looked round, instinctively putting an arm up to shield his head. Tesfaye was pelting down the slope towards him, another stone in his hand. Yohannes and Hailu stood up, looked nervously at each other, and backed away.

'Cockroach! Rat!' yelled Tesfaye, hurling the other stone, which grazed Mamo's shoulder. 'Why aren't you looking after my cows? Who says you can sit here all day singing dirty foreign songs from your mother's slag shop bar?'

The blood rushed to Mamo's head. His fist tightened round his stick. He was gearing himself to rush at Tesfaye when Hailu let out a yell.

'The cows! Look!'

The second stone that Tesfaye had thrown had rolled down the hill and hit the black cow's forelock. She had started back nervously, frightening the others, who were trampling about at the edge of the stream.

Hailu and Yohannes raced down towards them, holding out their sticks, trying to reach each of their cows in turn to soothe them and guide them away, and Mamo, fear of the farmer overcoming his fury, followed them automatically.

His head still in turmoil, he missed his footing and fell headlong, grazing the skin off both his knees. His stick flew out of his hand. It hit the normally quiet brown cow, who was standing behind the black one, and who now lurched forwards, butting the black cow's rump with her horns. The black cow, nervous as usual, rolled her eyes and arched her back, then side-stepped, and Mamo could only watch in silent horror as she lost her footing and fell sideways down the bank, landing with a drenching splash in the stream. Frozen, he waited for her to scramble to her feet again, but she didn't move. She lay in the water, her huge belly bulging grotesquely, opened her mouth and began to bellow with agonised, uncowlike intensity.

'Look what you've done! Look!' screamed Tesfaye, as much fear as anger in his voice as he jumped over Mamo with a flying leap and plunged into the stream. 'Come and help me! We've got to get her up!'

Mamo staggered to his feet, hardly feeling the pain in his knees, not noticing the blood dripping down his shins. Tesfaye was trying to lever the cow up, pushing at her with all his strength. Mamo joined him, and they heaved and strained against her, ignoring her anguished bellows.

She didn't help them. She lay like a dead weight, her legs kicking feebly.

'Come on, you, push!' Tesfaye was shouting. 'Get her up!'

It was no good. The cow had stopped bellowing and her head had fallen back into the water. As Mamo watched, her tongue flopped out of her mouth, her eyes stopped rolling, and death began to glaze them over.

There was a shout from above and the farmer came running down the path.

'What's happened? What are you doing? Get her out!' he yelled.

Then he took in the animal's unmistakable stillness. With a howl, he lifted his stick and advanced on Mamo.

'It was all his fault, Father,' Mamo heard Tesfaye say in a rapid, high-pitched voice. 'He – he threw a stone at me, and scared her, then he threw his stick at her.'

'Liar! Liar!' screamed Mamo.

'Mamo's right. Tesfaye threw a stone first,' Mamo heard Yohannes say indignantly, but no one took any notice.

The rage in Mamo's head was so hot that he hardly felt the farmer's first blows. He was struggling to get past him, to reach Tesfaye, to stuff his lies down his throat and make him grovel to his father. But the stick was falling on him so fast and so cruelly that he could think only of protecting himself, of covering his head with his arms and trying to run away.

He didn't manage to take a step. The man knocked him to the ground.

'You dog! You filthy animal! I'll kill you!' the man was shouting wildly, as the stick struck brutally again and again, raining blows on his arms and legs, thwacking against his back, his head and his face.

Then, with a crack as loud as a gunshot, the stick snapped in half. It seemed to enrage the farmer even more. He flung the two ends aside, grabbed Mamo by the shoulders, and dragging him to the stream, plunged his head under the water.

He's going to drown me. Oh God, help me! Oh God, don't let me die! was Mamo's last thought, then everything was wiped from his mind as he fought to hold his breath.

He was about to burst, about to give up and allow the water to enter his lungs and drown him, when his head was suddenly released. He came up spluttering, and was flung backwards on to the bank. As he struggled for breath, every part of his body throbbed with pain, and he felt as if he would faint.

He sat woozily on the ground, his head down on his knees, only dimly aware of the confused noises all around: the receding footfalls of the cattle as they were driven away, and the subdued retreating voices of Hailu and Yohannes.

After a long time, he lifted his head, wincing at the pain across his shoulders. He looked round cautiously. Everyone had gone. He was alone.

A dreadful desolation entered his heart.

I can't go on, he thought.

He had a strange feeling that his soul was coming loose from his body.

If it comes right off, he thought, and floats away, where will it go?

He saw in his mind's eye a picture of God, like one of the frescoes he had seen in a church in Addis Ababa. God looked like an old father, with his arms open and a loving smile on his face.

Maybe it would be like going home, he thought, to a family.

He looked up at the sky. The blue immensity seemed to swirl around his head, but the light sent jagged darts into his eyes, making his head ache even more painfully. He looked down again and noticed that the strength was beginning to seep back into his arms and legs.

'No,' he said out loud. 'Please, God, don't do this. Take my soul.'

But it was too late. His body was taking charge again, drawing his soul back in like a child pulling on the string of a balloon.

Mamo suddenly felt violently angry. For a moment, escape seemed to have been within his grasp, and now it had been snatched away. And then, in his head, he heard Tesfaye's voice again, from that very first day, when they had taken the cattle out together.

'That sort of plant's poisonous,' Tesfaye had said. 'You'd better watch it, city boy.'

Mamo had kept an eye out after that, for the occasional clump of poisonous plants, and he knew where the nearest one was, right now. It was growing luxuriantly down by the stream, near the place where the dead cow still lay. He had helped Hailu and Yohannes to hack it down several times, but it kept on putting up fresh shoots.

He didn't wait for second thoughts. He stood up shakily and hobbled down to the water's edge. He picked a clutch of the new leaves, which were sprouting obstinately from the plant's deep roots, and stuffed them into his mouth.

Take me. Be my father. Take me away.

The words ran round inside his head like a drum beat.

The leaves tasted so bitter that, against his will, he almost spat them out again. Instead, he scooped up water from the stream in his cupped hands and drank, swilling them down.

'Now, now,' he whispered, waiting to feel once again the delicious lightness as his soul drifted away from him, hoping to see the father with the open arms.

Instead, he felt a horrible trembling sensation begin to shake him, and a cloudy mushiness invaded his mind. Before he fainted, his last thought was, 'I shouldn't have done it.' And then, like the flicker of a flame in a dying fire, 'No! No! I want to live!'

The morning his mother flew away to England, it felt to Dani as if the bottom had dropped out of his world. Numb with misery, he had hung around her room while Zeni turned out drawers and cupboards, packing clothes and shoes and medicines into a huge suitcase, and Miss Watson hovered by Ruth's bed, checking her pulse from time to time and looking over the injections and pills in her small black bag.

'You're going to come back soon, aren't you, Mamma?' he whispered to her, sidling up to her bed. 'You're not going to die over there?'

She turned her head wearily towards him, and he was shocked at how ill she looked. Why hadn't he noticed the dark shadows round her eyes and the grey tinge to her lips?

'No, I'll be all right. Work hard, darling. Try to please Baba. Be nice to Meseret.'

Then Miss Watson had shooed him out of the room.

The very worst moment of his life, so far, was when Negussie had limped out to open the compound gates, and the car, with his mother, his father and the nurse inside it, had swept out into the street and disappeared. He'd had to fight hard to hold back tears. He tried to follow in his mind the car's route to the airport. Now it would be turning out into the main road. It would have stopped at the traffic lights. It would be going round Meskal Square. It would be going under the arch now, turning on to the airport road.

How long would it be before Father came back alone? Two hours? Three? And what would happen then?

He went back into his room and sat down on his bed, not knowing what to do. The everyday sounds of the house were all around him. He could hear the splashing of the hose which Negussie had brought out to water the flowers. In the street outside, a vegetable seller was passing by, calling out his wares. Meseret's voice came from the room next door. She was singing softly in a monotonous drone as she played a babyish game. He could hear Zeni too. She was talking to the cook. They were walking round the side of the house, approaching his window.

'What do you think?' Zeni was saying. 'Is she going to make it? She looks so sick, poor lady.'

The cook cleared his throat and spat.

'Not much of a chance. She's got that look my mother-in-law had before she passed away, God rest her. How could she survive the journey? And that English nurse was only a girl. What good can she do?'

Zeni gave a sharp sigh.

'I suppose you're right. There'll be changes around here then. I'll be looking for a new job, for a start. She was so sweet, it was her that kept me here. I don't fancy working just for him, I can tell you. He terrifies the life out of me.'

They moved on, and their voices faded round the far side of the house.

Dani sat still on his bed, staring at the wall, trying not to think.

At last he heard the familiar rattle of the metal gates, and Ato Paulos's firm tread as he strode into the house. Dani braced himself, hoping that his father would walk past his door and on down the corridor to his room, or that Meseret would come running out to hug him, and distract his attention. But the footsteps stopped, the handle of his door turned, and Ato Paulos marched into his room.

He stood looking down at Dani, the usual frown on his face.

'Well, and what do you expect me to do with you?'

His voice was softer than usual. He sounded genuinely puzzled.

'I don't know, Father,' Dani said, trying to fill the silence.

'I've tried everything I can think of. Threats, bribes, punishments. Nothing works.'

Dani looked sightlessly at the floor.

'It's impossible to deal with you here,' Ato Paulos went on, looking with irritation at the mess on Dani's desk, and the clutter of old toys and drawings beside his bed. 'It's too soft. Too easy. There really is no alternative.'

A cold feeling was settling in Dani's stomach.

'No alternative to what, Father?'

'I called Feisal today,' Ato Paulos said. His eyes didn't meet Dani's. He was staring at a stain on the wooden floor. 'He's coming to fetch you tomorrow.'

Dani felt the blood drain from his face.

'No, Father! You said, only if I failed the exams! The results aren't even out yet!'

His father reached down into the pocket of his jacket and pulled out a slip of paper.

'They came today. You scraped through a couple, did well in Amharic, I grant you, but the rest – hopeless. Appalling!'

For once his voice was sad rather than angry. It pierced Dani like a bayonet.

'I'll try again. They'll let me resit them. I promise, I'll work harder, I'll—'

'No.' Ato Paulos stood up. 'I've been too soft for too long. When I make a threat, I carry it out. I've already written to the school, withdrawing you. A year of proper discipline, with Feisal . . .'

'A *year*?'

'I'll visit you from time to time. You'll be looked after. But there'll be no more nonsense. No mooning about daydreaming, making up silly stories. A proper regime of work.'

'I can't, Father. Please don't send me away. I *can't*.' Dani's voice was barely audible.

His father came over to the bed, dropped a hand on his shoulder, and shook it lightly.

'It won't be that bad. There's no need to make a fuss about it. Feisal's strict, but he's fair, and he'll make a man of you. Please believe me, Dani, I didn't want to do this, but I really think it's for the best. You'll thank me one day.'

Dani hardly noticed him leave. He jumped off his bed and stood in the middle of the room, his knees shaking and his head light with fright.

There were lions in the countryside all round Jigjiga, and ferocious bandits armed with Kalashnikovs. A boy at school had heard someone talk about it. It was blisteringly hot, and the food was awful, and there were scorpions in the houses.

But even the lions and bandits and scorpions would be bearable if he didn't have to be with Feisal. Feisal would bully and terrorise him. Feisal would mock him and hold him up to everyone else's ridicule. He would rather die than live with Feisal. He would rather run away.

Run away! That's what I'll do! he thought. I'll go to Auntie Tsehai. No, Father would find out and make her send me back. I'll find someone else to stay with. Not Ato Mesfin. He'd say I had to go home. Someone in my class at school. Someone from my old school. Anyone. That nice waiter at the Hilton. Someone will take me in. It would only be for a while, till Mamma comes home.

He swallowed, trying not to think about what would happen if she never came back at all.

An idea suddenly came to him.

Giorgis! That quiet boy in my primary school. We used to do really nice things together. And he doesn't live with his parents, just with his uncle. An uncle wouldn't bother about me, or get in touch with Father. I went to Giorgis's house once. I can sort of remember where it is. That's it! I'll go to Giorgis's!

He was pulling things out of drawers already, making a pile on his bed.

I'll need clothes and stuff, and some spare shoes, and the money Mamma gave me. I've got fifty birr at least.

The door behind him opened suddenly, making him jump.

'What are you doing?' Ato Paulos said.

'Packing,' Dani said nervously.

A rare smile crossed Ato Paulos's face.

'Good,' he said, trying to hide his surprise. 'Good boy.' He hesitated. 'I have to go to the office now. Feisal's arriving tonight. I'll see you both off in the morning.'

He was about to close the door.

'Father,' Dani said urgently.

'Yes?'

'About Mamma. Is she going to – be all right?'

Ato Paulos frowned.

'Yes, yes of course she is. That's why I've sent her off to London.'

'When's she coming home?'

'As soon as she's well enough. Not long. I don't know.'

He went out and closed the door.

He doesn't believe that, thought Dani. He knows she's going to die. He just won't say so.

He heard his father leave and the gates clang shut behind him. His heart was pounding and his palms were sweating.

If I'm going to go, he thought, I've got to go now, before he gets home and Feisal arrives.

He pulled an old sports bag off the top of the cupboard in the corner of his room and stuffed his clothes into it, then picked up his blue baseball cap and rammed it on to his head. He looked around one last time, and his eye fell on his desk. Should he leave a note? Try to explain? But what was there to say?

He opened the door a crack and looked out. Meseret had wandered round to the back of the house in search of Zeni. He could hear her funny little voice raised in excitement as she tried to explain something. He wanted suddenly to go after her, to pick her up and give her a cuddle. Instead, he turned the other way, towards the front door.

It was open. In the harsh sunlight outside, he could see the little kiosk where Negussie slept beside the big gates. He could tell it was empty. Negussie must have gone round to the kitchen too, or perhaps he was sleeping under the big tree at the side of the house, making the most of his employers' absence.

This was his chance then. It was now or never.

Dani stood for a long moment, hesitating painfully, breathing in the familiar smells of home, the faint whiff of his mother's perfume, the sharpness of onions frying in the kitchen, the slight mustiness of the old brown rugs. Then he crept down the front steps, and, his bag bumping clumsily against his knees, raced across to the gates. He opened them as quietly as he could and was suddenly outside in the lane, alone.

Milk dribbling into his bruised mouth made Mamo choke. He opened his eyes. The face bending over him seemed a long way away, then very near, then it broke up into shimmering fragments. He closed his eyes again.

He heard Yohannes say, 'There's still some of that stuff in his mouth, Father, look.'

Someone pulled down his lower jaw and he felt a finger hook round the last of the leaves that were clinging to his tongue. Then a man's voice, which was somehow familiar, said, 'Lift his head. Gently. We must get more milk inside him.'

He didn't choke this time. He let the warm fluid trickle into his mouth, and swallowed.

'Good,' the man said. 'Help me lift him on to my back, Yohannes.'

As they moved him, Mamo fainted again.

When he opened his eyes, he was lying on a cowskin in a strange house. Light from the setting sun shone through the open door, hurting his eyes. A woman was squatting near the fire that burned cheerfully in the middle of the floor, with a couple of small children near her feet.

From outside he could hear a furious voice.

'You've no right. He's mine. Good money I paid for him, and all he's done is lose me my best cow.'

It was the farmer. A shiver ran through Mamo. He shrank back from the light against the curved wall of the round house. The movement sent a wave of nausea through his stomach. He closed his eyes again and lay still.

'I know, neighbour. I'm sorry.' Yohannes's father was speaking softly, soothingly, trying to calm the farmer down. 'But what could I do? I thought the boy was going to die. He still might.'

'Eating poisonous leaves! I don't believe it.' The farmer spat angrily. 'I'm warning you, he's a crafty one. You're so soft you'd believe anything of anybody. He's just trying to get sympathy and escape his punishment.'

'I thought you'd punished him already,' Yohannes's father said drily. 'His face is so battered he can barely see out of his eyes. It'll be a while before he can walk again, even when he's flushed out the poison.'

The farmer growled out something which Mamo couldn't hear.

'I tell you what,' Yohannes's father said pleasantly. 'Let him stay with me till he's on the mend. I owe you a favour, after you brought that barley back from the market for me last month. As soon as he's on his feet and can work again, I'll send him back to you.'

'On his feet?' exploded the farmer. 'He'll be on his feet in the morning if he knows what's good for him.'

'Oh, I don't think so,' Yohannes's father said. 'Come and look at him yourself.'

Mamo heard their feet cross the beaten earth floor towards him. He lay still, his eyes closed, too weak and shaky to dare to open them, not sure if he would faint again.

The farmer drew in his breath.

'Well, what would you have done?' he said defensively. 'He destroyed my best cow. He's useless, I tell you. I wish I'd never set eyes on him.'

'Then leave him here,' Yohannes's father said. Their voices were retreating as they went outside again. 'I'll look after him.'

Mamo felt a rustle of clothes beside him and managed to look up. The woman had come over to him. She had pulled a low stool across and was sitting beside his cowskin mat, holding a glass of milk out to him.

'Drink it,' she said kindly. 'It'll stop the poison harming you. Sip it. Slowly does it. I'll hold your head up if you like. That's better. You silly boy, what did you do such a thing for?'

Something seemed to give way inside Mamo. Something loosened. Tears edged through between his swollen eyelids and ran down beside his ears. He turned his head away from her and sobs racked his chest.

For the next few days, he hovered between sleep and wakefulness, between despair and a faint rebirth of hope. At first he could barely move. Convulsions of shivering and bouts of sickness would overcome him, and each painful bruise protested every time he stirred.

But suddenly, on the third day, he felt life flow back into him, a new life, different from the old one, as if he really had died and come back to earth again as another person, and he was overcome by a strange euphoria, as if he had entered an enchanted world of happiness.

For the first time in his life he felt surrounded by love. Yohannes's mother fed him and washed his cuts. She talked to him gently, asking him about his mother and Tiggist. When she went to fetch water, she left him to mind the babies, to call out to them if they went too near the fire, and when she came back she smiled and thanked him.

The best time was in the evening, when Yohannes, full of the day's events, had brought the cattle home, and his father had come in from his day's work. The family would sit round the fire and eat while the little ones nodded sleepily, and then they'd talk, mulling over the events of the day, telling stories, discussing the next visit to the market. And Mamo, when he was able to sit up, would be drawn into the circle. He'd sit with them, like a guest, eating what they ate, laughing when they laughed. His eyes would go from one face to the next, watching, almost breathless with love, as the firelight flickered on their coppery skin.

On the twelfth evening, as the fire died down and Yohannes's mother stood up and yawned, ready to unroll the bed mats and lie down to sleep, Yohannes's father came over to Mamo and sat down beside him. He put a hand on Mamo's knee.

'You are well now,' he said.

A cold hand seemed to tighten round Mamo's heart. He said nothing.

'Tomorrow you must go back.'

Mamo squeezed his eyes shut, as if to keep out what the man was saying.

'I know it's hard for you, but you can't stay here any longer.'

'I can't go! Please keep me here, with you!'

Mamo's sharp cry made Yohannes and his mother look round. Then they turned away again.

'You know I can't do that.' The man hesitated. 'Try to understand your master. He lost his eldest son last year. Did you know that?'

Mamo shook his head.

'The boy was only a year older than you, and a great help to his father. His death made him feel bitter. He's had bad luck since then, too – flooded fields, a fire in his grainstore – he does his best.'

'They'll kill me if I go back,' Mamo said hoarsely. 'They hate me. Especially Tesfaye.'

'Tesfaye misses his brother. He can't bear to see another boy in his place.'

Mamo clenched his fists.

'Please,' he said. 'Please.'

Yohannes's father picked up the end of Mamo's *shamma* and tucked it round his shoulders.

'Go to sleep,' he said. 'You'll feel better about it in the morning.'

But in the morning, Mamo woke with a lump as heavy as a stone in his chest. He couldn't even eat the breakfast he was offered. Choked with tears, he muttered a few incoherent words of thanks, and walked stiffly away out of the compound, feeling more miserable with every step he took.

He saw the farmer's cattle straggling down the hill towards the river from a long way away, and recognised Tesfaye, who was herding them. His pulse quickening with fear and anger, he made himself walk on.

They met where the lane from the homestead joined the broader path at the bottom of the hill. Mamo, braced for angry words, for insults and flying stones, was taken aback by the nervous, almost guilty look in Tesfaye's eyes.

'Are you all right now, then?' he said, looking away.

'Yes.'

'Good. Then I'll get off to school. Here, take my stick if you like.'

He handed his stick almost politely to Mamo and ran back home to put on his uniform and fetch his books.

The day was not unbearable. Falling into the old routine with Hailu and Yohannes, Mamo could put out of his mind, for quite long periods of time, the dread of returning to the farmer and the hated compound of his master. When the shadows began to lengthen, he lingered by the stream for as long as possible, knowing that there would be only hostile faces and the most meagre supper waiting for him when he'd driven the cattle home.

At last, he could put it off no longer. He almost missed the difficult black cow, who had always veered off the path, as he drove the others round the corner of the lane. He looked up when he came to the last stretch, and his heart gave a painful thump as he saw that the farmer was standing by the gate of the compound, his arms draped over the stick across his shoulders, waiting for him.

He reached the top and shepherded the cows inside, then cried out as the man's finger and thumb caught his ear in a vicious grip, and yanked him down to his knees.

'Any more trouble from you, one more thing goes wrong, and I'll kill you, do you hear? And there'll be no more whining off to the neighbours, making a fool of me. Stay away from them or you'll really know what it feels like.'

He let go of Mamo's ear, went into the house and shut the door, leaving Mamo outside in the gathering cold and darkness.

The door opened a few times during the evening. Once or twice Tesfaye came out. He seemed about to speak to Mamo, but never did. The girl brought him a corn cob for his supper, and a glass of water. The woman went round behind the house to fetch something and went back inside without speaking to him.

Huddled in his *shamma* under the eaves of the cowshed, Mamo saw himself suddenly as if from the outside, a pathetic figure, lonely, in a place he hated, with people who despised him.

Anything, any place in the world is better than this, he thought, so why do I stay?

The question came back, twice, three times, and suddenly the answer was there.

I won't stay. I'll go away.

He felt light-headed with excitement. Before, he'd been afraid of running in case, out there in the unknown countryside, he might starve to death before he could find the way home to Addis Ababa. He wasn't afraid of death any more. Death was a simple thing, just a separation of the soul from the body. It wouldn't matter if he died.

I'll go tonight, he thought. Now.

He was about to jump to his feet and run out of the compound, but caution held him back. The farmer would come after him. He'd paid out money. He wouldn't want to lose his investment.

He forced himself to sit and wait until the intermittent conversation in the house stopped, then he crept towards the compound gate and opened it.

'Who's there? What are you doing?' the farmer called out sharply from inside the house.

Mamo's blood seemed to curdle.

'Nothing. Going for a pee,' he called back.

He waited for a few moments, and shut the gate again. Then he went to the cowshed and opened and shut the door. The farmer would think he'd gone inside to bed.

He stood motionless for ten long minutes, until he heard loud, regular snores coming from the house, then, much more cautiously, he opened the compound gate and slipped outside.

And then he was off, running as if a demon was after him, down the lane and away. As he ran he tried to pick out, in the light of the rising moon, the long pale track that would take him from this hated place to the road, which in its turn would lead to Addis Ababa.

Chapter 6

Dani was conscious, as he hurried away from the familiar gates of his home compound, that people were noticing him.

'Where are you going?' the woman in the little kiosk shop a few metres down the road called out to him. 'Don't you want any sweets today?'

He'd run to her shop hundreds of times, ever since he could remember, to buy a few cents worth of sweets, while Negussie stood by the compound gates watching out for him.

'Not today. In a hurry,' he called back, breaking into an awkward trot.

A group of shoe-shine boys were sitting on the corner where his street joined the main road.

'Hey!' one of them shouted. 'Let's do your shoes.'

'You can't polish these,' Dani called back, smiling nervously. 'They're trainers.'

'Then give us a birr.'

They started coming towards him. He hadn't thought out which way he should go, left or right, but to get rid of them he turned left.

Dani had never been out alone in the city before. Ibrahim had always taken him to school in his taxi, and when he'd gone out with his parents, to visit relatives or family friends, or gone with Mamma, when she was well enough, to the pool, or to the cafés and shops in the centre of town, they'd been in the family car. He hadn't realised how long it would take to walk to the next busy road junction. He'd never noticed before how rough the verges of the road were, with sharp stones and potholes to trip him up. He wished he hadn't stuffed so many useless clothes in his bag. The weight was making his back ache.

It's only till I get to Giorgis's house, he told himself.

Three huge worries were nagging at him. The first was the fear that his father would see him, would suddenly appear out of nowhere, emerge from a building and snatch at his arm, or sweep up alongside him in the car, and drag him into it. He kept a lookout all the time, his eyes scanning the road ahead, turning his head constantly to look over his shoulder.

The second thing was that he couldn't quite remember the way to Giorgis's place. He'd only been there a couple of times, ages ago, and the area where Giorgis lived was a maze of back alleys and side turnings.

He shut his mind to the third thing. He wouldn't think about what he'd actually say to Giorgis and his uncle until he got there. He wouldn't worry, either, about Giorgis not remembering him, after so long.

At last he reached the road junction. He put his bag down and wiped the sweat off his forehead with his sleeve. He was hot and very, very thirsty.

He turned into a busy shopping street, walking more slowly now. He and Mamma had often come here. Their favourite café was just past the next tall building. Mamma would usually order coffee, and he'd have a Coke and a big piece of vanilla cake.

He pulled the brim of his cap down over his face. It was risky here. He might easily bump into someone from school, or one of Father's colleagues or Mamma's friends, but it was the only route towards Giorgis's part of town that he knew. He would just have to keep a sharp lookout, and dive in through a doorway if he recognised anyone.

He passed the pastry shop where he and Mamma had often stopped for a drink and a snack on one of their shopping expeditions. He couldn't help pausing for a moment and looking in at the laden counter, covered with his favourite cakes and biscuits. His mouth watered, but he knew it would be madness to go inside. All the waiters knew him.

The thought of food made his mouth water. He was really hungry. They must have had lunch at home hours ago. Come to think of it, they must have noticed by now that he'd gone. Zeni would have hunted for him everywhere. She'd probably phoned Father at work. They'd have found that his clothes and his bag were missing. They'd have realised he'd run away.

A small gleam of pleasure, shining through his worry, made him almost smile. They'd be really anxious. Father might even be feeling sorry. Perhaps, if he went home, Father would realise he'd been cruel, change his mind, and send Feisal back to Jigjiga on his own.

The gleam faded. Father wouldn't be sorry. He'd be furious, in a terrible rage. There was no going back now.

He hurried on.

At the end of the street he stood uncertainly, not sure which way to go. He didn't see the car slowing down on the other side of the street, but he suddenly heard a familiar woman's voice.

'Hey, aren't you Dani? How's your mother? Is it true she's gone to England?'

It was Mrs Sara, one of Mamma's friends.

Panic struck him. Without looking round, he took off into the nearest narrow alley, that ran steeply down the hill away from the road. He was running as fast as his plump legs and heavy bag would let him.

A stitch in his side slowed him down and he stopped, panting for breath. He looked back up the alley, half expecting to see a crowd of angry people pursuing him, but the alley was empty except for a small child, who was holding a string attached at the other end to a goat, and who hadn't seemed to notice him.

What now? What next? he thought, taking off his cap to wipe away the sweat that was sprouting from his forehead.

He turned round and began to plod up the hill again, but stopped after a few steps.

It would be crazy to go back up there. He'd been lucky to get away from Mrs Sara, but he'd be bound to run into someone else he knew. His best option was to keep going on down the hill, and hope that the alley came out somewhere recognisable.

It was much further down the hill than he'd expected, and the alley took so many twists and turns that he was soon hopelessly confused, but he stepped out at last on to a big main road and knew, after looking up and down it a couple of times, more or less where he was.

His heart sank. He was still miles and miles from the area where he thought Giorgis lived, and not very far from home. And he was exhausted already. He'd never walked so far or carried anything so heavy in his whole life. He was famished too, and terribly thirsty.

I must eat something, he thought. I've got to keep my strength up.

There was a little bar on the other side of the road. It was quite unlike the smart pastry shop up the hill, with its mirrored walls and Formica-topped tables, its smiling waiters and bubbling coffee machine. This was no more than a shack, a dark, dingy little place, with a slatternly woman standing outside.

Hesitantly, feeling horribly out of place, Dani crossed the road and went inside. There were a few rough stools set about on an uneven mud floor around a couple of rickety tables. A man was eating some coarse-looking *injera*, taking swigs of some cloudy liquid from a grimy glass. A couple of ragged children stood watching him, flies clustering round their eyes.

Dani's stomach rose. He muttered something to the woman and hurried outside, then walked away fast, ignoring his developing blisters.

The road was wider here. He saw familiar buildings ahead – the big central bank building, the national theatre, some old hotels. He'd passed through here often, in the car.

He was walking along the front of the Ethiopia Hotel, and his footsteps began to drag. What had Mamma always said?

'The old Ethiopia? But it's so *dowdy*. No one goes there any more, not since the new Sheraton opened.'

He'd be safe in here, then, from meeting any of her friends. There'd be a restaurant, or a bar at least, where he could get a nice drink and something to eat. He could say his mother had told him to meet her here, but to order something and start eating if she was late.

The thought of sitting down to a decent meal and drinking some ice-cold Coke drove everything else out of his mind as he walked up the shallow steps into the dim interior.

No one seemed to notice him. He saw the bar area and turned into it, chose a seat in the far corner where his back would be to the door, and sat down gratefully against the comfortable padded upholstery.

A waiter appeared beside him at once.

'Yeah, I'm waiting for my mum,' Dani said, as casually as he could. 'She said to go ahead and eat.' He was eagerly scanning the menu as he spoke. 'I'll have a club sandwich, and French fries and a big Coke. And some ice cream afterwards.'

The food was delicious. He relished every mouthful, feeling almost cheerful as he ate it. He'd never done anything like this before, never gone to a hotel and bought himself a meal. It made him feel grown-up.

But when the bill came, he had a nasty shock. It used up almost half his supply of money. He pulled the notes out of his pocket and put them down reluctantly on the little tray the waiter was holding out.

'What's happened to your mother, then?' the waiter said. 'She didn't come.'

Dani nearly said, 'No, she's in England,' but he stopped himself just in time.

He sat slumped back in the chair for a long time, not wanting to go outside and face the streets again, resting his tired legs and sore feet, and as the minutes passed, a horrible realisation crept up on him.

He couldn't possibly go to Giorgis's house and ask to be taken in. However had he imagined, for one moment, that he could? He hadn't seen Giorgis for years and years. Giorgis might not even recognise him. And even if he found the house again, which most probably he wouldn't, why on earth would Giorgis's uncle welcome him and let him stay? He'd do what every other grown-up would do – phone Ato Paulos, and get him to come and take Dani home.

What am I going to do then? Dani thought. What on earth am I going to do?

The waiters were beginning to give him funny looks. They were talking to the maitre d', who was looking over towards him. There was nothing for it. He'd have to go.

He stood up, his heart beating fast, suddenly desperate to stay in the comfortable, orderly shelter of the hotel, but a moment later the glass doors had swished shut behind him, and he was outside on the pavement.

He looked up and down the street, standing irresolutely, not knowing which way to turn.

It was good luck for Mamo that the moon was nearly full. It shone with such clear brilliance that it cast deep shadows on the ground and hurt his eyes when he looked at it. By its light he could pick out the track ahead quite easily.

He ran for a long time, until his legs ached and his head began to spin, then he slowed down to a fast walk, breaking into a trot whenever he had gathered enough breath.

His great fear was that he wouldn't find the way.

It was easy at first. There was only one path, which was clearly marked, the earth beaten bare and hard by the constant passage of human feet and animal hooves, and he began to feel confident. He allowed himself to daydream.

He'd find his way home easily, once he was back in Addis. If Tiggist had given up the house, she'd probably be at Mrs Faridah's shop, and if she wasn't there, Mrs Hannah would know where she'd gone. Even if she'd got a live-in job somewhere, she'd still make sure he had a place to stay and help him to get started on something.

Everything would be just fine, as soon as he was back there, in Addis. He'd be able to listen to music outside the shop again, and see some of the boys he'd known on the street corner. He grinned as he thought of the noise and life he'd missed so much, the passing cars and trucks, the buses full of people, the glimpses of TV through the windows of bars, the constant buzz and news and hum.

He pulled himself up with a start. The track had dwindled to almost nothing. And straight ahead, looming up out of the hillside, was a cluster of thatched houses. A sudden furious barking made him jump with fright. He must have wandered off the path, towards a homestead, and the dogs had got wind of him.

Angry with himself for being careless, he ran back down the way he'd come, but a cloud had come over the moon, and he couldn't pick out the path more than a few metres ahead.

He shivered. How long had he been gone? How many hours were left till dawn, when he would be missed? The farmer would set out after him at once. He'd ride the donkey, whipping it mercilessly to make it trot. He'd travel fast, and catch up with Mamo before he could reach the road.

Blindly, Mamo began to run. Several times he came to a dead end and had to double back, feeling his way, his bare feet instinctively seeking out the worn smoothness of the path.

He had a horrible feeling, a nightmarish feeling, that he was trapped in a kind of maze, doomed to run around in circles while the night wore away, and that when the day came he'd be dead with exhaustion, or out in the open, easily caught, and hauled back to misery.

He was almost ready to give up and flop down to the ground when the moon came out again. Floating serene and impersonal across the sky, it lit the whole vast landscape. And there, far away but still visible, sliding across the countryside like a bright white stream, was the tarmac road.

A sob of gratitude rose in Mamo's throat and he began to run again, blundering wildly through fields of standing grain, forcing his way, oblivious to the scratches, through thorn hedges, skirting round farmsteads, jumping over gulleys and ditches, frantic with worry in case the moon should go in again and leave him in the dark.

He was no more than half a kilometre away from the road's silver ribbon when he heard the terrifying *whoop! whoop!* of a hyena. His body shrivelled with fright. The hyena sounded as if it was straight ahead, between him and his goal.

Instinct made him want to turn and run back away from danger, but he made himself go on. He hadn't come this far, he hadn't dared everything, only to turn back now. He pulled a thick stick out of a nearby hedge, then bent down and picked up some heavy stones. If the hyenas came for him he'd be ready to fight them off.

All the horrible stories he'd ever heard about hyenas rushed into his mind. They'd snatch a limb off you, biting it clean through. They'd go for your belly, disembowelling you with one snap of their massive jaws. They'd follow and follow you, wearing you down, till you were too weak to fight them off.

But they're cowards, too, Hailu had said boastfully. I know how to scare a hyena. My uncle told me. You wave a stick at them and throw stones. They just run away.

The road was nearer now, but so was the whooping sound. Mamo could even fancy he saw their ugly, limping forms, slipping from shadow to shadow, waiting for him.

He took a firmer grip on his stick, and whirling it round his head, he ran on with all his might. The hyenas seemed to melt away and their howling stopped.

When eventually he stumbled out of the last field, felt the smooth cold tarmac under his feet and breathed in the half-forgotten smell of oily tar, an intense feeling of joy exploded in Mamo's mind.

It lasted no more than a few minutes. The road stretched ahead, endlessly long and completely empty. It was still the dead of night, and only the rustling of leaves in the cold wind disturbed the silence. No vehicles would venture out until just before dawn, and even when they did, who would stop for him, a ragged boy?

What would happen if he couldn't get a lift? By mid-morning the farmer would have reached the road and started alerting people. They'd be on the lookout for him.

No one can force me to go back, he told himself. He's got no rights over me, not really. But he wasn't sure if that was true. He felt the malign influence of the farmer spreading across the countryside like a net. It would trap him, as sure as anything, if he didn't get away soon.

I'll have to start walking, he thought. I'll have to walk all the way to Addis.

He set off along the road, but after a few paces he stopped. Which direction was Addis anyway? And which side of him was the small town where Merga and he had got off the bus? If he ran slap into that he'd be done for.

Anyway, his strength, still not fully recovered, was giving out. He'd eaten virtually nothing yesterday and had been running and walking all night.

Discouraged, he squatted down on the grass verge and dropped his head on to his knees.

It was all for nothing, he thought. I'll never get away. They'll take me back, I know they will.

He remembered the poisonous bush.

I'll eat it again if I end up back there, he told himself, only I'll make sure it works next time.

But he knew he wouldn't. He'd been given a new life last time and he wouldn't be able to throw it away again.

He lifted his head and listened. At least the hyenas seemed to have given up on him. Their blood-curdling calls were fading into the distance.

He sat for a long time, feeling worse and worse. Hunger, thirst and exhaustion were making him weak, and the cold wind was biting into him through his thin rags. Strange thoughts flitted through his mind, confusing him. The moon had set now and it was completely dark.

He almost didn't notice the sound of a truck approaching. Its roar merged with the strange half dream playing in his head. He was looking at a great rushing river, and if he could just step into the boat bobbing around in the middle of it, it would carry him somewhere beautiful where his own forgotten father, who looked strangely like Yohannes's, was waiting for him with his arms held open.

The truck's headlights, stabbing through the dark, roused him. Almost too late, he jumped up and ran out into the glare, shouting at the top of his voice. The truck veered sideways and the driver angrily sounded his horn, sending a long blast echoing through the night. And then it was past him and its red tail lights were growing smaller and smaller, mocking him, like a pair of evil eyes.

Mamo felt furiously angry. Without knowing what he was doing, he began to run after it, yelling, 'No! Come back! Take me!'

He didn't see the stone that tripped him up. It sent him flying and he landed with a sickening crash, grazing the skin off his hands and feet, tearing another hole in his thin ragged shirt and cutting a slash down his cheek. He lay half stunned for a while, then cautiously sat up. Blood was trickling down his face and now it was mixed with tears. He didn't try to stop them coming. He sat on the road and let despair wash over him, not even noticing that he was shivering with cold.

The second truck came as the first hint of grey was spreading along the horizon. Mamo didn't bother to get off the side of the road. He sat still and did no more than raise a pleading hand. The truck saw him nearly too late, and had to swerve to avoid him. He looked up and saw the vague outline of the driver gesticulating angrily to him, and then it too was past.

Two more trucks came by, then an early bus appeared in the distance, coming up very fast, its orange-and-gold livery gleaming dully in the first faint light of day. Scared, Mamo crawled off the road and hid from it behind a tree. They couldn't possibly be searching for him yet, and anyway no one would recognise him, but supposing someone did? Supposing someone who knew the farmer caught sight of him, and made the bus stop, and dragged him away?

The sky had slowly been turning from grey to blue while the band of pink on the horizon expanded and deepened. Blazing stripes appeared over the distant hills, and suddenly the great red rim of the sun came up. Its rays struck Mamo's back and he realised how cold he'd been. He turned gratefully towards it.

The sun seemed to warm his mind too. A new determination took hold of him. He would force the next truck to stop. He wouldn't let it go without him. Somehow or other, he'd make sure he was on it.

He heard it while it was still a long way off, when its gears were grinding up a distant hill, and he gathered himself, not sure what to do, waiting for inspiration. Then it came into sight, lumbering slowly under its heavy weight down the road towards him. The sun was glancing off its windscreen so that he couldn't see the driver's face.

In a moment it would be past him, like the others.

Without thinking of the danger, driven by desperation, Mamo ran right out into the path of the huge machine and stood in the middle of the road with his arms outstretched.

The truck's brakes squealed but its massive weight carried it on, the tyres skidding on the tarmac. Mamo stood still, watching the wall of white metal and sparkling glass roar down upon him. Mesmerised, he couldn't have moved, even if he'd wanted to. The blood was pounding through his heart, in his ears, round his head.

The truck shuddered to a halt at last, its hot radiator inches from Mamo's chest, but Mamo didn't see it. He had fainted.

He came to a moment later. The driver had climbed out of his cab and was staring down at him, his full lips tight with anger, a furious frown creasing his pitted forehead.

'You idiot! You fool! What the hell are you doing? I nearly killed you!'

Mamo opened his eyes and stared up at him woozily.

'Please,' he said, 'take me to Addis.'

The driver was looking at him more closely now, taking in the bloody smears on his cheeks, the lacerations on his hands, and the old bruises that still showed through on his face and arms.

'How did you get into this mess? What happened to you?'

Mamo licked his parched lips.

'I've got to get away from here. Please, if you're going to Addis, take me with you.'

Understanding softened the man's face.

'Running away, are you? All right. Can you stand up? You'd better come with me. Can't have you jumping out on any more poor truck drivers. I nearly died of fright back there.'

Mamo tried to stand up, but his head felt too light and his legs buckled under him. The driver bent down and hauled him to his feet.

'You don't have a fever, do you? I don't want any infections in my cab.'

Mamo managed to shake his head.

'No,' he whispered. 'Just hungry. Nothing to eat or drink. Been running all night.'

The driver pushed him up into the cab and Mamo sank back against the padded passenger seat.

I'm in a dream, he thought. This isn't really happening.

He closed his eyes. The driver put the truck into gear and it groaned into life.

It was only the second time in Mamo's life that he'd been in a moving vehicle, but in the oddest way he felt as if he'd come home. A delicious ease relaxed his whole body, and he slipped gratefully into sleep.

He woke with a start. Someone was shaking his shoulder, and the noise of the engine had stopped.

'What . . .?' he said, struggling to sit upright, suddenly scared. 'Where . . .?'

'It's all right.' The driver was smiling at him. 'It's breakfast time, that's all. Come on, or aren't you hungry, after all?'

Mamo half fell out of the high cab and walked groggily after the driver towards a busy bar. Its outside wall was painted scarlet, and the mortar between the breeze blocks was smartly picked out in white. He stopped in the doorway, feeling awkward. A haughty girl came up to him.

'What do you want? They don't let beggars in here. Hop it.'

'He's with me,' the driver called across to her. 'What are you waiting for, son? Come and sit down.'

Mamo had never been served in a bar before. He had hung around the place where his mother had worked, looking in through the window or running odd errands for the manager, but the thought of sitting at a table like a proper customer made him feel really weird. He was horribly conscious of his filthy ragged clothes, his bare feet and his bloodstained face.

'The tap's out the back,' the driver said. 'Go and clean yourself up.'

There was a bar of soap balanced behind the tap on the water drum in the backyard. Mamo washed his hands and face, relishing its smell. Even if only a few bits of him were clean, he still felt more human.

The bar was crowded with truckers and early travellers, but the food had already arrived at the driver's table. There was a plate piled high with crusty white bread, a dish of six or seven fried eggs and saucers of butter and honey. Coils of steam rose from two tall glasses of milky coffee, with a thick layer of sugar settled at the bottom.

Mamo sat down and stared at the food. Surely the man wasn't going to let him eat? Surely this wasn't for him?

But the driver was smiling at him.

'Well?' he said. 'I thought you were hungry.'

He took a piece of bread, dunked it in the brilliant orange egg yolk and held it up to Mamo's face. Like a child, Mamo opened his mouth.

After that first heavenly mouthful, Mamo's hunger almost overwhelmed him. He tried to hold back, tried not to stuff the food in, tried to leave a fair share for the driver, but he couldn't help himself. He ate voraciously, feeling for every last crumb when the plate was empty, and falling on the second plateful of bread, which the driver had laughingly ordered, as hungrily as if it was the first.

Replete at last, he drained the final drops of sugar-thickened coffee from his glass, put it down, and smiled at the driver with adoration in his eyes.

'You are my saviour,' he said.

The driver didn't hear him. He was clapping his hands for the bill.

'On your feet,' he said, turning back to Mamo. 'We've got a long way to go.'

It was amazing, thought Mamo, how different the world seemed by day, when you were full of breakfast and warmed by the sun. Looking out of the window at the bright green of the fields and the brilliantly coloured dresses of the women, who were walking to market along the side of the road, he could hardly remember how terrible the night had been, how lonely and cold, and frightening, and full of despair.

'Who are you, then?' the driver said, breaking in on his thoughts. 'Tell me about yourself. I don't even know your name.'

'It's Mamo, but there's nothing to tell,' Mamo said shyly. He was awed by the magnificence and generosity of his rescuer.

'Come on. Not everyone ends up like you, thin as a leaf, half starved, covered in blood, jumping out in front of trucks.'

It took a while for Mamo to get started, but slowly he found his voice. He told the story of everything that had happened to him, and it seemed to him almost as if it had happened to someone else.

'And then I reached the road,' he said at last, 'and no one would stop, and I was desperate, and then you did, and you saved me.'

The driver didn't say anything, and looking up at him Mamo saw the sun glinting on drops of water on his cheeks.

'Did I say something wrong?' he said anxiously. 'Why are you crying?'

The driver swallowed. His hands were gripping the steering wheel so hard that his knuckles stood out pale.

'You didn't say anything wrong. I know your story. Bad things happened to me when I was young. I had to run away too.'

He didn't say anything else, and he asked no more questions. Tiredness overcame Mamo again. His head lolled back against the seat and his eyes closed of their own accord.

Chapter 7

It had taken Tiggist a few weeks to settle down in Awassa. Everything was really strange here. The town was stretched out along the shore of a huge lake, with sinister black storks nesting in the enormous trees by the water's edge. The main street was a wide boulevard which ran up the hill away from the lake, and had all kinds of elegant shops and cafés. People came down from Addis Ababa to have their holidays here. They strolled around in nice clothes, relaxing.

She'd thought, when they'd rushed down here in such a panic, that Mr Hamid was just about to die, but he seemed to have turned the corner, for the time being, anyway. He was still very ill though. The problem didn't seem to be his eye, like the watchman back at the shop had said. It was something no one wanted to talk about.

'He's got a bad chest,' Mrs Faridah answered awkwardly, when people asked her how he was. 'He's never got over his war injuries.'

Tiggist hardly ever saw Mr Hamid. He lay in a darkened room and when she peeped in all she could see was the brightness of his eyes, glittering like diamonds in his skull-like head, and one skeletally thin hand which plucked at the sheet. She heard him coughing often.

'Nothing to do with the war, whatever she says,' she overheard one of the neighbours whisper. 'Aids, that's what it is.'

Mrs Faridah was so busy looking after her husband that Tiggist had Yasmin more or less to herself. There was no shop to work in here, but the house (a very nice one on the edge of town) had to be kept clean and the cooking had to be done. There was a servant, a girl called Salma, who was supposed to do all that.

Salma was friendly, a bouncy, plump girl with strong arms and a big voice, and Tiggist didn't mind helping her out. She liked it. The two of them shared a room and spent nearly all their time together. Salma was a good cook. Her *injera* was fine and smooth and her stews were delicious, with rich, red gravy and plenty of flavour. Watching her, Tiggist was learning how to cook really well herself. She'd never learned much from Ma.

One morning, as Tiggist and Salma were sitting on the back steps of the house, picking little stones out of a tray of lentils and talking and laughing as they usually did, Mrs Faridah marched outside, banging the door behind her. She went over to Yasmin, who was playing beside Tiggist's feet with a piece of string and a broken comb.

'Mamma's little girl,' she crooned, scooping her up and giving her a fierce hug.

Yasmin let out a yell and wriggled angrily, stretching her arms out towards Tiggist, who jumped up and went across to take her.

Mrs Faridah looked coldly at her over Yasmin's still furiously rocking head.

'You can leave her with me today, and I'll thank you not to interfere. Go up to the pharmacy at the top of the hill and find out what's happened to those medicines I ordered. And take off that ridiculous bracelet. Do you want people to think you're a tart?'

Shocked, Tiggist stammered, 'Yes, madam, I'll go as soon as we've finished the lentils.'

Mrs Faridah frowned.

'Are you deaf? I said go, and I meant now.'

Tiggist ran off, her face burning. What had she done? Why was Mrs Faridah cross with her? Was she going to get the sack?

She ran most of the way up the hill and all the way down again, and handed the medicines nervously to Mrs Faridah, still gasping for breath. Mrs Faridah took them without a word. Yasmin had calmed down, Tiggist was relieved to see, but as soon as she saw Tiggist she held out her arms to her and started wailing again.

'Now go round to the back and clean the toilet,' Mrs Faridah said. 'It's a disgrace.'

Tiggist's anxiety deepened. What had gone wrong?

She ran about all afternoon, doing one task after another, hearing in the background Yasmin's fretful crying. When night came at last she crept into the tiny room she shared with Salma and lay down beside her on the mat.

'What have I done? Why's she so cross with me? She was always lovely to me before.'

'Jealous, I reckon,' Salma answered with a yawn. 'Yasmin wants you all the time, and she can see we're friends and like having a good laugh and she has to spend all her time with that grumpy old bag of bones.'

'Yes, but that's not my fault.' Tiggist felt indignant. 'I can't help it if Yasmin likes me best. She's used to me, that's all, because Mrs Faridah leaves her with me all the time. What does she expect?'

'I know, but you'd better be careful.' Salma dropped her voice to a whisper. 'Mrs Faridah can be like that. She's fine to start with but she can go off you and get suspicious. Then you really have to watch your step.'

Tiggist hardly slept a wink that night. She had been feeling so secure and happy in her job that she'd stopped worrying about the future at all. She'd assumed that she'd go on working for Mrs Faridah for ever. Now the prospect of being alone and destitute again was looming up out of the future.

She mentally counted her little hoard of savings, carefully stowed in the tin box on a high shelf in the corner of the room. It hadn't grown much recently. She'd got into the habit of spending more freely, buying little presents for Yasmin and bits of cheap jewellery for herself. She'd have to stop all that. She'd have to save again in earnest, in case she suddenly found herself out of a job.

For the first time in ages she thought about Mamo. She'd got used to imagining that he was as happy and settled as she had been, but now she began to wonder. Well, there was nothing she could do for him. She had too many worries of her own.

The next morning she didn't put on her new earrings or her brightly coloured scarf, and took care when she was out in the courtyard to keep her voice down. There was no problem stopping herself from laughing. There was nothing to laugh about today.

As soon as she'd got Yasmin up and dressed, she picked her up and went to find Mrs Faridah.

'Yasmin wants you,' she said, her eyes cast down modestly. Then she bent down and whispered in the little girl's ear, 'Go to Mamma. She's got something nice for you.'

Her heart was beating fast. She was terribly afraid that Yasmin wouldn't go, would cling to her instead, and she let out her breath in relief when Yasmin stopped clutching her skirt and tottered across to her mother.

Mrs Faridah picked her up and smothered her face with kisses, but at that moment a groan came from Mr Hamid's room.

'Go back to Tiggist, darling,' Mrs Faridah said to Yasmin. 'Mamma will see you later,' and she gave Tiggist a small smile.

Phew, thought Tiggist. I'll have to watch out. I'll have to be really careful.

Instead of rushing off to the kitchen to find Salma, as she usually did, she went round to the other side of the house, set Yasmin to play with her old baby bonnet and sat a little way apart, anxious and watchful.

***

Dani stood outside the Ethiopia Hotel paralysed with indecision. He didn't notice the beggar until a scrawny hand plucked at his sleeve. He jumped and looked round. A little boy, barefoot and wearing the filthiest rags, was looking up at him with pleading eyes.

'No father, no mother,' he murmured, holding out his hand. 'Very hungry. Stomach zero.'

Dani flinched and stepped back, almost bumping into another beggar, an old blind man who had come round behind him.

'For the sake of Jesus,' the old man chanted, in a singsong voice, 'for the sake of Mary.'

'God bless you,' stammered Dani, using the formula his father always employed to fob beggars off. 'Thanks be to God.'

He picked up his bag and set off, walking away from the busy square down a long half-empty road. He felt as if a pit had opened out at his feet, a terrifyingly dizzy drop, and that he might fall over the edge and be catapulted down to nothing.

'I wouldn't ever beg,' he muttered out loud. 'I couldn't. I'd rather die.'

He walked for a long time, his mind in turmoil, not noticing where he was going, until the pain of his blisters and the tiredness in his legs were so bad that he couldn't ignore them any longer.

Where am I going? he thought. I can't walk for ever.

He looked round. It was late afternoon now and the sun was dipping low behind one of Addis Ababa's tree-covered hills. A cool breeze had sprung up. The long unfamiliar road curved uphill past a high wall behind which tall old trees were growing. A few people were passing by, walking purposefully home from work, intent on the promise of supper and rest, but only an occasional car seemed to pass this way. There were some small houses on the opposite side of the road from the wall. The sound of voices and the clatter of dishes came through the open doors, and woodsmoke from their cooking fires drifted across to him.

Tears prickled behind his eyes.

'I'm totally alone,' he thought.

Without realising it, he had stopped walking. There was an old tree stump at the side of the road under the wall, and he dropped his bag and sank down on to it. He shivered. The cold wind was getting stronger. He unzipped his bag, pulled out a sweater and slipped it on.

At home, he thought, Zeni'll be calling Meseret to come and eat her supper, and Father will be on his way back from work. Negussie will be waiting by the gates, ready to open them.

He was overcome with an intense longing to be there, and leaped to his feet.

That's what I'll do. I'll go home. I'll go to a main road where there are taxis, and find one. I've got enough money for that. And when I get home I'll stand up to Father. I'll refuse to go to Jigjiga. I'll just say I won't. I'll *make* him understand.

He could see his father's face, stern and unyielding, and Feisal, looking over Father's shoulder, a triumphant grin on his face. Slowly, he sank back down on to the tree stump again.

The sun had gone down now, dropping quickly away below the horizon, and the light was fading rapidly.

I can't stay here all night! Dani thought incredulously. I'll go to one of those houses over there and ask if they'll take me in. Someone will. Someone will help me.

But he felt numb, and couldn't move.

The last home-bound worker had passed a while ago and the street had been empty for some time. Now, though, someone was coming. Dani could hear running footsteps and a strange high-pitched voice. The footsteps stopped some way away then started again, now quick, now slow, coming closer all the time. The man was singing snatches of an unfamiliar song, then stopping to laugh uncontrollably, then mumbling and singing again.

Dani's hair lifted on his scalp.

A madman, he thought. What if he sees me? What will he do?

There was nowhere to hide. Dani was about to pick up his bag and run away when the man appeared out of the darkness, a few metres away.

'Hey ho hey, my brother,' he said, stopping to peer through the dark at Dani. 'His Majesty the Emperor's returned. Didn't you know? Why are you sitting there? Everyone's gone to the palace. Come with me.'

He shot out a long arm to take hold of Dani's and Dani jumped up and cowered away from him. The man's eyes were bright in his dark face and Dani could see that his hair, uncut and uncombed, stood out in rough corkscrews all over his head.

'No, thanks,' Dani managed to say. 'I've been to the palace. There's no one there.'

'What?' the man stared at him, astonished. 'Where've they all gone?'

'I don't know. Home,' said Dani, his voice shaking.

'Home? Home sweet home, home and off, off we go,' the man said, dancing a few steps, then he began to run on up the road.

Dani had hardly had time to let out a breath of relief when he was back again.

'Was His Majesty there? At the palace?' the man said, sounding bewildered. 'Did you see him?'

'I – no,' stammered Dani. 'He's gone to Jigjiga.'

He said the first place that came into his mind, hoping it would satisfy the man. It did.

'Jigjiga,' he said. 'Jigga jigga jagga jig,' and he ran off with a burst of new energy.

Dani found that he was trembling all over and his knees felt weak.

He might come back and turn nasty, he told himself. I've got to find a place for the night.

He walked slowly on up the street, looking across at the small lights burning in the windows, trying to screw up his courage to knock on a door.

But they'll think I'm crazy. They'll tell me to go home.

Someone else was coming up the road now. He could hear brisk footsteps drawing closer and closer. Who could it be this time? Another wild man? A policeman? Feisal? His father?

Blindly, Dani snatched up his bag and began to run, keeping close to the wall. The person behind him was coming up fast, calling out something, he couldn't hear what. An unreasoning panic was gripping Dani, a desperation to get away.

The wall on his left was whitewashed and clearly visible even in the dark, and so was the black gap that suddenly appeared in it. Without thinking, Dani dived through it and crept behind the wall.

The footsteps went past. The man called out again and Dani, listening properly this time, realised that he was only shouting goodnight to someone in one of the houses. He felt foolish for a moment and nearly went back out into the road, but instead he stepped further into the enclosure, through the thicket of trees near the wall.

He was in a cemetery. White marble tombs climbed up the hill above him. It was obviously a place where the rich were buried, because there were no simple headstones here. Each grave had a marble box the size of a coffin standing above the ground, with various kinds of sculptures and stone monuments above them.

Dani felt a shiver sweep right through him, starting from somewhere deep inside. Ever since he was little, Zeni had chilled his blood with tales from the graveyard, stories of ghosts and hauntings and restless spirits. She wouldn't have stayed here for a single minute, whatever the danger outside. She'd have grabbed hold of him and yanked him back out through the wall.

But Dani took another step further in. He felt curiously unafraid. There was something peaceful here, a kind of gentleness. Instinctively he knew that no one else was in this place and that he was quite alone. There was no living soul that he needed to fear, no grasping beggars or wild men or questioning policemen or angry fathers.

If Mamma's died on the journey, he thought, she'll soon be in a place like this. There are probably mothers of other people in here.

The thought comforted him. For the first time since she'd gone away he could almost feel her presence, not anxious, as it had so often been in real life, but loving and teasing.

'Oh, Dani,' he could hear her say. 'What have you got up to this time? Darling, silly Dani.'

He began to wander backwards and forwards through the lines of tombs and as he did so the safe feeling began to fade. The trees at the edge of the cemetery cast odd shadows which moved as the wind stirred their branches. Zeni's spooky stories came back uncomfortably clearly and in spite of himself he felt his skin creep.

He moved back towards the gap in the wall where the trees were thicker. For some reason it felt better here. The darkness was denser, but more friendly. There was more of a feeling of Mamma.

The dim light caught on a big old tomb house nearby. He went up to it and saw that it was made of white marble. It must have been put up for a grand person. Above it was a cross, and all round it Amharic words were engraved.

The slab of marble closing off the foot end had fallen down. Dani peered inside and could see nothing but old leaves and dusty grit. The tomb was empty. No one seemed to have been laid to rest here. He bent down for a closer look. There was nothing sinister, no bones or anything like that.

He hesitated. It would be really, really weird sleeping in a tomb. It might actually be wrong, as if it was tempting the devil, or it might be terribly unlucky, or there might be a sickness in there that he could catch. On the other hand, there was no doubt that it would be warmer inside the little marble house than it was out here, where the wind was getting right in through his sweater. He wouldn't go inside yet, though. He'd stick it outside for as long as he could.

He rummaged around in his bag and pulled out a sweatshirt and his new, green, silky bomber jacket. It was an expensive one with a designer label sewn on the front. He didn't like the idea of wearing it in a place like this where it would get dirty. Zeni would scold him for that.

No, she won't, he told himself. I won't be there to be scolded.

He sniffed, and then felt unstoppable sobs rise in his chest. He let them come and cried for a long time. Then, worn out, he lay down along the side of the tomb, as far out of the wind as possible, pillowed his head on his bag and shut his eyes.

Dani had been right about his father's reaction. Ato Paulos came home from the office just after night had fallen, as he usually did, to find the whole household in a twitch of anxiety. He extracted from Zeni the news that Dani hadn't been since that morning, and that no one knew where he'd gone, and his expression terrified her so much that she nearly dropped the pile of clean laundry she was carrying.

'What do you mean, gone?' he barked at her. 'Where? Who to? Come on. You must know.'

Zeni felt a cold sweat break out on her forehead.

'I don't, sir,' she said. 'None of us saw him. He didn't say anything to any of us. I was busy with Meseret, plaiting her hair, and Negussie was watering the plants behind the house. Dani must have slipped off when no one was around.'

'Slipped off? What rubbish! He's gone to say goodbye to a friend, that's all, before he goes to Jigjiga. I won't have any secrets in this house. Tell me at once where he's gone.'

Zeni took a step backwards.

'Honestly, sir, I don't know. He was in his room this morning. I heard him opening and shutting his cupboard door once or twice. Then Meseret called me and . . .'

Ato Paulos pushed past her and thrust open the door of Dani's room. Its untidiness offended him as usual and he was about to close the door again when he hesitated. Dani had been packing clothes into a sports bag this morning. Where was it now?

He made a quick search. The bag had gone. He went towards the door, about to call Zeni back and ask her if she'd seen it, but stopped. If, as he was beginning to suppose, the little idiot had run away, he would have to handle things carefully. Feisal was due to arrive at any moment. He didn't want to appear a fool in front of his own old sergeant.

He picked up a plastic ruler that had been lying on Dani's desk and rapped it angrily on the surface. His hands were so tight with tension that the ruler snapped in two. He flung the pieces down.

Where would Dani have gone? What friends did he have? None had ever come to the house, as far as he knew. Dani's lack of popularity was one of the many things about his son that had always offended him.

Tsehai! He'll have gone to her! he thought, his relief mixed with exasperation as he thought of Ruth's younger sister, who lived on the far side of Addis Ababa with her feckless husband, and whose giggling inanities never failed to drive him wild with irritation.

He strode out of Dani's room and crossed the hallway to the sitting room. The telephone was on a glass-fronted cabinet full of china ornaments, near the window. He dialled Tsehai's number.

'*Abet?*' said a slow, unfamiliar voice.

'Woizero Tsehai,' said Ato Paulos. 'Is she at home? Can I speak to her?'

'Not at home!' the voice shouted. It clearly belonged to someone unused to speaking on the telephone. 'They have gone out of town. I am the caretaker.'

It was the first of many fruitless calls. Ato Paulos began confidently, expecting every time to hear that Dani was there, but as he worked his way through the list of relatives and family friends, his certainty began to wane, and by the time he'd spoken to the tenth puzzled, curious person he was rigid with frustration and embarrassment.

'Wait till I get my hands on you, young man,' he muttered to himself. 'You'll see what happens when you try to make a monkey out of me.'

He was sitting on the carved stool by the telephone, leafing through Ruth's phone book and trying to think who else he could call, when the phone rang, making him jump.

He picked it up quickly, convinced it was bringing news of Dani. Instead there was faint crackle and a moment of silence, then Ruth's voice, as clear as if she was in the next room, came floating through the airwaves.

'Paulos? Hello? It's me, Ruth,' she said.

He swallowed, momentarily unable to speak.

'Ruth!' he said at last. 'Are you all right? Where are you?' He knew his voice was harsh with anxiety and he stopped.

She gave a little laugh.

'I'm fine. I'm in the clinic, in a nice room. Nurse Watson's still with me. I'm seeing the surgeon tomorrow. It's so strange to be in London without you.'

'How was the journey?' he said quickly, anxious to stop her asking questions. 'Did you manage all right? Are you totally exhausted?'

'A bit tired, yes. I felt a little faint after we took off, but Nurse Watson gave me a couple of injections and then I was better. I slept most of the way. Everyone was very kind. How is —'

'You're not to worry about a thing,' he said quickly, trying to sound breezy. 'We're all OK. Meseret's had her supper and is going to bed. Dani's somewhere around.'

'Is he . . .?'

'I told you. Everything's fine. Now you must rest, my dear. You've got a big day tomorrow. I've called your cousins over in Hendon. They're both coming to see you in the afternoon. I'll try and call you again then. Goodnight. Sleep well now.'

'Goodnight? It's only four o'clock here,' she said, but he was already replacing the handset.

He stood up. Talking to his wife had unsettled him even more. An unaccustomed fear was clouding his mind, making him uncertain of what to do.

I'll have to contact the school in the morning, I suppose, he thought, letting his anger warm him again, and ask them where he's staying. They'll get it out of him. He'll be with one of the boys in his class. He's got to be. There's no other explanation.

Outside, the compound gates were squeaking as Negussie opened them on their rusty hinges.

Feisal. That must be him arriving, Ato Paulos thought, his heart sinking. What on earth am I going to say to the fellow?

Chapter 8

Mamo stood on the corner of the street, breathing in the remembered wafts of the city, the cloying sharpness of exhaust from old trucks, dust kicked up from the road verges, woodsmoke from a million cooking fires. He had forgotten how busy Addis Ababa was, how many people crowded the streets and how much noise they made. He'd forgotten the music, too, radios crackling out songs and dance tunes from the bars and from loudspeakers fixed to the roofs of buses. For the past months he'd lived in a world of quietness where the cry of a buzzard miles away would make you turn your head and a stranger was an object of fascinated speculation.

He had felt euphoric when the driver had set him down near Mercato, the city's teeming market place.

'Going back to your sister, are you?' the man had said, leaning out of his cab window and smiling down at Mamo to say goodbye.

'Yes,' Mamo had replied sunnily. 'She'll be amazed. She probably thinks I'm dead or something.'

The driver had fished into his pocket, pulled out a ten-birr note and put it into Mamo's hands.

'Good luck,' he'd said, and before Mamo had had time to stammer out more thanks, he'd put the heavy truck into gear and had driven away.

Mamo had watched the truck till it was out of sight. He'd had only one idea in his head – to find Tiggist – but saying goodbye to the driver had made him feel as if he'd lost his only friend in the world and he was suddenly uncertain about everything.

What if he couldn't find Tiggist? What if he did and she couldn't help him, anyway? Perhaps he should have asked the driver to take him on, to take him on the road with him, and teach him to be a mechanic or something.

He shook himself. It was too late for that now.

It was quite a long way from Mercato to Mrs Faridah's shop and by the time Mamo arrived there his magnificent breakfast was only a distant memory. He was hungry again. He was growing more anxious too. His pace quickened as he came near the shop, and he ran the last few metres.

The boy with the withered leg was leaning against the vegetable stand under the shady awning.

'Hello,' Mamo said shyly, awed by the boy's green overall and horribly aware of his own ragged clothes. 'Is Tiggist here?'

The boy shook his head.

'Gone to Awassa,' he said succinctly. 'With Mrs Faridah. Husband's sick.'

Mamo felt his stomach tighten.

'When's she coming back?'

'Dunno. Been gone for months. He's managing the place now.'

He jerked his head sideways, and Mamo saw that a smartly dressed man was standing in the doorway, frowning at him.

'But Tiggist's my sister,' Mamo said stupidly. 'She can't be in Awassa. I need her.'

The boy shrugged.

'Can't tell you any more.'

'What if – do you think he'd take me on?' said Mamo, looking over to the doorway. 'I'd do anything. Does he need someone?'

The boy scented competition and his eyes narrowed.

'How should I know? Ask him yourself.'

But the man was waving his arms at Mamo as if he was shooing away a fly.

'Get out of here,' he called out. 'Scram.'

'I only wanted . . .' Mamo began, but the man was advancing towards him now. Mamo backed away.

The shock made him unsteady as he walked back along the uneven pavement. He couldn't take it in. He couldn't believe that Tiggist wasn't there!

He stopped and looked over his shoulder, about to go back and ask again, but the sight of the manager, still watching him, stopped him. It must be true, what the boy had said. Tiggist had gone. A horrible mixture of fear and loneliness was making his chest feel tight. It had never crossed his mind that Tiggist would have left Addis. He'd thought she might not be at Mrs Faridah's. He'd told himself he might have to look for her. He wouldn't have minded that. He'd have spent days doing that. But Awassa! Awassa was miles away, way down south past the lakes! He'd never be able to get as far as Awassa.

He wouldn't want to, anyway. He was an Addis boy. This was where he wanted to be.

He thought for a moment of going to visit Mrs Hannah. She might be able to get a message to Tiggist, send her a letter or something. But he shook his head at once. Mrs Hannah couldn't write, and even if she'd been able to, where would she write to? He didn't know Mrs Faridah's address. And supposing he did get a message to Tiggist? What could she do? She was there and he was here. He'd just have to accept that she'd gone. He'd just have to manage on his own.

Without realising it he'd walked towards the corner where he'd often spent his days hanging out with some of the other local boys.

'Mamo!'

His heart jumped. Someone was calling him. Someone had recognised him!

He spun round.

'Hey, Worku,' he said, a grin spreading over his face. 'It's you!'

The younger boy ran up to him.

'Where've you been, Mamo? You haven't been around for months and months.'

Mamo grimaced.

'I was in the country. I got taken away. Had to work for a farmer.'

'You've got really tall,' Worku said, looking him up and down. 'And thin.'

'Where's Getachew?' Mamo said eagerly, looking round. 'And Mulugetta?'

The thought of seeing his old friends was wonderful. He wouldn't be alone any more.

Worku looked at him incredulously.

'Didn't you know? I thought everyone did. Getachew got into trouble. The police picked him up.'

'Getachew's in prison?'

'Yes. Since last month. And Mulugetta's mum's married again. He goes to school now.'

'Oh.' The ground under Mamo's feet had seemed firmer for a moment, but it was shifting horribly again. He stared down at Worku greedily, as if this small boy, who'd only been a hanger-on to the older ones in the group, was the most important person in the world. 'What about you, then?'

'My dad's come back' Worku said proudly. 'He says I've got to stop hanging round the streets. He's working in a furniture shop. I'm helping him. I have to polish up the wood. I'm only here because he sent me out to buy some meths. Look.' He held up a bottle of purple liquid.

'Oh,' Mamo said again.

Worku was already running away.

'See you,' he called back over his shoulder.

Mamo sat down on the kerb. His knees had suddenly felt too weak to hold him up.

What am I going to do? he thought. Where am I going to go?

It was mid-afternoon already. The sun was still high in the sky but the heat would soon be gone. Mamo shivered when he thought of the night to come. It was always cold in Addis Ababa when the sun had set. If only he'd thought before he'd run away! If only he'd brought his old *shamma* with him! His thin shirt and cotton trousers would give him no warmth at all.

The driver's ten-birr note still lay in his pocket and the thought of it encouraged him. He'd try to buy an old blanket or a coat with it. There were loads of places in town where people sold things second-hand. He'd be sure to get something nice.

He'd think about food later. For the moment, keeping warm was the most important thing.

Finding a blanket that he could afford was harder than he'd thought. He had to walk a long way, looking out for someone selling second-hand stuff cheap at the side of the road. He struck lucky at last. He'd spotted quite a good blanket, reasonably solid without too many worn patches, and he was bargaining for it when the woman selling it saw a policeman in the distance. She scrabbled her things together and without further argument agreed to his price and handed him the blanket, even giving him a few coins as change.

He tucked his find under his arm, holding it tightly, and went across to the bakery on the far side of the road, handing over his last coins in exchange for two stale rolls. Then he went outside and walked aimlessly, looking for a quiet place to sit.

He was in a busy shopping street. He'd often come here in the past and he'd usually stopped for a moment to look longingly in through the window of the pastry shop near the corner, wondering what the delicious piles of cakes and pastries might taste like.

A plump boy wearing a baseball cap low over his eyes was looking into the window now. He was wearing smart clothes and carrying a heavy bag.

Mamo hesitated. The boy looked as if he had money. Maybe he'd be good for a few coins. Mamo hadn't ever begged before, but he'd have to start getting used to the idea. He moved towards the boy who, without seeing him, picked up his bag and walked off. Something in the way his shoulders drooped told Mamo that he wouldn't be likely to give anything today.

Mamo shrugged and walked on in the opposite direction from the boy.

He knew of old that there was nowhere peaceful in a busy shopping street to sit. If you went into a shop doorway the owner would come out at once and hustle you away. If you squatted against a wall, the local street boys would warn you to get off their patch.

At the far end of the street was a minibus stand. The conductors were leaning out of the sliding doors, shouting out the destinations in hoarse voices. People were crowding round, trying to board the little buses, or looking up the street waiting for the next empty one to arrive. No one would notice him here in all this confusion.

He moved away from the kerbside on to the piece of open ground behind and sat down, leaning his back against a wall of bare breeze blocks. He hadn't realised until this moment how tired he was, how his turbulent night, and the journey and the clamour of the city had worn him out.

He was almost too tired for food but he ate one of his rolls, although its dryness made him even thirstier. He told himself to get up and look for water, but found he was too exhausted to move. Instead, he wrapped his blanket round his shoulders, let his head fall back and closed his eyes.

When he woke up it was getting dark. He sat and stared, bewildered, at the scene in front of him.

The bus stand was busier than ever and the street beyond was crowded with cars. Everyone was going home from work.

The thought of home, of the old shack and the promise of food, most nights, anyway, and a proper mattress under a real roof, and the friendly presence of Tiggist, and even, when she'd been in a good mood, of Ma, made him feel dreadfully miserable. He sniffed and wiped his dirty sleeve across his eyes.

Thirst distracted him. He badly needed to drink.

He looked round. There was a run-down little bar on the corner, an old-fashioned place with a mud floor and a few simple wooden benches ranged along the wall. He went to the door and coughed gently to attract attention. The tired-looking woman, serving home-made beer to a few elderly customers, looked up.

'Please,' he said. 'A glass of water.'

She brought him one. He drank it, and held the empty glass out for more. Clicking her tongue impatiently, she refilled it, and he drained it gratefully.

The cool water cleared his head and he began to walk slowly along the street. He felt oddly reluctant to leave the bus stand. It had begun to feel almost familiar. It wouldn't do, though, for the night, which was coming on fast.

He was on a quieter stretch of road now. Apart from small kiosks on the street corners there were no shops, only small houses set back behind corrugated-iron fences, with open stony ground between them and the road. Surely he could find a quiet corner here where he could sleep in safety?

He chose a place that seemed quite sheltered, in a curve where the road bent round, and he sat down on a stone. The evening breeze was blowing now and he was cold already. He draped the blanket round himself, took out his second bread roll and began to nibble it. He tried to eat as slowly as he could but within a few minutes it had all gone.

But I've done it, he told himself, suddenly feeling triumphant in spite of everything. I got away from them. I made it to Addis. I'm free.

He sat for a long time, watching the rising moon turn the corrugated-iron roofs on the hillside opposite first into dull grey, then into shining silver. He was trying not to think about what he'd do tomorrow.

He didn't notice the police car slowing down beside him, but boots crunching on the stony ground made him turn his head. The sight of a policeman's khaki uniform sent a chill of terror through him. Could the farmer have followed him all the way to Addis? Could Merga be on his trail again? Were the police looking for him?

He was up and off like a startled bushbuck, his bare feet flying over the sharp stones. He veered off the road into a side turning and found himself going up a hill. Blindly he raced on. He was dimly aware that there was a long high wall on his left, behind which tall trees were growing, and that a row of small houses was on his right, but in his panic all he could think of was danger from behind.

He was halfway up the hill when he heard the sound of a car behind him. It must be them! It must be the police! Any moment now their headlights would pick him up and they'd be after him like cats chasing a rat!

He dashed off the tarmac and ran across the rough verge to the shelter of the wall. If he stood quite still perhaps they wouldn't spot him under the overhanging branches of a tree. Then he saw, a little further on, that there was a gap in the long whitewashed wall. With a sob of relief, he darted up to it and bolted inside.

The sound of someone panting close by disturbed Dani's light, restless sleep. He was wide-awake at once and sat up, grabbing his bag and holding it to his chest.

A few metres away stood a wild-looking figure: a tall, thin creature, whose torn trousers barely reached his ankles. It had whipped round at the sound of Dani's movement and stood staring at him, perfectly still but seemingly poised for flight.

'Who are you?' whispered Dani, unsure, for a horrible moment, whether this thing was of the living or the dead.

'Who are you?' echoed Mamo, who was frozen with fear. The apparition in front of him seemed to have risen straight up out of a tomb.

Neither of them spoke for a moment, then Dani moved his feet, drawing them in closer and scraping his shoes along the ground.

The sound reassured Mamo. A ghost wouldn't have made a normal noise like that. He looked at Dani more closely. In the fading moonlight he could see now that he was only a boy.

He took a step closer. Dani shrank back against the cold marble tomb.

'It's OK,' Mamo said with a shaky laugh. 'I'm not a ghost. I thought you were.'

Dani's grip on his bag relaxed a little, then tightened again. This person might not be a ghost but he could easily be a thief. He cleared his throat nervously and looked from side to side, wondering if he could get to his feet and make a dash for it if the stranger suddenly lunged at him.

Mamo noticed and understood.

'I'm not a thief either, if that's what you're wondering.' He felt offended. 'I'm just . . .' He didn't want to say that he'd been running away from the police. 'I'm on my own,' he finished lamely.

'Oh.' Dani screwed up his eyes, trying to see the boy's expression, but Mamo's back was to the moon and his face was completely shadowed.

Now that Mamo was sure that the boy sitting against the tomb was a living human being, he felt better. The boy looked harmless, terrified in fact. He wouldn't be the sort of person to stay where danger lurked.

He crossed the last few metres to the tomb and sat down beside Dani on the stone platform below it.

Dani could make out Mamo's face now. This boy didn't look dangerous at all, just scared. Dani put his bag down.

'What's your name?' he said.

'Mamo.'

Dani realised too late that he'd have to give his own name, and he hesitated. If Father had got the police out looking for him, it would be better to give a false one.

'I'm Girma,' he said.

A night bird calling out harshly in a tree on the far edge of the cemetery made them both jump. They were each aware of the hairs standing up on their heads.

'Aren't you scared, being in here at night?' whispered Mamo.

Dani thought about Mamma and how she'd felt close when he'd first come in through the gap.

'I don't think so. Are you?'

Mamo remembered with startling clarity how, when he'd been by the stream, he'd felt his soul separating from his body.

'No. Not really.'

Dani realised with surprise that he didn't want this strange boy to go. To be with someone else who was lost and alone was making him feel a bit stronger.

'You can sleep here too if you like,' he said. 'It's not so bad if you keep on this side, out of the wind. I thought I might have to go in there,' he jerked his head backwards towards the tomb, 'but I didn't want to.'

Mamo shuddered.

'No.'

A glint of something wet on Mamo's foot caught Dani's attention.

'Is that blood? Have you cut yourself?'

Mamo picked up his foot and examined the bare sole.

114

'Must have done. There were lots of sharp stones back there. I had to run over them.'

'I should have brought plasters and stuff,' Dani said fussily. 'I didn't think of it.'

Mamo looked curiously at him.

'What are you doing here? You don't look poor like me.'

Dani wished he'd held his tongue.

'It's complicated. What about you?'

Mamo thought back over the last few days and realised that he didn't want to talk about it, either. An overwhelming weariness was creeping over him again.

'I've got a blanket,' he said. 'If we spread it over both of us we'll keep warmer.'

Dani was blinking rapidly, as he always did when he was uncertain. It was clear from the boy's smell that he hadn't washed for a long time. His filthy clothes were probably full of lice and fleas. Dani could see the fastidious curl on Zeni's lips and hear his mother's anxious command to come away. But the cold was getting to him now, penetrating even through his bomber jacket.

'All right,' he said, swallowing his disgust.

They shuffled about for a while, arranging themselves and the blanket. Mamo, utterly exhausted and used as he was to sleeping on the hard ground, fell at once into a deep sleep but Dani, who had slept every night of his life on a comfortable bed under a clean sheet and blanket, lay staring up at the sky, from which the light was slowly draining as the moon finally dipped down behind the trees.

Chapter 9

A loudspeaker crackling nearby woke Dani with a jerk. He rolled over and sat up, pulling the blanket off Mamo, who clutched at it wildly and sat up too. The two boys stared at each other, appalled, as the realisation of where they were came back to them.

'That noise, it's so loud,' Dani said thickly. He couldn't believe that he'd slept under the same blanket as this filthy ragged boy, from whom yesterday he would have averted his eyes in disgust.

'It's the church. It's Sunday,' said Mamo, who also could hardly believe that he'd fallen in with the kind of rich kid he'd only ever seen driving round town in a car, or stepping into a hotel or a shop. He peered at Dani more closely through the thin dawn light.

'Haven't I see you before?'

Dani shook his head.

'Yes, I have. Yesterday. You were standing outside the pastry shop in Piazza.'

Dani felt uncomfortable and suddenly suspicious. Had this boy been following him?

'What were you doing there?' he said, sounding more hostile than he'd intended.

'Looking. Same as you.' Mamo felt his temper flaring up. 'You don't need to be rich to look at things.'

Dani felt embarrassed and sank back into himself.

'I'm not rich.'

'Yes, you are.' Mamo put out his hand and touched the expensive soft material of Dani's bomber jacket.

'I mean I'm not rich any more,' said Dani awkwardly. He'd have to give this boy some kind of explanation, he could see. He might as well get it over with. 'I've run away from home, if you must know.'

'Why?'

'My mother's . . . My father . . .' Dani didn't know where to start, but he saw that Mamo had settled himself comfortably and was looking expectant, like a child waiting to hear a story. He began slowly, not knowing how to put everything into words, and came to a sudden stumbling halt.

Mamo was frowning at him incredulously.

'You ran away just because of that? Because your pa beats you and you didn't pass your exams?'

'No!' Dani felt his face go hot. 'I told you. He wants to send me to Jigjiga, to this guy, Feisal.'

'But you'd get fed there and everything,' Mamo said, 'and have a place to sleep and go to school, and you wouldn't have to work or beg or anything.'

'Yes, but . . .'

'If someone gave me food and sent me to school I wouldn't mind how much they beat me.'

Dani winced at the scorn in Mamo's voice. He hunched his shoulders.

'You don't understand. You don't know my father.'

Mamo was silent for a moment.

'What are you going to do now?' he said at last. 'Have you got any money?'

'A bit.'

'How much?'

'Twenty birr.'

'Oh.' Mamo looked impressed. 'But even twenty birr won't go far. Not when you've got to eat.'

'I was going to go to my friend's house,' Dani said, 'but I didn't – it wouldn't work. I can't go there after all. I didn't mean to end up here like this.'

He felt his throat tighten, and tried desperately to control it.

'Why don't you go home, then?'

Dani shuddered.

'I can't. Not now. He'd kill me.'

'Who? Your pa?'

'Yes.'

'So what are you going to do?'

'I don't know.'

Neither of them said anything. The loudspeaker from the church behind the trees was blaring out chanted prayers. The sun had risen and its first rays were warming them.

'What are you doing here, anyway?' Dani asked at last.

Mamo felt a little spurt of pride. When he'd told his story the first time, the truck driver had been so touched he'd ended up with tears in his eyes. It would be easy to impress this soft rich kid. He sat back against the tomb, feeling his muscles relax gratefully in the warmth of the sun, and embarked on his tale, embellishing it here and there with little flourishes to give it a more heroic twist.

The effect was gratifying. Dani listened open-mouthed, his eyes full of respect.

'You ought to write all that down,' he said. 'It's like a real story.'

The gloss on Mamo's confidence dimmed a little.

'Can't write much,' he admitted. 'I didn't even finish grade two.'

'What are you going to do, then?'

Mamo wrinkled his nose as he thought, and Dani felt suddenly anxious. He'd only just met this extraordinary boy but already Mamo felt like someone he could cling to.

'I'd like to get a job, I suppose,' Mamo said at last, 'but I don't suppose there are any. I won't be lucky like Tiggist.' He shrugged. 'I'll have to manage for a bit. Beg, guard cars, get tips, save up for a shoe-shine kit.'

As he spoke he felt more confident again. Compared to this poor creature he'd do just fine.

'Right,' Dani was saying. He was trying to visualise himself begging and guarding cars and shining shoes, and the thought was so scary and horrible that he shut his eyes.

The blare from the loudspeakers cut out suddenly and in the silence Dani heard a loud rumble from Mamo's stomach. He realised that he too was desperately hungry. Unbidden, the thought of breakfast at home swam up before his eyes: fresh papaya, and bread and eggs and milk. Butter and honey. Coffee and tea. He hadn't always bothered with it. He'd often told Zeni grumpily that he didn't want anything, and munched sweets in the taxi on the way to school.

He opened his eyes and saw that Mamo was looking at him.

'I'll get going now, then,' Mamo said. 'Got to find something to eat.'

He stood up.

'No,' Dani said, scared at being alone. 'Please don't go.'

'Come with me, then,' said Mamo.

'I can't. Father will have got the police and everyone out looking for me. I've got to hide.'

'All right. Stay here.'

Mamo was looking away towards the gap in the wall, already beyond it in his thoughts.

'Wait,' Dani said desperately, digging his hand into his pocket and coming up with a ten-birr note. 'Why don't you get something to eat with this and bring some back to me.'

'Oh. All right.'

Mamo twitched the note out of Dani's fingers and was off at once, dodging between the graves towards the wall.

As soon as he'd disappeared, doubts began to creep into Dani's mind. He must have been crazy to give an unknown beggar boy half his remaining money! He'd never see it again.

He got to his feet and began to walk up and down, cursing himself. How could he have been so stupid and naïve? And that story the boy had told him, it couldn't possibly be true. False uncles luring him away and selling him off like a slave! Living on nothing but corncobs and prickly pears! Deliberately eating poisoned leaves and jumping in front of trucks – it was totally insane.

And I shouldn't have told him about the police looking for me, Dani thought, a new worry jabbing at him. What's to stop him going to them and telling them where I am? Father might even have offered a reward. All that rubbish Mamo told me, I bet it's just a blind. He's probably a police spy. He'll be with the police right now, and they'll be coming here any minute. They'll put a cordon round the cemetery, and close in, and then they'll pounce.

For a moment, the thought was almost appealing. He'd be like a fugitive in a film. And then, when he'd surrendered at last, after a heroic struggle, he'd be driven home, and Father would be haggard with worry.

'I never knew how much I cared for you, son,' he'd say, hugging him like he hugged Meseret.

But the picture faded at once. Father would be humiliated, not relieved, and humiliation was the thing he hated most in the world. His anger would be terrifying.

Dani swallowed. He'd let his imagination run away with him again. How could the police encircle the whole cemetery? They wouldn't bother, not even with Father pushing them on. But one or two of them might come back with Mamo, if Mamo really was a spy. He'd better be careful and take cover.

He picked his bag up and walked through the tombs up the hill towards the far side of the cemetery. There were more big trees here. It would be easy to hide and keep watch from their shade.

He sat down on the ground and waited. Whether Mamo came back or not, this wouldn't be a bad place to spend the day. He couldn't go back out into the streets, not after yesterday's narrow escape with Mrs Sara. He'd have to stay hidden till after dark. It would be a long day, just waiting, with nothing to eat and drink and no one to talk to, but if he had to, that's what he'd do. In the meantime he'd think, and see if he could work out a plan.

He thought hard for a while, going through all the possibilities and trying to make some sense of it all, but it was like doing a bit of difficult homework. His mind just skidded over on the surface and jumped about in unexpected directions, and the minute he stopped concentrating he started daydreaming, living out in his imagination in impossible and heroic stories.

He gave up in the end, picked up a couple of little stones and sat vacantly, tossing them from one hand to the other, his whole body slumped in depression.

A scrabbling noise made him look up. He couldn't see the cause and the hairs began to rise on the back of his neck. The sound came again, from a pile of earth that had recently been dug over a little way away.

Nervously, Dani stood up and went over to investigate. Anything in a place like this was better than uncertainty.

What he found was the last thing he was expecting. A tiny golden-haired puppy was struggling to climb out of a pit in the ground. It was too weak to do more than pat the loose earth with its paws, but it managed a feeble whine when it saw Dani.

Dani bent down to look at it more closely. Blood was clotting on one of its ears and it was pathetically thin. He hesitated. Mamma and Zeni had bred in him a fear and distrust of dogs. Older ones usually attacked you, and even puppies could give you worms and infect you with rabies.

The puppy whined again. It looked much too small and helpless to be dangerous. Dani reached down his arm, caught it by its shoulder and hauled it up out of the pit. It snarled pathetically and tried to nip his hand. Hastily,

Dani put it down on the ground. The puppy stood up, and it was too shaky to walk. It lay down again and looked up at Dani, its nose twitching as it tried to learn his smell.

'Can't do anything much for you,' Dani said, rolling a pebble past the puppy's nose and watching its feeble efforts to reach out and pat it. 'I haven't even got anything to eat myself.'

He was glad, though, that he'd found it. Now that Mamo had been gone so long he'd given up hope that he'd ever come back. Even a starving little puppy was company of a sort.

Mamo, walking down the road away from the cemetery, felt a sort of optimism. It was great to have a ten-birr note in his hand again. He could buy plenty to eat with it. He and that boy (Girma, he'd called himself, though Mamo had known at once that it wasn't his real name) could have a feast with ten birr.

His mouth watered as he planned what he would buy. *Injera* would be the best thing, with some spicy sauce if he could find a place that sold it really cheaply. With the rest of the money he might be able to get some of yesterday's stale bread for a few cents, the way Tiggist used to.

He had worked his way round the outside of the cemetery wall now and found himself at the entrance to the church. A broad flight of stone steps led up to the wide, open area that surrounded the circular building. People in snowy white *shammas* were coming down them, pausing at the top to kiss the hand-cross which a black-caped priest was holding out to them.

Clustered round the bottom of the steps was a crowd of beggars. They were mostly old women, some wearing nuns' caps, but a few children were there as well – and one boy.

Mamo was about to walk past them when the boy, whose head had been bent forward in an attitude of pious submission, looked up.

'Getachew! Is that you?' cried Mamo.

The boy squinted up at him against the light, and grinned.

'Hey, Mamo. I haven't seen you for ages.'

Another group of people was coming down the steps, and Getachew let his head fall again.

'For the sake of St Michael,' he whined. 'For the sake of Gabriel.'

A woman with tear-stained cheeks was handing out plastic bags of food to the beggars. She put one into Getachew's hand.

'For the sake of Christ, another for my poor mother,' he murmured, looking up at her pleadingly. Nodding, she gave him a second bag.

Getachew murmured his thanks, stood up and bowed respectfully, then he slipped away from the crowd, following Mamo. When they were out of sight he danced a little jig and flung one arm round Mamo's neck.

'Where've you been all this time?' he said. 'I thought you'd gone for good.'

'And I thought you were in prison.'

Getachew's face darkened.

'I was. I was stitched up by that lousy Feleke.'

'Who?'

'He started hanging around with us after you'd gone. He was a right little coward. He nicked some stuff off a street stall and got caught, and pinned it on me. I'd been living with my uncle up till then, but he didn't want to know once the police arrested me. I can't go back to him now.'

He thrust one of the bags of food into Mamo's hands.

'I got this for you.'

Mamo smiled delightedly, and took the bag.

'Do they do that every Sunday?' he said. 'Give out food, I mean? I didn't know.'

'No. It's the forty days ceremony. Some big guy must have died forty days ago, and his wife's doing the whole thing. Donating food to beggars. You have to keep your ear to the ground to know when a forty days is coming up and which church to go to. Come on. Let's go somewhere quiet where you can eat.'

Mamo hesitated. He wanted more than anything to go with Getachew. He hadn't known him very well before, but he could tell that he was just the sort of friend he needed now. Getachew knew his way around. He knew the streets, and was a born survivor. He'd managed before on his own, for weeks at a time sometimes, when his uncle had got angry with him and thrown him out. Getachew would be a great person to go around with, not like that rich kid back at the cemetery. But Dani's ten-birr note was in his pocket. He promised to get him some food.

'There's this boy,' he said awkwardly. 'A real weirdo. We spent the night in the cemetery up there. I promised to buy him some food. He gave me the money for it and everything.'

Getachew stared at him.

'You spent the night in a cemetery? Are you crazy? I don't dare go past the walls even in the daytime.'

Mamo smiled. He'd have felt the same before he'd eaten the poisoned leaves and nearly died. Everyone he knew would have felt like Getachew. It struck him for the first time that Dani, too, hadn't minded being in the cemetery all night. That was one thing at least that they had in common.

It was Getachew's turn to hesitate now. He held up the second bag of food.

'I'd give them both to you but I've got to take one back to my *joviro*.'

'Your *joviro*? What's that?'

'My gangmaster. I'm in a gang now.' He looked proud. 'Our *joviro*'s great, but he's really strict. If you don't take back what he sends you out to get, and share it out with everyone, he'll throw you out, or set all the others on to you. I'll tell him about you if you like. Maybe he'll let you join us.'

'Thanks,' said Mamo, taken by surprise, not knowing how to respond.

'See you later, then,' said Getachew, turning to go.

'Yes.' Mamo was reluctant to let him go. 'I'll take this to Girma and come back here straight away. I'll wait for you.'

'All right.' Getachew was already running off towards the busy main road.

Mamo talked to himself impatiently as he retraced his steps to the cemetery.

'I'm a fool,' he muttered. 'I should have gone with Getachew. Maybe they'd have let me into their gang. I just wish Girma hadn't given me his ten birr.'

He was nearly back at the gap when something bright caught his eye. He grunted with satisfaction when he saw that it was an old plastic bottle. The cap was missing, but it would still be useful. Now all he needed was to find a water supply.

He reached the tomb where he and Dani had spent the night and went round behind it. Dani wasn't there. Instead of being relieved, as he might have expected, Mamo was disappointed. He'd wanted to show off to Dani that he could get food without paying for it and making a bit of a thing about giving him back his money. There was something else too. Now that Dani seemed to have gone, Mamo realised that he'd liked him.

Gone back to his precious father, I suppose, he thought resentfully. I don't blame him, and he slapped his hand against the marble tomb to relieve his feelings.

Dani had been preoccupied with the puppy but he raised his head when he heard the smack of Mamo's hand.

'Mamo!' he called out, shouting more loudly than he'd meant to in his relief and pleasure. 'I'm up here. Did you get anything to eat? I was afraid you wouldn't . . .'

He was going to say 'come back', but he stopped, not wanting to offend Mamo, who was running up between the tombs towards him.

'There,' panted Mamo, as soon as he was close. 'I got breakfast and I didn't spend a cent. Here's your ten birr back.' He held out the note and the plastic bag with a triumphant flourish.

'Brilliant. What is it?' Dani said, greedily eyeing the bag. 'How did you get it?'

But Mamo had seen the puppy. He squatted down beside it.

'What's this? Whose is she?'

'Mine now, I suppose.' Dani was opening the bag. 'I found it over there in that pit they've been digging.'

'In a grave?' said Mamo. He was fondling the puppy's uninjured ear.

Dani wasn't listening. He had opened the bag and was stuffing a piece of *injera* into his mouth.

'Mm,' he said. 'This is good.'

'It's to share,' Mamo said awkwardly. 'It's for us both.'

Dani's face went hot.

'Oh. I'm sorry. I didn't think.'

He gave the bag back to Mamo, who smoothed a place on the ground, pulled the food out of the bag and laid it out neatly on the plastic. Dani could see now that there wouldn't be much between the two of them. He would have eaten three times that amount in any normal meal at home.

The food looked almost lavish to Mamo. He wasn't sure why, but the moment seemed somehow important. The sad face of the woman who'd given it to Getachew, or Getachew's kindness in begging an extra bag for him, or just the fact that he was sharing it with Mamo, had made it seem special. Almost sacred. He sat back and crossed himself, as he had seen Yohannes's parents do, back in the country, before they began their meal.

Dani, watching curiously, was impressed by his air of ceremony. He'd wanted to grab at the food and wolf his share at once, but he made himself hold back and eat slowly from the common pile.

He had forgotten the puppy until Mamo took a piece of *injera*, nudged the puppy's mouth open and dropped it in. The puppy gulped it down, moved its feathery yellow tail and gaped for more. Mamo hesitated, but took the last piece of *injera* and tore it in half. He gave one piece to Dani, and the other to the puppy.

The puppy swallowed, yapped once and licked Mamo's hand. Mamo laughed delightedly.

'I bet she's thirsty,' he said. 'She needs water.'

'So do I,' said Dani. 'I'm parched.'

Mamo was on his feet already.

'I'll go and look,' he said, picking up his plastic bottle.

He was halfway back to the gap in the wall when he paused. The only water source he knew was by the bus station, where he'd been able to drink yesterday, but that was miles away. He'd scout around here first, on the off chance of finding something closer.

He set off round the inside of the cemetery wall. The corner where he and Dani had slept, and the place at the top of the hill where they'd been sitting, were at the farthest points from the main entrance. He could see the gates now. They were shut and looked as if they were padlocked. Just inside them was a little hut where the caretaker must stay.

Moving as quietly as he could, Mamo edged round towards the hut. The caretaker must have a water supply nearby. And even if he didn't have a tap of his own, he'd have a jerrycan somewhere around. Water wasn't like anything else. It wouldn't be stealing to take a bit.

Mamo reached the corner of the hut and peeped round to the other side. He froze. A man was lying on a string bed outside the hut, seemingly asleep.

Mamo waited for his heart to stop hammering. The man was completely still. The breeze was fluttering his clothes without him even noticing.

Perhaps he's dead, Mamo thought, shuddering. He's a body and they've brought him here to bury him.

But the man turned a little and sighed in his sleep.

Mamo dragged his eyes away from him and looked round. Against the far wall was a metal barrel with a tap at the bottom. Water was slowly dripping on to the earth below, turning it a rich dark brown.

Licking his cracked lips, Mamo tiptoed past the man on the bed, and holding his breath held the bottle at an angle below the tap, then eased it open. The water trickled almost soundlessly into it. Mamo heard a sound behind him and looked round. The man had turned again and was lying on his back. He was still asleep.

The bottle was full now. Carefully, Mamo closed the tap and moving as cautiously as he could, stole away. He looked back when he was well clear and thought he saw a flicker in the man's quiet face as if he had been watching and had quickly closed his eyes again, but he lay so still that Mamo thought he must have been mistaken.

Putting his spare hand over the mouth of the bottle to stop the water splashing out, he bounded joyfully back to Dani, thrilled with his own cleverness.

The food had cheered Dani for a moment, but the minute Mamo had gone off to look for water, his spirits had plunged again. How could he have let himself get into this terrible situation? He was completely dependent on Mamo, for food and water and everything. If Mamo deserted him he'd either have to go back outside and get picked up by the police or stay, a prisoner, right here in this cemetery until he starved to death.

The puppy whined and tried to nuzzle Dani's hand. He pulled it away.

'Sorry,' he said. 'I told you, I haven't got anything for you.'

Mamo came back at last, the full bottle in his hand. He looked capable and pleased with himself. After the first surge of relief, Dani felt more useless than ever.

'Where did you find it?' he asked, looking at the bottle but not daring, after his mistake with the food, to ask for a drink.

'The old guy up the gate,' Mamo said, squatting down beside the puppy. 'He's got a barrel behind his hut. He was asleep. I was really scared but I sneaked round behind him. I'm sure he didn't see me.'

Dani didn't notice the little hesitation in his voice. He was licking his lips and thinking of the water.

'Pour some into my hands,' Mamo said, cupping them under the puppy's nose.

'Why?'

'For her. The puppy. Can't you see she's dying of thirst?'

Dani wanted to say, 'So am I,' but he poured a little water into Mamo's palms. The puppy sniffed at the water, then began to lap, drinking more and more eagerly, then licking round Mamo's fingers to retrieve every drop of moisture.

Mamo laughed delightedly.

'Good dog. Clever Suri,' he said.

'Suri?'

Mamo looked at him apologetically.

'I thought it would be a nice name for her. Sorry, she's your dog, isn't she? You found her. You'd probably like to call her something else.'

The puppy was snuffling round Mamo's hands, wagging her tail.

'She's not my dog.' Dani's voice was cracking with thirst. 'You can have her if you like. She likes you best, anyway.'

Even the dog knows Mamo's more use than me, he thought gloomily.

As if in thanks, Mamo handed him the bottle. Almost reverently, Dani lifted it to his lips. The cool water seemed to bless his mouth. It was the best drink he'd ever had.

He realised almost too late that he was drinking too much, and made himself stop. He held the bottle out in front of him and looked at it. He'd drunk a little more than half.

'Sorry,' he mumbled, handing it back to Mamo. 'Where's the guy's hut? I'll go and get some more.'

'No. He'll see you.'

'I'd be careful, like you were,' Dani said defensively.

Mamo looked at him, and Dani, thinking he saw contempt in his eyes, flushed.

Mamo turned his attention back to the puppy. He picked her up and turned her over in the palm of his hand, looking at Suri's soft tummy. The hairs here were sparse and paler, almost white, and the pink skin showed through. Mamo tickled the soft flesh and the puppy squirmed and yapped.

A strange feeling was invading Mamo. The softness and warmth of the puppy in his hands seemed to be creeping up his arms, making him feel soft too. He'd never felt like that before.

'Hey, Suri,' he said, turning the little dog over again and holding her up to his face. 'You're my dog, OK? I'm going to look after you.'

Suri wriggled and tried to reach out with her tongue to lick Mamo's cheek. Mamo laughed delightedly.

'You're coming with me,' he said, standing up. 'We'll go and see Getachew together.'

Dani had been staring down at the ground but now his head shot up again.

'Where are you going?'

'To see a friend. He got us the food.'

'Oh.'

'I'll see you later, maybe.'

'When?'

'I don't know. Tonight, perhaps. Are you going to sleep here again?

'I suppose so. Where else?'

'See you, then. Come on, little one.'

Dani's mind was scrabbling round frantically, trying to think of a reason to keep Mamo back.

'Wait a minute,' he called out, when Mamo had already gone a few paces. 'I could give you a shirt. One of my shirts. I've got three in my bag. It's got a pocket. You could put Suri in it. Easier than carrying her in your hands all the time.'

Mamo hesitated. The shirt tempted him, but it would tie him to Dani, like the ten birr had done. He wanted to feel free. But Dani had already unzipped his bag, and now he was rooting around in it. He was pulling out a beautiful yellow shirt with white buttons and a neat little breast pocket. It was the most magnificent garment Mamo had ever seen close up. He looked at it, looked away, and looked back at it again.

'Go on,' said Dani. 'I mean, you got us that food and the water and everything. If you need something else, maybe I could give it to you. Tomorrow.'

He was bribing Mamo shamelessly, and his voice wavered with embarrassment. Mamo looked up from his rapt contemplation of the shirt. The expression in Dani's eyes reminded him of something, and it took a moment before he realised that Suri had looked like that, dependent, helpless, pleading. He felt a faint echo of the soft feeling he'd had when he'd held Suri in his hands, and he smiled.

'Don't worry,' he said. 'I'll come back. I really will. I'll leave my blanket over there where we slept and you can look after it for me. And I'll get some more food for us this evening. I've got to go and see Getachew, though. He's with a load of other boys. He knows where to get food and stuff. He can really help us. Might even get us in with them.'

The word 'us' chimed in Dani's head like a bell. He smiled, comforted, and held the shirt out again.

'Go on, take it. Please.'

Mamo put Suri gently down on the ground, took the shirt gingerly and held it up against himself. He twisted his head and craned his neck, trying to see how it looked. Then he lowered it and smoothed the thick satiny cotton between his grimy calloused fingers.

'It's lovely,' he said, trying to find the right words. He handed it back to Dani. 'Keep it for me. I can't wear it out there. It would look like I'd stolen it or something. The pocket's much too small for Suri, and anyway, she might tear it. But I'll put it on tonight, when it's just us. Look, I'll see you later, OK?'

He scooped up Suri, and was gone.

Chapter 10

Dani's mood, which had swung up and down all morning, settled now into a state of gnawing anxiety. His watch told him that it was only ten o'clock. He couldn't believe it was so early. He couldn't believe, either, that this time yesterday he'd still been at home, had only just waved goodbye to Mamma, and was bundling his things up ready to bolt. He seemed to have been gone for a lifetime, an eternity.

He stood up and began to walk about, his legs as restless as his mind. Giorgis had been a bad idea. He couldn't have gone there. But surely there was someone else he could think of, some kind adult, or a child even, from his own world, who would take him in and hide him, keep Father at bay anyway, until Mamma came home?

He'd gone through everyone he knew already, over and over again, but now he tried again. No one from school, nor from the family, nor any of his parents' friends could be trusted. They'd all go straight to Father. But what about the nice doorman at the Hilton? He'd known him ever since he was a baby. Or the vegetable seller on the street corner, near home, where he'd often gone to buy bananas and things for Zeni? He sighed. He was being stupid. Why would people like that risk getting into trouble for him?

He sat down again. There was no point in thinking. He might as well just sit and wait for Mamo to come back.

An ant crawled up his leg, then another and another. He was sitting near a whole column of them. He shifted himself a few metres away. It was totally quiet in this cemetery. There'd be nothing to do all day, and now he didn't even have the puppy to play with. Perhaps, if he was lucky, there'd be a funeral later that he could watch. At least it would give him something to do.

He realised he was still hungry, and thirsty again too. He had to get hold of more water. He couldn't be expected to sit around in this hot place all day with nothing at all to drink.

I'll go and get water myself, from the hut, he thought, excited by the idea of doing something independent. Mamo's not the only one who can sort himself out. I can be quiet and sneaky too, whatever he thinks.

Mamo had left the bottle propped up against a grave. Dani picked it up and set off up the hill from where Mamo had come back with the water. It was hotter now. He could feel the sun beating down on his head through the thin cotton of his cap.

He'd been looking down as he walked, keeping the glare out of his eyes, and when at last he looked up, he saw that the gates were closer than he thought. He stopped and ducked behind a monument. How could he have been so careless? The caretaker could easily have spotted him already.

His pulse quickening, Dani peeped out from behind the stained marble. No one seemed to be around. He waited for a moment, then tiptoed forward. He could see now that the padlock was hanging loose off the gates, which were slightly ajar. The caretaker must have gone outside. This was his moment, then. All he had to do was make a quick dash to the hut, find the barrel, fill his bottle and run away.

He was gathering himself to dart out from his shelter when a strong hand suddenly clamped down on his shoulder. Dani yelped in terror, and his head shot round. An old man was standing right beside him, glowering at him from under a heavily scarred forehead. One eye was filmed with blindness but the other was unblinking and fierce.

'Who are you?' he said.

'I didn't mean any harm.' Dani was trying to wriggle free. 'I was coming to ask if you'd give me some water I – my aunt – her tomb's over there.'

He waved his hand towards the far side of the cemetery.

'Where's your friend?'

'What friend?'

'The one who was sleeping beside you last night. Curled up, the two of you, like a couple of stray dogs. I saw you when I did my rounds.'

Dani felt a small glimmer of hope. Why hadn't the caretaker kicked them awake and sent them packing. Perhaps he'd turn out to be friendly, after all.

'Is he coming back, that other boy?'

Dani tried to read the man's expression, to find the right answer.

'I don't know. Yes, I think so.'

The caretaker's eyes dropped to the bottle in Dani's hand.

'What did you do with the first bottleful he took?'

'I – we drank it. We were thirsty.'

'And I suppose you've come back for more.'

'Well . . .'

'Think this is a hotel, do you? Free bed and water?' But his voice was grumbling rather than angry.

The word 'free' triggered a response in Dani. He felt in his pocket.

'I've got some money. I can pay you for the water if you like.'

'You've got money to pay for a drink of water? Where did you get it? Are you a thief?'

'No!' He managed to wriggle free at last, and stepped back. The man was looking him up and down, examining his clothes.

'All that new stuff you're wearing, where did you get it from?'

Dani's face was hot.

'Mamma – my mother bought them. I'm not a thief.'
The hope he'd started to feel was turning to panic. He
might be arrested by the police! They might send him
to prison!

'If you're not a thief, what are you then?'

The old man was leaning forward to look at him more
closely. It was hard to read the expression in his one
good eye.

'Just a boy. My mother's sick. She's gone to England.
My father – I didn't pass . . .'

He stammered to a halt.

The caretaker straightened up, easing his back with
one hand.

'Run away, have you? So why did you come in here?
There's not many who choose to sleep among the dead.
Scared stiff, they usually are.'

'There was a crazy guy out in the street, following me.
I was frightened and I just ran in through the gap down
there to get away from him.'

'What crazy guy? Who?'

'He said His Majesty the Emperor had come back.'

A smile spread over the old man's face, changing his
expression. Dani could see now that his good eye only
looked fierce because of the way the scarred skin had
puckered round it.

'That was only the Lost Prince, as he calls himself.
Think's he's the Emperor's long-forgotten son. He
wouldn't hurt a fly. Lost his mind when his truck blew up
under him in the Somali campaign. He's a fine man. Brave
as a lion when he has all his wits. He's as gentle as a lamb.
You didn't need to be scared of him.'

He put out his hand for the bottle and Dani found
himself passing it over.

'Don't need to be scared of me, either. Ran away myself
once, when the fighting got too hot. Hiding's no fun after

a while. I won't know you're here if you keep out of the way and don't harm anything.'

He turned his back on Dani and started walking towards his hut. He limped badly, and Dani could see that one of his legs was crooked, as if it had once been broken and hadn't been properly set. After a few paces, he turned round.

'Well? Do you want your water or not? I'm not bringing it back to you here, if that's what you think.'

'Oh yes! Oh thank you!' Dani said, flooded with gratitude. He caught the old man up. 'You won't tell anyone, uncle? You won't give me away?'

'Don't know who to tell. You'll come to your senses after you've been here for a night or two, and go home if you know what's good for you. Still, you must have your reasons, if you'd rather sleep in a tomb than in your own house. I know myself, which most people don't, that there's more to be feared from the living than the dead.'

They'd reached the barrel now, and the old man, leaning on it to take the weight off his bad leg, held the bottle under the tap.

'A few fills a day you can have, but I've no wish for you to run me dry. Go on now, get off with you before the first lot of mourners come and see you here and get me into trouble.'

Mamo wasn't surprised when Getachew didn't come to the church entrance, but he was disappointed. He squatted against a wall nearby and settled down to wait.

It wasn't as if he had anywhere else to go, or anything else to do. He'd go back to Dani later, of course, and get the ten birr off him to spend on food for them both, if he didn't manage to find something else in the meantime, but he was glad to be away from Dani for a bit. It was sort of fascinating, being with a rich kid like that (Mamo had had to stop himself craning forward to stare when Dani had unzipped his bag) but unsettling too. Dani was so careless about things, so casually selfish, the way he'd drunk more than half the water, and started in on the food. And why had he run away in the first place? It couldn't only have been because his ma was sick and his father was threatening to send him away. No one would leave a rich home like his for such pathetic reasons.

He's so lucky, he's got no idea, Mamo thought resentfully.

And yet there was something he liked about Dani too. Perhaps it was because although he was rich and educated he was quite humble in a way. He hadn't minded showing Mamo that he needed him.

He does, he really does need me, Mamo thought, rescuing Suri, who had ventured too near a donkey tethered at the side of the road. The idea pleased him. It made him feel more confident.

When Getachew comes, he told himself, I'll see if he can get us into his gang, if it's a good one. It'd be better than just being on our own.

He had only a hazy idea about what the gang would be like. Some of the kids he'd known before had tagged along with groups of street boys, but they hadn't really belonged. They'd all had families, of a sort, to go home to at night. The real gangs, he knew, lived on the streets all the time, sleeping in the same place, sharing out what they'd got and looking out for each other. Some were good and some weren't.

Getachew seems OK, Dani thought. He was really pleased to see me. He'll get us in.

To pass the time he began to croon quietly to himself. Being able to sing out loud was the only good thing he remembered about the country. Being able to hear music again was one of the best things of being back.

A couple of hours must have passed before Getachew at last appeared. Mamo saw him when he was still a block away. Three other boys were with him, two about the same size, and one much smaller.

That's them, Mamo thought. He's brought his lot with him.

Nervously, he got to his feet, tucking Suri out of sight inside his shirt.

Getachew greeted him quietly, without his usual exuberance, then stepped back to stand with the others.

'Million wants to see you,' he said.

'Who's Million?' asked Mamo.

'Our *joviro*. The boss.'

The other three had already turned and were walking away. Getachew and Mamo followed them.

'Did you tell him about me?' Mamo said. 'What did he say?'

'He wants to see you, that's all. I said you were OK, a friend, respectful, didn't go in for fighting. He said he'd meet you. Look you over.'

Mamo swallowed.

'What does he make you do?'

'Different things. Beg, guard cars, you'll see. He's good, Million is. He sorts us out. Makes decisions. That's why we elected him.'

'What do you mean, elected?'

'What do you think? We chose him. Even Buffalo did.' He pointed to the thickset shoulders of the biggest of the three boys walking in front. As if he'd heard his name, the boy turned. His face was heavy and unsmiling. He stared at Mamo, then turned round again and walked on.

'That's not his real name, Buffalo, is it?' Mamo asked Getachew quietly.

'It's what we call him.'

'He doesn't like me.'

Getachew shrugged.

'That's just Buffalo. He doesn't like strangers. He's all right. Got a bit of a temper, that's all. He and Million have been together for years, since they were really small.'

They had crossed the main road now and were heading downhill towards a busy crossroads. Mamo was feeling more and more scared. What would it mean, being in a gang? What would he have to do?

There was a policeman at the crossroads, standing on the corner, his starched khaki uniform easy to see from a good way away. The three boys in front instinctively bunched together, and Mamo sensed a greater wariness in Getachew, walking beside him. Mamo's first instinct had been to run, as he had done yesterday, but being with the others was making him feel braver.

That would be the best thing about being in a gang, he thought. I wouldn't feel so scared all the time.

They passed the policeman, keeping their eyes turned away from him. A little further on, the pavement broadened out. There were a couple of elderly women here with a few vegetables displayed for sale on squares of sacking in front of them – handfuls of chilli peppers and onions, and neatly arranged pyramids of potatoes.

Some way behind them, a boy was sitting on an old rubber tyre, his back against the wall. He was wearing a flowered shirt and blue trousers. A stick that looked at first glance like a cigarette stuck out of his mouth, and one of his front teeth was chipped.

He put his hands in his pockets and thrust his legs out in front of him when he saw the others approach. They squatted down in a ring around him.

'This is Mamo, Million,' Getachew said. 'The boy I told you about. He's OK. A really good friend of mine.'

Million leaned his head back against the wall and looked sideways down at Mamo. His face was lean and sharp.

Mamo looked at him once, quickly, then dropped his eyes, but he had seen the calculating look in the *joviro*'s face, and his pulse beat faster.

'Where did you come from?'

Million's voice was surprisingly high and light.

'I'm from Addis. But I was taken away to the country. Sold. I ran away, and came back here.'

'You a thief?'

The question, coldly asked, stung Mamo, and he lifted his head.

'No! I don't want to be, either.'

Million rolled the stick round to the other side of his mouth.

'We're not thieves in this gang. Anyone wants to steal, they're not with us.'

Mamo nodded.

'You steal, we beat you. You come with us, you do what I tell you. What have you got?'

'Got? Nothing,' said Mamo.

'What's that in there, then?' said Million, pointing at the bulge in Mamo's shirt, just above the waistband of his trousers.

Mamo reached in his hand and pulled out Suri. The puppy had been asleep. She yawned, showing a pink tongue and two rows of sharp little teeth. The others leaned forward, and even Million sat up to look.

'She's my dog,' Mamo said, resisting the urge to cradle Suri away from their curiosity. 'She's called Suri.'

'Is she a guard dog?' Million said.

The smallest of the boys laughed, then was taken by a coughing fit that shook his small body.

'She couldn't be, not yet, Million,' he said. 'She's too little.'

Million put a finger out to touch Suri's rough coat.

'When she's bigger she'll have to work for all of us. Guard our blankets during the day.'

It took a minute for his meaning to reach Mamo, then he looked up at Million, a wide grin on his face.

'Does that mean you'll have me, then?' he said.

Million's face had been softened by a smile as he'd watched Suri squirming around in Mamo's hands, but he made himself look severe again.

'We'll see. You can stay with us for a day or two. Then we'll decide. You'll have to obey our rules. No thieving. No fighting. Sharing everything. What you beg or earn or find you bring to me. It's for everyone. Where I decide to go, you agree. Where I say we sleep, you sleep. OK?'

Mamo nodded. He felt almost breathless with relief.

'The police might try to get me,' he said reluctantly, afraid his confession would make Million change his mind. 'They might be after me because I ran away.'

'Where did you run from?'

'I don't know where it was. Hours and hours away from Addis on the bus. But the man who sold me, he lives here. He might see me.'

He had to stop himself looking over his shoulder.

Million considered, and Mamo felt a kind of lightness in his head, almost making his neck feel longer. It was as if he'd been carrying a heavy load around with him and someone was lifting it off. He had a leader now. Someone to respect. He wouldn't have to make all the decisions any more.

At last, Million shook his head.

'No danger,' he said. 'Too far away. And this man who sold you. Was he your relative?'

'He said he was my uncle, but he wasn't.'

'Then he hasn't got any power. He can't touch you again.'

He put his hands out as if he wanted to take Suri, but the puppy bared her teeth.

'It's good to have a dog,' Million said. 'She'll bark if anyone disturbs us in the night.'

Suddenly, Mamo remembered Dani. He bit his lip, undecided. What did he owe that rich kid, after all? They'd only met last night, a few hours ago. Dani was a different sort of creature, from a different world. He didn't need Mamo, not really. Any time he wanted to, he could go right back home, eat as much food as he liked and sleep in a safe warm bed, even if it did mean getting a beating from his pa.

He was surprised to hear himself saying, 'Million, I've got this friend.'

Million was watching while the little boy teased Suri with his forefinger, waggling it in front of her nose then drawing back from her snapping teeth. He looked up and frowned at Mamo.

'Who? What friend?'

'He's a rich kid,' Mamo said awkwardly. 'I met him last night. We slept in the cemetery.'

Million raised his eyebrows.

'The *cemetery*?'

'Yes. It was because we were both so scared.' Mamo wished he hadn't mentioned the cemetery. It had made a bad impression on all of them. 'This boy, he's run away from home because he's frightened of his father.'

Million was shaking his head.

'No rich kids. They're bad news. The police go out looking for them. Think we want to draw attention to ourselves?'

'He's got a bag of stuff,' Mamo said, feeling like a traitor. 'He'd share it out. He offered to give me things, if I helped him. He's got twenty birr, too.'

The third boy, who had said nothing so far, shifted his feet in the dust.

'What sort of stuff?'

'Clothes,' said Mamo. 'New ones. Really, really nice. And other things, I think. I don't know.'

'Sounds lovely,' the little boy with the cough said wistfully. 'Is he nice?'

'Yes,' said Mamo, hesitantly. 'Yes, he is nice.'

'See him, Million,' grunted Buffalo. 'Let's check him out.'

The third boy was nodding eagerly.

'We know what *he* wants,' Getachew said, smiling round at the group, trying to raise a laugh. 'This sad guy's always on the lookout for shoes,' he said to Mamo. 'Got hungry feet, or something. We even call him Shoes. It's his nickname. He hunts through rubbish all the time, looking for old shoes. He's got a total thing about them.'

'I haven't got a thing about them,' Shoes said indignantly. 'I look for everything.'

But the others were laughing, as if it was a favourite old joke.

Mamo was watching Million.

'All right,' Million said at last. 'Bring him here.'

Mamo hesitated.

'He won't come. He's scared of the cops. He won't leave the cemetery.'

'We're not going in there,' the little boy said with a shudder.

'You heard Karate,' Million said. 'If your friend wants us to see him, he's got to come to us.'

Mamo stood up.

'OK. I'll go and tell him then. Shall I bring him back to you now? Will you still be here?'

'We might be,' Million said casually. 'It depends.'

'Oh.' Mamo shifted from one foot to the other. 'Then where?'

'If we go, we'll come back,' Million said. He swept his arm out to indicate the broad pavement, the road in front and the crossroads just beyond. 'This is our place. We'll be back here tonight, anyway.' Suddenly, he turned on the others. 'What are you all waiting for? Think the birds are going to drop your food down from the sky? Shoes and Buffalo, go round to the New Flower restaurant. Ask at the back for scraps. Getachew and you, Karate, go and beg at the traffic lights, and don't forget what I told you. Old cars give more than new ones, and old people more than young ones.'

***

The worst thing, Dani thought, worse even than the prospect of going hungry for the rest of the day, was having nothing to do. He had never known time to pass so slowly.

At this moment, he thought, at school everyone will be going into maths.

He could almost feel the draught on the back of his neck from the crack in the window frame under which he usually sat, and hear the teacher's grating voice.

I bet Makonnen finished all the homework he gave us last week, and gets top marks for it, he thought.

Remembering the smug look on Makonnen's face, and the contemptuous expression in his eyes whenever he'd looked at him, Dani felt a little better. He'd almost started missing school.

They won't be wondering where I am yet, he told himself. They'll just think I'm off sick or something. But they'll miss me soon. Everyone'll know soon that I've run away.

Normally he'd have let his mind spin off into a satisfying daydream at this point, but somehow he couldn't just now. He was too uncomfortable. His hands were sticky, and he felt sweaty and dirty all over. He was longing for a shower.

I could change into clean clothes, I suppose, he thought, mentally reviewing the contents of his bag.

But the effort seemed too great.

I'll be even dirtier by tomorrow. I'll save changing till then.

He had scooped up another handful of small stones and had been idly playing with them, aiming them at a trunk of a tree some way away. After a while he could hit it three times out of four. Bored, he gave up.

Every few minutes he looked at his watch. He couldn't believe how slowly the hands crawled round its flat, white face. He took it off and held it up to his ear, convinced it was broken, but the ticking was as steady as ever.

I can't stay here for ever, he thought. Even if Mamo comes back and helps me get food. Even if the caretaker goes on being nice to me and gives me water. I'd go crazy. I really would.

Thoughts of home kept trying to edge into his mind. He pushed them away. The mixture of fear and longing they conjured up was too awful to bear. He wouldn't think of Mamma, either.

She'd be ashamed if she could see me now, he muttered to himself.

A swamp of despair seemed to be sucking him down. It made him feel heavy all over. He didn't want to think any more. He tried to empty his mind and sat dully for a long time, slumped against a tomb.

Hunger eventually spurred him to sit up. It was hours since the handful of *injera* he'd shared with Mamo at breakfast time. Now the pangs were getting worse and worse. He'd never felt real hunger before yesterday. It was as if there was something inside him, something independent, calling out to be satisfied.

He took a last swig out of the water bottle, draining it, then stood up. He wouldn't go outside into the road, but there'd be no harm in going back to the gap in the wall and looking through it. He'd be able to see if Mamo was coming back. He might even have a brainwave about what to do next.

He picked up his bag and walked down between the tombs to the trees near the wall, then dropped his bag cautiously and approached the gap. He could hear voices coming from the row of small mud houses on the far side of the road. Women were calling out to each other and a baby was crying.

He peered out, looking cautiously up and down the road. Whatever the caretaker had said, he didn't fancy the idea of seeing the mad Lost Prince again. He settled himself on a stone behind the lowest part of the broken wall. He could easily duck down out of sight if anyone came by.

A loud squawking noise in a tree overhead made him look up. A pair of big black birds was quarrelling noisily. One of them suddenly swooped down to the road, snatching at the body of a dead mouse, which had been stiffening beside the tarmac. The other flung itself down from the tree too, and they began to tussle over the little grey body, threatening each other with furious flaps of their wings.

Dani watched them, half envious. Birds were free and independent. They could do what they like, find their food anywhere, fly freely in the sky. They didn't have to depend on each other, get depressed and lonely, worry about the future and hang around waiting for other birds to come and help them out.

He was so absorbed in the fight he didn't hear footsteps approaching and only the sound of loose stones rattling against Mamo's feet as he picked his way across the fallen rubble of the wall made him look up.

He felt a flush of relief and pleasure.

'Have you brought anything to eat?' he burst out before he could stop himself.

A quick frown twitched Mamo's forehead, making Dani feel anxious. He'd made a mistake again.

'Million says he'll see you,' Mamo said grandly.

'Who's Million?'

'My *joviro*.'

'Your *joviro*? What's that?'

'The leader of my gang. He's trying me out. If they like me, I'll be one of them. After a day or two, he says.'

'A gang? What do you mean, a gang?'

Dani shivered, suddenly scared. He'd seen loads of gangster movies on TV. Gangs were run by criminals, he knew that much. They were really hard and had running battles with the police in old buildings. The gangsters usually ended up dead.

Mamo didn't know how to answer. He stared at Dani, perplexed. It was hopeless talking to this rich kid. He didn't seem to know anything about anything. It was like being with a baby or something. The most ordinary things were strange to him. Even Suri, whose warm body he could feel wriggling around inside his shirt, seemed to have more of a clue.

'They're boys, like us,' Mamo said at last. 'Got nowhere to go. They stick together. Million's the *joviro*. He tells them what to do.'

Dani could picture Million already, a sinister figure in a sharp suit with wads of money in his pockets and a gun in his holster.

'Sends them out to steal, you mean?'

'No!' Mamo was exasperated. 'It's not like that. No stealing. He says anyone who steals gets punished and thrown out.'

'Oh.' Dani's mental picture fractured and disappeared. 'What does he make them do, then?'

Mamo hesitated. He didn't want to tell Dani that Million had sent the others off to beg.

'How should I know?' he said at last. 'I've only just joined. I told him about you, about how we were together. He said to tell you to come and see him.'

'What, leave here and go outside, you mean?' said Dani, looking back over his shoulder into the cemetery, which suddenly looked like a safe haven.

'Yes. They won't come here. They're scared. They wouldn't believe we were hanging out here. That we slept here all night even.'

He felt proud as he said it, and catching Dani's eye he smiled. Dani smiled back. The cemetery and the feelings that made them unafraid of it, their strange meeting in the dark by the tomb, and the night under the shared blanket was a bond that neither of them could put into words.

Mamo turned back to look out at the road.

'Well, are you coming or aren't you?'

'I don't know,' said Dani. 'What if the police see me?'

'Look.' Mamo felt impatient. 'Are you going to stay in here for ever? Grow up here? Get old? Die? You've got to go out sooner or later. I can't go on bringing you food any more, anyway.'

Dani's heart plummeted. He hadn't realised how totally he'd been relying on Mamo. He thought of how he'd bribed him last time with the promise of the shirt, and put his hand out towards his bag again.

Mamo was following his own train of thought.

'Once you're in a gang,' he said, explaining carefully as if Dani was a small child, 'you do things just for the others. You share everything with them.' It was his turn now to look down at the bag. 'Everything you have, belongs to the whole group. You can't sneak off and take stuff to some guy who isn't in the gang.'

'Oh,' Dani said in a small voice.

Now that he'd cleared the gangster idea out of his head, he was beginning to see the kind of gang Mamo was talking about. He'd watched them often on street corners, from behind the safe glass windows of a car. They were the raggle taggle groups of street children, barefoot, dirty and bold, who clustered round the cars at traffic lights, thrusting claw-like hands in through the windows, begging in sing-song voices.

I couldn't! I never could be one of them! he thought, panic clutching his stomach. I'm not like them. I never would be. Anyway, they'd take my bag and everything in it. I wouldn't have anything at all then.

Mamo suddenly pushed past him and ran up into the cemetery. He ducked down behind the tomb where they'd spent the night and bobbed up again holding his blanket.

'Here,' he said, bounding back to Dani. 'Give me your baseball cap and wrap this blanket round your head and shoulders. You'll be safe walking round the streets then. No one will recognise you.'

'No, I don't – I can't . . .' protested Dani feebly, wanting to snatch back his cap, which Mamo was already arranging at a jaunty angle on his own dusty head.

But the blanket was already round his shoulders, and Mamo had picked up his bag and was walking off with it, through the gap in the cemetery wall, out into the street.

His heart thumping painfully, Dani followed him.

Chapter 11

Tiggist was scared all the time of offending Mrs Faridah, but she couldn't help feeling a bit sorry for her too. Mrs Faridah was looking tired and worn. Her husband's voice, weak but demanding, constantly called her into the sickroom. There were phone calls also from Addis Ababa, where her brother-in-law seemed to be having problems in running the shop.

Tiggist was learning to watch Mrs Faridah closely, trying to judge her moods, working out her own strategy for staying out of trouble. She was careful now not to show too much affection to Yasmin when Mrs Faridah was around, and pushed the little girl towards her mother whenever she could.

Salma watched her with amusement.

'You worry too much,' she said one morning, as they sat together in the courtyard, washing sheets in a tub of water. 'Mrs Faridah would be mad to get rid of you. You're brilliant with kids. Yasmin's so good when she's with you.'

The little girl had been trying to climb on to Tiggist's lap. Tiggist wiped her soapy hands on her skirt, and put her arms round her. Then she buried her face in the soft skin between Yasmin's neck and her plump little shoulder, and made a funny growling noise. Yasmin squealed with delight and wriggled free. Tiggist looked round anxiously in case her mother had heard, then relaxed as she remembered that Mrs Faridah had gone out to the market.

'Aren't you scared in case she gets angry and sacks you?' she asked Salma.

Salma shrugged.

'She can't. Mr Hamid's mother employs me. Anyway, I wouldn't put up with anything from her. I'd just go home to my mother.'

Tiggist said nothing. Salma glanced up from the stained pillowcase she'd been scrubbing and saw the desolate look in her friend's face.

'Oh, sorry,' she said. 'My big mouth again. Here, help me with these sheets.'

The girls wrung out the sheets, twisting them between their hands and sending showers of drips down to wet the concrete. They were draping the first one over the washing line, which ran from the old tree in the corner of the compound to a hook in the side wall of the house, when they heard someone rattling the compound's iron gates.

'I'll go,' said Salma.

She ran across the concrete courtyard and opened one of the gates. Tiggist, who had bent down to pick up the second sheet, looked up curiously.

A young man was standing there. He was greeting Salma in the usual Ethiopian way, tapping his right shoulder against her right one, then his left shoulder against her left one, then they touched right shoulders again. Now he was reaching into his pocket and bringing something out, putting it into Salma's hands.

Salma's got a boyfriend! Tiggist thought incredulously. She never told me!

The young man was too far away to see clearly, but he looked really nice. He wasn't handsome exactly, a bit too thickset and heavy-browed for that, but even at this distance it was easy to see that there was something solid and kind about him.

Lucky Salma, Tiggist thought enviously.

Salma was laughing now, and pointing across to Tiggist. Embarrassed, Tiggist lifted the sheet up to hide her face and started arranging it on the washing line. After a few minutes, unable to hold her curiosity in any longer, she peeped round the side of it to see if he was still there.

He was, and he was looking straight at her. A slow smile was spreading across his face.

Tiggist ducked back behind the sheet again. She heard the metal gate clang shut, and Salma's flip-flop sandals slap on the concrete as she ran back again.

'You've been very quiet about him,' said Tiggist teasingly. 'You didn't tell me you had a boyfriend.'

Salma burst out laughing.

'He's not my boyfriend. He's my brother! He brought me some medicine my mother's made up for me, for my skin rash. Did you like him? Did you really? He liked you, I could tell. He kept asking me about you.'

Tiggist felt a slow blush start somewhere in her chest and rise up towards her face.

'He can't have liked me. He hardly saw me.'

'He did. Enough to say he thought you were pretty, anyway. I told him all about you.'

'What? What did you tell him?' Tiggist asked anxiously.

Salma giggled and squeezed her friend's arm.

'I told him you were really bold and naughty and liked going out with men, and that you'd got dozens of boyfriends and would do anything for a laugh.'

'Salma, you didn't!' said Tiggist, appalled.

'Of course I didn't. I told him you were very sweet and loved kids and had a kind heart and that you were very shy,' Salma said. 'Yes, and that you're my best friend.'

The blush had spread right through Tiggist now.

'Oh,' she said.

She was dying to ask Salma more questions but she didn't dare. Luckily, Salma didn't need any encouragement.

'His name's Yacob,' she said. 'He's much older than me. He finished tenth grade at school. He's not like my other brother, who just went off to Addis and never came back. Yacob's the slow, steady kind. We always tease him about it at home. But he's been great since my father died. He's looked after Mum and my little sisters. Done all kinds of jobs to pay their school fees. He even got me this job with Mr Hamid. Now he works in that electrical shop, the one up near the church. You know it, don't you? He's been learning everything he can, how to do repairs and stuff. He's saving up so he can open his own place one day. That's what he wants. A little shop of his own where people can bring their radios and TVs and he'll fix them. He'd have new stock too, once he could afford it. He keeps talking about it.'

'Oh,' said Tiggist again. A lovely vision had risen before her eyes, of a little shop window with electrical goods in brightly coloured boxes nicely displayed, radios and fans, irons and cassette players, with maybe some fairy lights winking round the edges to set it all off, like in a shop she'd often passed in Addis Ababa.

There was something she badly wanted to ask, but she had to screw up her courage to bring out the words.

'I expect he's got a girlfriend, then,' she said at last. 'What's she like?'

'Yacob? A girlfriend?' snorted Salma. 'Of course he hasn't. I told you. He's really slow. Especially about that kind of thing. Really shy. Up to now, anyway.' She gave Tiggist's arm another delighted squeeze. 'He'll fall for you, though, I bet he will. Hey, this is going to be fun.'

Walking along the road, his head wrapped up in Mamo's blanket, Dani felt strangely distant, as if he was watching a film of himself playing some weird character. It was scary, but a relief, to have left the cemetery. He'd been in there less than twenty-four hours, but it had seemed like years. He was back in the real world now. It wasn't the usual world at all. With Mamo's blanket disguising him, he felt like a different person, as if he'd left his old self with the dead people back there, and had been born into a new life as someone else.

He'd had a vague picture in his mind of where Mamo must be taking him, and of the gang he was supposed to be joining. He was prepared for it to be a poor place, some kind of shack perhaps, a little bar, or a roadside shelter. Mamo said the gang members were only boys, but he bet they'd be really tough-looking guys, who would expect him to be tough too, to undergo some ritual, or to fight them, like they would on TV.

He was building the gang up in his mind to be so huge and fearsome that when at last Mamo stopped walking, and Dani looked up, he assumed Mamo had simply paused for a minute, and he waited for him to walk on.

But Mamo gestured towards some boys squatting by the roadside.

'I've brought him, Million,' he said. 'This is Girma.'

Dani, who had forgotten the false name he'd given Mamo, looked round, expecting to see someone behind him. Then he suddenly remembered, and turned back to look at the gang.

He couldn't help recoiling in distaste, and stepped back, almost toppling off the kerbstone into the road. This ragged little group, this pathetic collection of waifs, whose disintegrating rags barely covered their bodies, surely this couldn't be it, the gang Mamo was so keen to join, the group he actually expected Dani to join too?

Dani took a firmer grip on the handle of his bag and waited for someone to say something.

The boys were slowly standing up, one by one, and were staring silently at him. Only one, the sharp-eyed, lean-faced boy, who Mamo had called Million, hadn't moved. He was lounging back against the wall, staring with calculating eyes at Dani.

'You Mamo's friend?' he rapped out suddenly.

Dani had never been spoken to in such a way by a person like Million. Such people had always approached him obsequiously, palms held out for money. He was afraid, but

155

felt too proud to show it, and lifting his chin he looked down his nose, trying to look haughty, the way his father did.

'Yes,' he said. 'Mamo and I . . .'

'What's your name?'

'Girma,' said Dani, grateful to Mamo for reminding him.

'Your real name?'

Dani looked sideways at Mamo, who dropped his eyes. He didn't know what to say.

'Never mind,' said Million, leaning forward. 'What are you doing here, on the street, a rich kid like you?'

Mamo had put Suri down on the ground. The little dog was snuffling round his bare feet, whining. Getachew pulled a crust of bread from inside his *shamma* and held it under Suri's nose, laughing as the puppy snapped at it.

The diversion gave Dani a moment of relief to catch his thoughts.

'I had to leave home,' he said, 'for personal reasons.'

He was afraid that Million would press him, but he only nodded.

'Police after you?'

'I don't know. Maybe. I expect so,' said Dani. The idea made him feel momentarily important. No one would send the police out to hunt for any of these kids. But then he remembered his fear. The police meant Father, and Father meant Feisal.

Maybe I could persuade them to take me to their base and hide me there for a bit, he thought. Just till Mamma comes home.

'Look,' he said, his nervousness making him sound arrogant, which he didn't feel at all. 'All I want is a place to hide out for a while, just till my mother gets home from England.'

'From where?' said Getachew.

'What's England?' said little Karate.

'If we had a place to hide out,' Buffalo said, hunching a surly shoulder, 'we'd be using it ourselves.'

156

Mamo, who was looking from Dani to Million and back again, could see that things were going wrong. He was embarrassed. What would Million and the others think of him for dragging along this rich kid, with his soft hands and fat legs, who was showing no respect to anyone? He wanted to butt in and tell Dani to go off and find some other people to take him on, but he held back. Dani had offered him his yellow shirt. They'd lived through the night in the cemetery together. Dani had given him Suri.

'Like Buffalo said,' said Million, who hadn't take his eyes off Dani. 'We don't have a hiding place. We live here.'

Dani looked past him, taking in the fence against which Million was sitting, and the door set into it.

'I mean here, right here,' Million said, while the others laughed. He pointed to the patch of bare ground in front of him. 'If you don't like it, you can go somewhere else.'

Dani's knees suddenly felt weak. He put his bag down and sat on it. The blanket was making his head feel hot and he shook it off. Mamo stepped forward to retrieve it, holding back Suri, who was trying to worry it with her little sharp teeth. The others squatted down again one by one, except for Buffalo, who leaned against the wall with his arms crossed, staring down at Dani.

'But where do you sleep?' Dani said, still clinging to the idea that they had a base, a shelter of some kind, a hidden source of support, that they weren't telling him about.

'Million tells us where to sleep,' said Karate, who had shuffled close to Dani and was now right beside him. 'He decides. It's here, usually. He lets me sleep right next to him.'

Dani looked down at him. The little boy smiled back, and Dani noticed that his top two milk teeth had come out and the new ones were growing through.

'Oh,' he said. He was trying to imagine himself sleeping out in a place like this, just lying down on the side of the street, rolling in the dirt with these ragged boys, but his mind shied away from the thought.

Behind them, ignored by the boys, the traffic that had been cruising down the street was slowing to a standstill, blocked by an overloaded truck further along, whose axle had broken.

'Dani! Is that you? Dani?'

Dani felt as if his heart had stopped. He almost whipped his head round but stopped himself just in time. He knew that voice. It belonged to Mikhail, a cousin of his father, a gossipy, breathless, irritating meddler of a man, whom Ato Paulos loathed. Dani shut his eyes briefly, then looked pleadingly at Million.

Million stood up lazily and sauntered towards the car. Buffalo detached himself from the wall and followed him. Getachew and Shoes went after them, their hands held out. Little Karate darted between them, pushing his way through to the window of the car, the bottom of which was on a level with his chin. Mikhail was leaning out of it.

'No mother, no father,' Karate murmured with an air of practised misery. 'Very hungry. Give me one birr.'

They were blocking the man's view. He tried to look past them, but could no longer see the boy he thought he'd recognised. He pulled back from their outstretched hands and quickly shut the car window, put the car into gear and drove on.

'That's your real name then, is it? Dani?' Million said, coming back and standing over him.

Dani nodded miserably.

'Thanks for hiding me,' he said. 'Has he gone?'

'Yes. Who was it?'

The others, except for Buffalo, crowded round, eager to hear something interesting.

'My father's cousin.'

'Your father's cousin?' Million's voice was mocking. 'A guy as rich as that? Why don't you go to him, then? Ask him to take you in?' Suspicion was darkening his face. 'You haven't stolen anything, have you? You're not a thief, are you? If you are, you're out of it. We don't go around with thieves.'

Dani looked up, his face hot.

'No! Of course I'm not a thief! I told you. I can't go home because – it's personal.'

To his surprise, Million accepted this. He returned to his stone and leaned back against the wall.

'Well then,' he said. 'What is it you want from us?'

Dani shook his head. He didn't know. He wished he was back in the cemetery, just him and Mamo and the gruff old caretaker.

'Want us to hide and protect you, is that it? Like we did just now? You want us to get you food? We only just manage to eat ourselves.'

The mention of food made Dani's stomach lurch with hunger. It *was* what he wanted! To be protected and fed! To be looked after! The thought of eating what these boys probably ate, of sharing food that they had touched with their dirty fingers, made him wince, and the idea of lying down to sleep among them, with all the fleas and lice they probably had in their clothes, made his skin creep, but his need pushed everything else out of his mind.

'What do you want?' Million was saying again.

'Just to be with you, I suppose,' mumbled Dani. 'Like you said, food and protection, and being together, like I was with Mamo.'

The others were close in now, listening intently.

'In this gang,' Million said delicately, 'we share everything we have. What belongs to one belongs to all.'

'I know,' Dani said unhappily. 'Mamo said.'

He reached into his pocket and pulled out his small wad of notes. A few coins were left. He almost decided to hold these back, but fear of being found out and his own sense of honour made him fish them out too. He handed all the money to Million, who counted it carefully and put it into his pocket.

'Five birr for Karate's cough medicine,' he pronounced. 'Getachew, you take him to the clinic tomorrow.'

Mamo was watching Dani anxiously, afraid that, even though he'd handed over his money, he'd hold back the rest of his stuff. Dani looked as if he'd forgotten all about his bag. Giving up his money seemed to have thrown him into total dejection. He sat slumped, staring at the ground.

Karate broke the silence.

'What's in your bag, Dani?' he said sunnily. 'Have you got any trainers for Shoes?'

The others all laughed. Dani joined in awkwardly, then got off his bag and crouched clumsily beside it. Unlike the others, he was unused to squatting, and his chunky calves made it uncomfortable. He opened the zip slowly, trying to remember what he'd packed, hoping he hadn't put in anything too precious.

Before he'd had time to take anything out, Buffalo leaned forward, pulled the bag away from him and shoved it towards Million.

'He gets to open it,' he said shortly to Dani.

Dani smiled uneasily.

'There's a yellow shirt in there that I gave to Mamo,' he said. 'It's his.'

To his surprise, Million zipped the bag up again and stood up.

'Not here,' he said. 'Too public. We'll go down the lanes.'

Dani followed the others into the opening of a rough stony track that led down the hill away from the tarmac, into a maze of rough back lanes and small, one-roomed mud houses. He was too preoccupied to notice where they were going, and saw too late that he was lost. The realisation made him feel even more helpless and dependent.

Million stopped when they came to an open space where two tracks met. A tree here offered some privacy. They crouched down and he opened the bag. Everyone crouched down and he opened the bag. Everyone crowded round eagerly as Million began to pull out one thing after another.

The yellow shirt was at the top and Million handed it straight to Mamo. After that came a blue T-shirt, which went to Getachew, then a pair of black cotton trousers which Million put aside for himself.

A small hand crept into Dani's. It was Karate's, who was watching the share-out with painful anxiety, sucking in his breath with longing and admiration as each item came into view. But when first one white trainer and then another emerged, he dropped Dani's hand.

'Shoes! Shoes!' he crowed, and clapped.

Shoes solemnly took the trainers and forced his bare calloused feet into them.

'They fit me,' he said, and delight filled his eyes, overflowing into his whole face.

Dani had hated seeing his things being given away, and had been praying silently for Million to stop and hand his bag back to him, but he couldn't resist the happiness in the skinny boy's face. A new feeling, joyful, generous and reckless, was growing inside him.

'There's a sweater in there that would fit him,' he said, lifting his chin towards Buffalo, 'and please can Karate have the short-sleeved shirt?' He smiled down at the little boy. 'You'll really like that one. It's got pictures of elephants all over it.'

Mamo lay awake for a long time that night, looking up at the stars as they slowly wheeled across the black sky. Suri, tucked into the crook of his arm, stirred and snuffled from time to time, gripped in a doggy dream, and her little movements sent waves of warmth and tenderness coursing up Mamo's arm.

Mamo couldn't believe how everything had changed in two short days. Only forty-eight hours ago he'd been running like a hunted animal through the vast dark countryside. His feet and shins still smarted from the cuts and bruises of his escape. In spite of Yohannes's mother's nursing, he was still feeling, too, the after-effects of the poison. Every now and then a wave of nausea and dizziness came over him and he had to stop and wait until it passed.

But he'd made it! He'd done it! He was free!

Sometimes, during the past day, he'd been so overwhelmed with joy, with the relief of being rid of his hated master, that he'd almost wanted to leap about. But his mood had a funny way of swinging down again whenever he thought about the future.

He'd lost Tiggist. He had no family. He was alone in the world with no one to care if he lived or died, no one to feed him or look after him if he was sick.

At least, I *was* alone, he thought, turning his head to look along the row of dark heads, at the formless shapes wrapped in a dusty collection of old blankets and *shammas*. But I won't be any more if they let me stay with them.

The thought should have cheered him up, but it didn't.

What are they? Only *godana*. Street kids, he thought contemptuously.

He'd never imagined it would come to this. This was as low as you could go. There was nowhere to fall to from here.

And I'm lucky, he told himself, to have met up with Getachew on my very first day back, and to get in with Million, too.

He'd watched Million carefully all afternoon and evening, trying to understand him. Million was up and down a bit, frowning sternly one minute, as if he felt a sudden need to show he was boss, then just being one of the others the next. There'd been almost a party atmosphere when Dani had shared the stuff out of his bag. Everyone had tried on the clothes and preened themselves, looking over their shoulders to get the effect from the back, stroking the clean expensive material, pointing and laughing at each other and looking gratefully at Dani, who, after his first reluctance, had suddenly seemed not to care any more but had given away everything, right down to his socks.

Mamo, inspired by his new yellow shirt, had pulled Dani's baseball cap down over his eyes, struck a pose, and sung his favourite song.

'We're the survivors! Yes!

The black survivors!'

'Black survivors,' Dani had said in Amharic, with a twisted smile.

'Why do you say that?' Mamo asked. 'What do you mean?'

'It's what you said. The words of the song are in English. That's what it means in Amharic, "black survivors". Didn't you know?'

Mamo stared at him.

'I just copied them. I never knew what they meant. Can you really do English?'

Dani shrugged.

'Yes, of course.'

'Read it and everything?'

'Yes.'

Million had been listening, eyes a little narrowed. Mamo could see he was impressed, that he was thinking out how Dani could be useful.

But then Getachew had started prancing about.

'Look at me! I'm like a black American. Hey, Rasta! Give me five!'

He held up his hand and Shoes obligingly slapped it.

'Go on singing, Mamo,' Karate said. 'I really like it.'

After dark, Million had left Buffalo on their pitch to guard their blankets and had led the others to a restaurant further down the road. They'd planned to spend the evening in front of it, begging from the customers and offering to guard their cars for a few cents, but another group of boys had got there first, and they had to move away, settling like a row of dusty grey crows on a wall a little way further on. Much later, they'd gone round to the restaurant's back entrance.

Mamo had been amazed. Food, good food was being thrown away! Fine *injera*, and fried lamb, and beef bones with meat still clinging to them! They'd all had some, and Million had taken a share back to Buffalo too.

Dani had been strange and silent all evening. Mamo had watched him. He'd held back from the others while they were waiting at the side of the restaurant, not joining them on the wall, but standing apart in the shadows, looking hunched and miserable. When the cooks had come out with the spare food, and put it in the bins, he'd followed at a distance, and when Mamo had looked back at him over his shoulder, he'd thought Dani was going to be sick. Then Getachew had turned and offered him a handful of *injera*, and he'd suddenly lunged forwards, grabbed it and bolted it in one gulp, like a dog or a hyena. After that, he'd been like the rest of them, scrabbling for what he could get.

Karate, who was lying on the other side of Dani, started coughing. None of the others stirred. Even Dani, who was next to Mamo and who had been shifting around restlessly for a long time, didn't move.

The coughing fit lasted for ages, racking the little boy, who levered himself up on one elbow through the worst of it, then lay back, exhausted.

Mamo's mind was slowing down at last, moving towards sleep, but then he heard Dani's low voice, speaking to Karate.

'Are you OK, Karate?'

'Yes.' The voice was no more than a croak.

'That's a bad cough.'

'I know. It's got worse. Million's going to get me some medicine.'

There was a pause.

'What's your name, your real name?' Mamo heard Dani whisper.

'I don't know. My mother probably told me, but she died before I could talk properly and I can't remember.'

'Who looked after you?'

'Some other mothers. They were *godana* too. They picked me up when the van came to take my mother away to the cemetery. They called me Wondemu, but they said it wasn't my real name.'

'Where are they now, those mothers?'

'Gone. One of them, the nicest one, got sick. She died. She had a bad cough, like me. The others just left. I got really sick then. I was on my own. Then Million found me. He took me to the clinic. He said I could stay with him. I'm really useful, Million says. I'm a good beggar. People like little kids. They give me more than the others.'

Mamo smiled at the pride in his voice.

'You like Million, don't you?' whispered Dani.

'He's the best,' Karate said, 'except when he gets drunk. I thought he was going to buy *tej* this evening, after you gave us all your clothes, but he didn't. It's nice at first when he drinks, but then he gets angry and I get scared. He doesn't usually let me drink *tej*. He will when I'm older. But I have a bit sometimes. I really like *tej*. It warms you all the way through. They made me drink a lot once, just for a laugh, and I got really drunk. I can't remember but they said I was so funny. They tried to make me dance but I just fell over.'

He giggled, but his giggle turned to a cough. When he stopped at last he said, 'I like you a lot, Dani. And my shirt. It's my best thing I've ever had.'

A little later, just as he was drifting at last into sleep, Mamo was aware that beside him Dani was silently crying.

Long after Mamo had fallen asleep, Dani lay awake. The row of other boys, sleeping peacefully on the hard pavement, seemed inured to the discomfort. He couldn't understand why they weren't shivering with cold, like he was, and how they could relax against the brutal hardness of the ground, which was making him ache all over.

He couldn't get Karate's story out of his mind. His mother had died right there on the street with her baby clinging to her. How long had it been before someone had noticed, and taken Karate away? Had he sat there on his own for hours and hours?

Karate had snuggled up against him, and Dani saw that he'd put his thumb in his mouth. In spite of the awful germs that must be streaming out of the child's mouth with every breath he exhaled, Dani was too grateful for the warmth of the skinny little body to draw himself away. He was warmed also by Karate's friendliness.

He wasn't so sure about any of the others. Million was unpredictable. He might accept Dani into the group, or turn him out at any minute. Getachew seemed OK, though he wasn't sure if he could trust him. There was something strange about Shoes. He'd been almost hysterical when he'd got Dani's trainers, dancing and leaping as if he was possessed, but later he'd withdrawn, and become silent and distant, as if he was miles away. There was a funny smell about Shoes too, like petrol. He had a rag in his pocket, and every now and then he took it out and sniffed it.

Buffalo was scary. He was thin, like all of them, but built like a bull, with heavy shoulders and a low brow. He still had some growing to do, but he'd be a big man one day, a strong man. He exuded a sullen anger which only lifted when he spoke to Million. The acquisition of a sweater from Dani's bag had drawn a brief smile from him, but it hadn't lasted long.

I'll have to be careful, thought Dani. I'd better not get on the wrong side of him.

He shut his eyes and tried once more to go to sleep but Karate's story was in his head again. Only now it wasn't little Wondemu who was clinging to the dead mother, it

166

was little Dani. Dani was the one now who was wandering through the streets, abandoned by all the mothers, glad to be taken in under the wing of a ragged tribe of *godana*.

Chapter 12

Having fallen deeply asleep only a couple of hours before dawn, Dani could hardly open his eyes when the others started to get up, to fold into a pile their thin coverings, and begin to yawn and stretch. Even lying on the hard cold ground seemed at that moment more attractive than sitting up and facing whatever new horrors the day would bring.

He had no choice, however. The rest of the group was moving closely all around him, threatening to tread on him, and Karate was tugging at his shoulder.

'You've got to wake up, Dani. The police will be out soon.'

Dani sat up with a jerk. He felt terrible, with a thick head and a sour taste in his mouth, but at least his mind was working again.

The other boys were squatting in a line on the kerbstone above the gutter, down which a thin stream of water was trickling. It was coming from a bar nearby, where the owner was sluicing out his floor. The boys were scooping the water up in their hands to wash their faces.

No, thought Dani. I can't. Not in the gutter.

But Mamo was looking round at him, surprised, and Karate was beckoning to him.

'Hurry up, Dani. It'll all be gone in a minute.'

Dani stood up slowly, shaking out his stiff limbs. He brushed at his clothes with his hands, trying to shift the worst of the dust, then walked slowly towards the row of boys. As he'd hoped, the water had stopped running.

I'll get a proper wash later, he promised himself. I'll slip away from the others and find somewhere. They can't expect me to wash in street water like that. People like me don't.

The group seemed in no hurry to start the day. They ambled back towards the wall and sat down against it, getting up one by one to disappear round the corner to the patch of rough ground they used as a toilet. Dani had to steel himself before he went there, but this morning, somehow, it was easier than last night.

At least warmth was beginning to flow back into his cramped arms and legs. The sun was rising over the city streets and its rays were already deliciously hot.

Million shared out a hoard of bread rolls that he'd kept back from the restaurant bins the night before, and sent Shoes off to the bar to beg for some clean water. He came back with two old plastic bottles.

Dani felt a little better after he'd eaten some bread and drunk some water. At least now he knew to wait his turn, not to drink more than his share, or bolt his bread down. He was pleased with himself too, for avoiding a wash in the gutter.

I won't beg, whatever Million says, he told himself. I just won't. I don't care what any of them do to me. He felt indignation stirring him. Who is Million, anyway? Just an ignorant, illiterate tramp. Why should he tell me what to do?

Surreptitiously, he poured a bit of the drinking water from the bottle into the palm of one hand and splashed it on his face. It didn't wash it much, but the coldness made him more alert.

'What are we doing today, Million?' Karate asked, picking at a scab on his knee. He looked tired and heavy-eyed this morning, and was resting his head on his hands.

Million pursed his lips.

'It's a public holiday today. No point in begging downtown. Too few people about.' He fished in his pocket and pulled out a couple of Dani's coins. 'Mamo, go and buy some soap. There's a kiosk just round the corner. Two small bars. We'll go down to the river and wash. Do our clothes as well.'

Karate shivered.

'It'll be cold by the river. I'm freezing already.'

'Not you,' Million said. 'Buffalo's taking you to the clinic.'

Dani was too relieved about not having to beg, and pleased at the idea of a wash, to think about what the river would be like, but when he'd followed the others down a steep path and found himself standing on a broad flat stone, with the water gurgling sluggishly past his feet, he was astonished. He'd often driven across the bridges that spanned the many gulleys in Addis Ababa without even realising that streams ran beneath them.

The others were already stripping off their clothes, down to their underpants. Reluctantly, Dani did the same. He'd always hated being undressed in public, at school, for sports, or at the swimming pool. He knew everyone was secretly laughing at his round shoulders, big tummy and unmuscular legs. He looked sideways at the others. They were all thin, their shoulder blades sticking out as sharp as fins from their backs, but they were wiry too, their flesh lean and hard with muscle.

To his relief none of them were looking at him. They were politely keeping their eyes away from each other's nakedness.

The water was icy and made Dani gasp aloud. The others were squatting down, scooping up water in their cupped hands and dousing their heads and bodies, then soaping themselves all over. Dani forced himself to do the same. To his surprise, after the initial shock, the water didn't seem so cold. He'd never cared much about washing before, and Zeni had even had to bully him sometimes to take a shower, but then he'd never been really dirty. It was a pleasure to get the grit out of his hair, the stickiness off his hands and face, and the itchy sweatiness off his body. Although his teeth were chattering, he soaped and rinsed himself twice all over.

The others, who had put the new clothes they'd got from Dani to one side, were already dousing their old shirts and trousers in the water and rubbing at them with the soap. Dani had never washed clothes before, but he copied them, soaping, rinsing and squeezing like they did. Then, like them, he spread his things out on nearby bushes to dry.

The job done, they all squatted down on the stones near the water's edge, shivering less as the sun began to dry them.

Dani had been trying to ignore the rank, fetid, rotten smell that was wafting down from a huge pile of garbage at the top of the bank, but Million stood up after a while and began to climb up towards it. Getachew, Mamo and Shoes, only half dressed, followed him.

'Where are you going?' Dani called out to Getachew, who was the last to go.

'To look for stuff. You'll see,' Getachew said over his shoulder.

Disgusted, Dani saw that they had stopped at the rubbish pile and were poking around in it. Million had been bending over, but he stood up and was frowning down at Dani.

Resentfully, Dani stood up and walked slowly up towards the garbage pile. The smell was worse here, really disgusting. There were old bones mixed up with cabbage stalks and fruit and all kinds of other sludgy stuff, but in the drier bits there were piles of what looked like rags and old tins, the rusty springs of a mattress, broken boxes and pieces of plastic.

The others were already working efficiently. Shoes had picked up a plastic bag and was putting bruised bananas into it. Now he was turning over a pile of rags.

In spite of himself, Dani started to be interested. What was that blue thing over there? Part of a broken bucket? A punctured ball? A lamp shade? He went across and picked it up. It was only a plastic jug, its sides split right down to the base. But underneath it was an exercise book. The cover was smeared with ash and dirt, but when he picked it up and leafed through it, he saw that only a few leaves had been used. There was page after page of empty lined paper.

He looked round. Mamo's bag was already half full. Getachew had found an old sock. Million was peering into a large green bottle. Shoes didn't seem to have got very far. He was looking down dreamily into his plastic bag.

Feeling triumphant, Dani found a plastic bag for himself and put the notebook into it. Then, copying Mamo, he began to walk slowly forward, scrutinising the ground systematically.

Mamo, who had taken to scavenging at once, found the best thing. He turned it over accidentally with his bare foot. It was a hat made of wool, knitted in stripes of red, gold and green, the colours of Ethiopia. He held it up to Million, who took it from him, turned it round in his hands then put it on his head. It gave him a careless, rakish look. He bent down and picked up a shard of broken mirror lying near his feet, then studied himself, arranging the hat at different angles. He smiled at Mamo delightedly.

'This is good,' he said. 'A good hat for a *joviro*. You're the best at this job, Mamo, a real king. That's what we'll call you. The Garbage King.'

Mamo grinned delightedly. A nickname felt good. It made him special. He turned it over in his mind. The Garbage King. It sounded cheeky and tough.

'Garbage King, find me a hat too,' Getachew called out. 'Look at Million, he's like a black American now too. Hey, rasta man.'

They began to move back down the hill towards the stream, Mamo coming last, reluctant to stop the search.

'What have you found, Shoes?' Dani said. He hadn't dared address any of them by name before, except Mamo

172

and Karate, but he felt more confident now, especially with Buffalo out of the way.

'Bananas,' said Shoes, looking down into his bag. 'Very brown and squashy, but still OK.'

'No shoes?' Dani said teasingly.

'Don't need shoes any more,' Shoes said seriously, 'not now I've got these.'

He stuck his feet out in front one by one and admired them.

They reached the stream and felt their clothes. They were still damp but Million was putting his on.

'Mine are still wet,' said Dani.

'They'll dry on you,' Million said scornfully. 'Do you want us to wait here all day?'

'Hey!' came a voice from above. They looked up. Buffalo was leaping down the slope towards them.

'Where's Karate?' Getachew asked.

'They said he's really sick,' said Buffalo. 'They told me to take him to the nuns at Siddist Kilo. The nuns wouldn't let him go. Karate wanted to come back with me, but they made him stay.'

The news that Buffalo brought back, that Karate had been kept in hospital by the nuns, sobered the group down. They walked slowly back up to the road, talking about it.

'What did they say, Buffalo?' Dani asked anxiously, seeming to lose his awe of Buffalo in his eagerness to know.

'I told you. They said he was really sick. Asked me why I'd left it so long to bring him in.' He turned towards Million. 'He didn't seem so bad to you, did he?'

Million shook his head.

'I don't know. He was bad before and got over it. The nuns make a fuss of him because he's so little and cute.'

'He cried when I left him,' Buffalo said. 'Didn't want me to go. Said he didn't care if he was sick, he just wanted to come back to us.'

'We'll go and visit him later,' Million said. 'We'll beg some money and take him some sweets.'

He adjusted the hat, pulling it sideways over one eye.

'Where did you get that thing?' Buffalo asked.

'Mamo found it,' said Million, throwing an arm round Mamo's shoulders, and making Mamo shiver with warmth and pride.

Buffalo scowled, but said nothing.

They'd reached their pitch again. Shoes fished into his bag and pulled out the pieces of fruit. He handed them round. The boys ate carefully, relishing the sweetness, throwing the rotten parts away and laughing as Suri scampered after them. Less fussy than them, she wolfed down decayed bananas with every sign of contentment.

Million had taken up his usual place on his stone, with his back against the wall, while the others squatted round him. His new hat seemed to have put him into an expansive mood. He sat forward and said to Dani, 'What was that you found? I saw you put something into a bag.'

Dani fished out the notebook and passed it to Million, who leafed through it.

'Nothing in it,' he said, handing it back again.

'It's the paper,' said Dani. 'I thought I could use it. Write in it.'

'Write? What for?'

'I don't know yet.' Dani sounded defensive. 'Stories.'

'You know stories?' Getachew said eagerly. 'What sort? Can you tell us any?'

Dani nodded.

'Yes, if you like. I'll have to think a bit first, though, to remember them right.'

Million stood up, put his hand into his pocket and pulled out a few coins.

'There's still some left,' he said. 'Enough for some *injera*, anyway.'

The others all looked up at him. The bread rolls at dawn and the few mouthfuls of fruit hadn't gone far to satisfy their hunger.

'See you in a minute then,' Million said, walking off. Getachew started up after him.

'I'll come with you,' he said.

Shoes took out the rag from his pocket and held it to his nose. He began to rock backwards and forwards. Buffalo stared at the ground.

'That school you used to go to, where is it?' Mamo said to Dani, to pass the time.

Dani lifted his chin towards the hill above them.

'Up there.' He spoke shortly, as if he didn't want to think about it.

'Fancy uniforms, was it?' Buffalo said suddenly. 'Little blue sweaters? Bags with zips on them?'

'No,' began Dani. 'We . . .'

'What are you doing here, with us?' Buffalo interrupted savagely. 'Playing at slumming it? You could go back there tomorrow. What should we bother with you for?'

Dani seemed to retreat somewhere inside himself. He looked as if he wasn't listening any more. Mamo felt a spurt of anger.

'Leave him alone,' he said gruffly. 'He's got his reasons. No one lives like this for fun.'

Buffalo flicked his head round towards Mamo and Mamo realised, with a lurch of his stomach, that he had been Buffalo's real target all along.

'Too low for you then, are we?' His voice was tight. 'What are you trying to get in with us for? You're as bad as *him*.'

He jerked his thumb towards Dani.

Mamo felt like a gazelle who senses that a leopard is hiding in the long grass ahead. He'd have to be careful, or Buffalo would become his enemy. Buffalo would work on Million and have him and Dani chucked out of the gang.

'It's not like that,' he said unhappily. 'We just want – we just like being with you, that's all.'

But Buffalo had worked himself up into a rage. He was standing up now, dancing about on the balls of his feet, making shadow punches into the air. Mamo, his stomach fluttering, stood up too.

Buffalo's attack was so sudden that he was taken off guard and almost fell backwards. Then, a steely hand grabbed him above the elbow, while Buffalo's other arm caught him in a headlock. He struggled, kicking his legs out behind him, half suffocated, his arms flailing as he tried to land punches on Buffalo's back and sides.

He was vaguely aware that Dani had stood up too, that he was holding Suri out of harm's way and circling helplessly round them. He could smell a sharpness on Buffalo now, and felt the rage pouring out of him like heat.

'Let go!' he kept trying to say. 'Get off me!'

He managed at last to land a kick on one of Buffalo's shins, and followed it up quickly with a crack from his knee on Buffalo's thigh. Buffalo grunted with pain and his grip loosened slightly. Fury was coursing through Mamo now and he heaved against Buffalo's violent embrace, trying desperately to free his head.

Then, suddenly, he felt a sharp blow on his back. At the same time Buffalo let go and Mamo staggered backwards half stunned. Million was between them now, glaring at Mamo.

'What are you doing? What's going on? You fight, you're out, you hear?'

Mamo bit his lip and said nothing.

'You hear?' Million said again.

To Mamo's surprise, Buffalo said, 'It was me, Million. I got him going.'

Million turned to him and spread out his hands, exasperated.

'What? Why?'

Buffalo shrugged.

'He got on my nerves, him and that fat parasite there.'

'He's not a parasite,' said Mamo hotly, starting forward to attack Buffalo again.

Million held him off, then turned his head to frown at Buffalo.

'Why do you do it? All the time?'

Buffalo looked away.

'You know what I'm like.'

Million seemed to accept this. He made no comment. Mamo could see that he understood. He knew Buffalo had started it. He wouldn't lay the blame on Mamo. Mamo felt his anger begin to seep away.

Buffalo seemed to have forgotten his own rage completely. He looked quite calm again. In fact his face was even softening into a smile.

'It's my temper,' he said, as if he was talking about a being removed from himself. 'It gets me going.'

Million was standing beside Buffalo now, looking thoughtfully at Mamo and Dani. Mamo could see from the way that he and Buffalo were together that they were brothers, or as good as. If there was any trouble with Buffalo, Million would, in the end, always take his part.

It's just as well to know that, Mamo thought. It's best to know where we stand.

'Did you get any?' Buffalo said to Million, as if nothing at all had happened.

'Any what?'

'*Injera.*'

'Yes.'

They squatted down in a circle. Million took a roll of *injera* out of the plastic bag he'd been carrying and handed it to Buffalo, who passed it on to Mamo. With an inward sigh of relief, Mamo saw that something had shifted. The fight seemed to have resolved things for Buffalo. He and Dani would be accepted now.

Gratefully he took the *injera*, broke off a piece for Suri, and began to eat. He felt good. He might be a *godana*, a rubbish sifter, a piece of muck sticking to muck, but he was doing all right. He was one of a gang. An insider. The Garbage King had real friends that he could trust and the rest of the world didn't matter any more.

He had nearly finished his *injera*, relishing every crumb, when Getachew came flying down the road.

'Police! Quick! Run!' he panted. 'They're after me!'

A stitch was jabbing Dani's side and every breath he took hurt. He'd never run so fast in his life. The others had taken off like a flock of terrified goats at the word 'police'. They dived into a lane and hurtled down the hill, not slowing until they reached a piece of flat open ground a good half mile from their usual pitch.

They'd outstripped Dani at once and he'd only kept them in sight by making a desperate effort. Once he thought he'd lost them altogether and stopped at a fork in the maze of lanes in an agony of indecision.

Mamo had run back for him. Dani had seen his slight figure appear at the bend of the left-hand lane. Mamo had beckoned to him urgently and Dani had set off again at once, lumbering along, his whole body working as it never had before.

The group was standing in a knot behind a tumbledown corrugated-iron fence when Dani reached them at last. He bent over, gasping for breath. The others had recovered theirs. They were watching Million, who was interrogating Getachew. Even Suri seemed aware of the tension in the group. She had wriggled free of Mamo's arms and was yapping around Getachew's feet.

'So they just saw you walk out of the shop behind me, and they started to shout and run after you?' Million was saying suspiciously. 'Why would they do that?'

Getachew gave him a wide smile.

'You know the cops, Million. Do they need a reason?'

'No,' conceded Million, frowning, 'but we don't try to give them one.'

'So what are you all looking at me for?' blustered Getachew, hunching his shoulders and looking round at the others.

No one said anything.

'What's that in your pocket?' Million said suddenly. 'What's that bulge?'

Getachew stared down at his trouser leg as if he'd noticed it for the first time.

'What do you mean? Oh, this.' He sounded uneasy now. 'It's nothing. Just some things I picked up at the dump.'

'Let's see.' Million's voice was hardening.

'What is all this? You don't believe me?'

Million said nothing. He held out his hand and waited.

Defiantly, Getachew pulled a packet of a cigarettes and a lighter out of his pocket and dropped them into Million's hand.

Million looked up at him.

'You didn't find these in the dump. I saw them in the shop, on the counter, when I was buying the *injera*. You stole them.'

Getachew was looking scared now.

'I didn't! Honestly, Million . . .'

'You're a thief.' Million's voice was cold. 'We don't have thieves in this gang. You're out, Getachew.'

Getachew took a step backwards.

'No! Listen, Million. It wasn't like that. OK, so I didn't find them at the dump. They were on the counter at the shop, like you said, but I thought the guy in front of us had left them there and forgotten them. I was just – it's not stealing if someone's been stupid enough to leave their things lying about. It's – it's scavenging. Like at the dump.'

'No one left them behind. They belonged to the shopkeeper,' Million said, turning his back. 'Get out of here.'

'I won't! You can't make me. Please, Million, where will I go? It was just a mistake, that's all. Give me another chance.'

Buffalo had followed Million. He was talking quietly to him. Million turned round again.

'You want to stay with us?'

'You know I do.' Getachew's fists were tight balls of anxiety.

'What if you steal again? We'll be picked up. We'll end up at the police station. They'll beat the hell out of us. They've done it before for less.'

'I won't. Honestly. I swear to God.'

Million stood with his legs apart and his arms crossed, staring at him.

'Strip him down, Buffalo,' he said at last.

Buffalo went to Getachew and pushed him down to his knees. Then he pulled his shirt off over his head and tossed it to Shoes.

Getachew seemed to know what was coming. He bent forward and Dani, watching with fascinated horror, could see that his clasped hands were shaking.

Million was walking along the broken fence. He bent down and pulled out from behind it a long thin eucalyptus shoot. He twisted and tugged at it until it broke in half, then he stripped off its leaves and handed it silently to Buffalo.

The beating was hard. The stick brought welts up on Getachew's bare back. Mamo and Shoes turned tactfully away but Dani couldn't take his eyes off Getachew. Whenever his father had beaten him, Dani had cringed and cried, pleaded for mercy, then run to his mother in a storm of tears for petting and sympathy. But Getachew didn't even whimper. He knelt, back arched, accepting the blows as they fell.

'That's enough. Stop,' Million said at last.

Buffalo threw the stick away. Shoes handed back Getachew's shirt to him, and Getachew put it on, wincing in spite of himself as he moved his shoulders. He staggered as he stood up and righted himself with an effort.

'Last chance,' Million said curtly. 'Once more and you're out for good. You can go down to Mercato and thieve with the rest of them down there.'

'I won't do it again, Million, I promise,' Getachew said, his bravado gone.

Dani shivered. If ever he got punished like that he wouldn't be able to bear it so calmly. He hadn't realised that *godana* could be so strict about stealing. His father had always said that street people were thieves and con artists, that some of them were really rich and they just put on rags and went out to beg because it was easier than looking for work.

What other things do you get punished for in this gang? Dani thought. I'll have to watch it.

Million was looking round at the open ground.

'We'll have to sleep down here for a night or two,' he said. 'No point going back up to our pitch till things have calmed down. The ground'll be damp here, but that can't be helped. Dani and Garbage King, go back up there and fetch our blankets.'

'Please, Million,' Dani said, licking his lips nervously. 'I can't. The police will be on the lookout for me.'

Million nodded.

'OK. Mamo and Shoes, you go. Take your time. Watch out. We'll wait for you here.'

It was a long time before Mamo and Shoes came back. They'd approached the pitch cautiously, afraid that the police would be lying in wait for them. Two policemen were in fact standing nearby on the street corner, talking casually to each other, not seeming to be particularly interested in anyone, but a baleful presence all the same.

Mamo and Shoes moved away and sat on a wall at a distance, watching them out of the corner of their eyes.

It was the first time Mamo had been alone with Shoes and he didn't know how to talk to him.

'I don't think Getachew's really a thief, do you?' he said at last, breaking a long silence. 'I mean, not a proper one.'

Shoes was kicking his leg against the wall.

'I've seen him nick stuff before. Million doesn't know. Getachew had it coming.'

Mamo felt he had to stick up for Getachew. He'd known him for years, after all.

'He won't do it again. Not now.'

Shoes seemed to lose interest in the subject.

'He'd better not,' he said.

There was another pause.

'Have you been with Million and Buffalo long?' Mamo asked at last.

'Two years, I suppose. Since my stepmother threw me out.'

'Million's good, isn't he. A good *joviro*, I mean.'

'He's OK. There was another guy before. Isayas. We chose Million when Isayas went.'

'What happened to him? To Isayas?'

'He's still around. He does stuff down by the stadium. He stopped bothering about us when he started drinking all the time.'

It was an hour before the policemen moved on. The boys had stopped watching them and had begun idly following the progress of an argument between a taxi driver and a man who looked like a farmer up from the country. When they turned back, the policeman had gone.

They jumped down from the wall and slipped back towards their pitch. Their blankets and Dani's bag were still where they had left them that morning, neatly piled in a corner of the wall. Mamo looked round nervously as they bent to pick them up but no one was around to notice them.

It was obvious, when at last they got back to the group on the open ground below the lanes, that although

Getachew had been forgiven Million and Buffalo were still angry with him.

'What's been happening?' Mamo asked Dani in a low voice. 'They all tried to beg by the traffic lights over there,' Dani told him, 'but there's another gang around and they chased us away.'

'Were you there? Did you have to beg?' Mamo said, trying and failing to imagine Dani with the shuffling gait and cajoling voice of a beggar.

A rare smile lit up Dani's whole face.

'No. Million said I was too fat. I've never been grateful for all this stuff before,' he said, and he pinched the roll of flab round his waist.

'I don't want to beg, either,' Mamo said, 'but I'll have to, I know.'

It was good talking to Dani. They had things in common. They were both in the gang, but they were still a pair, too.

'I didn't thank you,' Dani said, 'for waiting when we were running away. I'd have got totally lost if you hadn't stayed back and beckoned me.'

Mamo smiled back at him. It was nice to be thanked. It hadn't happened to him very often. Then a thought occurred to him.

'What are we all going to do if we can't beg? I mean, what are we going to eat today? Are we going back to the restaurant?'

Dani shook his head.

'I don't think so. Million said we've got to stay away from the usual places. Lie low for a bit. Stick it out till they've forgotten.'

He spoke with more respect than before. Mamo nodded. Since Million had disciplined Getachew he'd felt in awe of the *joviro* too.

The rest of the day passed slowly. Million and Buffalo went back to the nearby road to try to strike a deal with the local gang. They came back late, when the sun was already beginning to set.

'What happened, Million?' Shoes called out when he saw them coming. 'Have you got any food for us?'

'Tomorrow,' Million said, squatting down with a sigh. 'Those guys on the road over there were OK in the end, when we explained we'd only be around for a few days. They said they'd show us a restaurant near here in the morning. The people there don't put the leftover stuff out till late. You have to get up and get it early.'

'So nothing more today then,' Mamo said, already mentally adjusting his mind to a hungry night ahead, and feeling superior to Dani who had let out a sharp 'Oh' of disappointment.

Chapter 13

It was five days before the group returned to their usual place on the street corner. They sniffed around it cautiously several times, then drifted back bit by bit, more alert than usual to any sightings of policemen.

It was a relief to all of them to be back. The streets here were their familiar territory, where nothing escaped their notice. They could predict the moment when the shop on the corner was about to dispose of tomatoes and guavas that were too far gone to sell, and when the baker was reducing the price on his stale bread. They had established rights on the guarding of cars that parked on a forecourt nearby, and were the resident beggars at the traffic lights further along.

Mamo had felt unsettled during the five days on the rough ground down the hill. There'd been too little to do, and not nearly enough to eat. It had been colder at nights as well. His feelings had veered up and down, almost frightening him sometimes with their intensity.

He tried to push them away. Whenever he thought about being a *godana*, a street person, he started falling into an abyss of anxiety and depression. And if he allowed himself to look into the faces of passers-by, especially those he begged from, seeing the mixture of pity and contempt in their eyes, he started to despise himself and feel worthless.

He could see Dani almost visibly changing as the days passed. His spare weight was dropping off him and the need to be constantly on the watch was making him sharper and quicker on his feet. He was acquiring too the worn, dusty, grey look that they all had. His old flashes of arrogance came more rarely now, and he was learning not to push himself forward when food came, but to take his turn and be more respectful to the others.

Sometimes Mamo was aware that he was changing himself. Something was hardening and sharpening inside him as if he was developing an inner core of metal. The longer he stayed out here on the street the more he was learning about how to survive, and the more certain he became that he could do it.

I'll never be trapped again. I'll never let anyone treat me like that farmer did, he told himself again and again.

They'd visited Karate once while they'd been away from their pitch, creeping into the hospital at Siddist Kilo to stand round his bed in awed silence. They'd felt nervous under the frowning eyes of the nuns in their stiff uniforms, and the hard walls and floors, the smell of disinfectant and the sound of doors clanging shut behind them made them all uneasy.

Mamo noticed that only Dani had seemed at home. He'd tied a piece of cloth round his head as a sort of disguise and had walked confidently up to Karate's bed, putting a hand down on the pillow as if he didn't even register how soft it was.

'We'll go up to the hospital again tomorrow,' Million announced when they'd repossessed their pitch. 'He might be ready to come out.'

It was a long walk up the hill to Siddist Kilo. Dani was more nervous this time. He'd wrapped up most of his face as well as his head, and skulked along by walls and fences, looking down at his feet. Mamo watched out for him, ready to warn him if anyone looked at him twice, but he didn't feel really worried. Dani already looked quite different from the plump, smartly dressed boy he'd first noticed gazing in at the window of the cake shop. People would be less likely to recognise him now.

Suri was getting too lively to be carried all the time. On their first visit to the hospital, Mamo had hidden her inside his shirt and taken her in with him, but today, when they reached the forbidding double doors, and he tried to tuck her away, she was so frisky she nipped his fingers.

'You'll have to leave her outside,' Dani said to him. 'They never let dogs into hospitals.'

'I can't. She might panic and run away. I might never find her again,' said Mamo, feeling cold at the thought.

'Tie her up to something,' Million said, pushing open the doors.

Mamo stood irresolutely as the others slipped past the doorman and went in. He didn't have any string and besides, he didn't like the idea of leaving Suri on her own.

'I'll stay here,' he called after them. 'Say hi to Karate for me.'

He squatted down against the wall to wait. It was interesting being in a new part of town. The university was just up the road and students were strolling up and down the wide boulevard with books tucked under their arms. Jacaranda trees were in bloom in the strip of garden by the hospital wall and every now and then a blue blossom floated down and landed beside him, to be pounced on and wrestled with by Suri as if it was a dangerous enemy.

It was nice here, peaceful and beautiful. For some reason, Mamo thought of Yohannes and Hailu. They must be out there in the countryside right now, herding their cows, throwing stones into the stream and playing one of their endless games.

He began to sing quietly, and was so absorbed in easing a stick out of Suri's mouth that he didn't hear the footsteps as the others came up behind him.

'That's nice,' Shoes said. 'You sing really nice.'

Mamo jumped and turned round, embarrassed to find that the whole group had been listening to him.

'No, I don't,' he mumbled. He'd been too shy to let any of them, except Dani, hear him sing before. 'How's Karate? When's he coming out?'

'He looks better,' Getachew said, 'whatever the nuns think.'

Mamo picked up Suri and stood up.

'What did they say?'

'The young nurse said he's really sick still. Very bad,' Dani said. He was looking worried. 'He's got to stay in hospital.'

'That's all rubbish,' said Getachew. 'He's miserable in there, you can tell. That's what's stopping him getting better. He'd be OK if they let him out. He was worse than this last time and he was fine after he'd come back to us.'

'That old one, she told me he wasn't going to make it,' Million said quietly, as if he was afraid that telling bad news out loud would make it worse. 'The medicine wasn't working on him any more, she said.'

Dani looked at him, shocked.

'What? But he was sitting up and talking and everything. You saw him.'

'I know, but she said there was something inside. Something really wrong.'

Mamo suddenly made up his mind.

'I'm going in to see him myself,' he said. 'Here, Dani, you take Suri. I'll catch you all up.'

It was quiet but echoing inside the hospital corridor and Mamo had to pluck up his courage to go on alone. He remembered from last time where Karate's bed was, and he found it easily. There was no one else around, except for a few sick children, hunched in their beds asleep, and an old woman rocking herself backwards and forwards in a corner, taking no notice of anything.

Karate was curled up in a tight ball under a blanket and tears were oozing out of his closed eyes on to the pillow.

He was holding a cloth in his hand and stroking his cheek with it. Mamo recognised the elephant shirt that Dani had given him.

He leaned over the bed.

'What's the matter, Karate? Why are you crying?'

Karate's eyes flew open and he struggled to sit up.

'I thought Million was going to take me,' he said, 'then the nurse came and said I had to stay.'

'But they're nice to you in here, aren't they?' said Mamo. 'I mean, they give you food and everything?'

'No one talks to you. You have to sleep all alone in your own bed. They get cross if you pee anywhere except in the special place. I'm so scared, Mamo. It's horrible. Take me with you. Please, please.'

Mamo looked round. He could see what Karate meant. You would be lonely in this place. The bare white walls and high windows were hard and stern. It made him shudder to think of spending even one night alone in this room, and Karate had been here for days and days.

'But they'll make you better if you stay,' he said, trying not to think about what Million had said.

'They won't. They never will. I get nasty dreams at night when I'm alone, bad things, I can't tell you, like animals and ghosts coming to eat me, and trucks running me over.'

He was beginning to sob, his small chest heaving.

Mamo put his arm around Karate's shoulders and squeezed gently. He didn't know what to do. What if he took Karate out of here, and then he died? But hadn't the old nun said he was going to die anyway? One thing was sure, being unhappy killed you quicker than anything else. Being with people you loved was the best kind of medicine. Yohannes's family had taught him that.

He bent down and whispered in Karate's ear, 'Where are your clothes?'

Karate stared at him for a moment, then his face lit up.

'They threw them away, except for this.' He held up his elephant shirt. 'I wouldn't let them touch that. They made me wear these stripy things.'

'Come on then, quick,' said Mamo.

He tore the blanket off the bed and wrapped it round Karate, then scooped him up into his arms. The little boy clung to him like a monkey, his arms round Mamo's neck and his legs round his waist. His heart thudding, Mamo ran with him to the door, raced down the long corridor and was out in the street a few seconds later.

The group was standing in a knot by the gate. Million saw him first and ran up, peeling Karate away from Mamo and holding him against his own thin chest.

'Good,' he said. 'I was just about to go back in there and fetch him out myself.'

For the last few days Dani had simply existed. He had shut his mind to the situation he was in and to all thoughts of the future and had lived only in the present, staying back when the others went off to beg, keeping himself in a quiet corner.

He'd lost count of how many days had passed since he'd left home. His father and mother, Meseret, Zeni, Negussie, the house, the compound, the big car, his school – they all belonged to another world, far away and long ago.

At the back of his mind he was aware that he was living off the others and that he couldn't do so for ever, but like everything else to do with the future, he pushed the thought aside.

The visit to the hospital shook him abruptly back into the present. He'd been in hospitals before, seeing Mamma when she'd gone in for tests and treatment. The wards she'd stayed in had been much newer and nicer than this charity place, but the atmosphere was still familiar. The clean corridors, enclosing painted walls and neat beds held no terrors for him. It was as if he'd stepped back for a moment into the real world.

Million seemed to have waived his iron rule on stealing and had accepted the theft of the hospital blanket. He walked fast at the head of his gang, moving defiantly on the balls of his feet along the crowded pavements with the other boys close to his heels.

'Here we are,' he said, when at last they reached their pitch. 'Home sweet home.' And he laughed at his own joke as he set Karate down, still wrapped like a cocoon in his blanket, next to his own sitting stone against the wall. Karate's eyes, large and burning in his pinched face, glowed gratefully up at him. His hand, protruding like a small claw from the blanket, was still clutching the elephant shirt.

'It's brilliant, Million,' he said hoarsely. 'It's much nicer here. Oh, they've taken down that sign by the barber's window. Yes and look, there goes the old man with the bicycle, the one who comes past here every day.'

Dani pulled Mamo aside.

'He can't stay out here all night,' he said. 'He's too sick. We've got to take him back to the hospital.'

Mamo stared at him.

'What do you mean? You saw how miserable he was in there. He's much better here with us.'

'But we haven't got any medicines or injections or anything. He'll be too cold. We won't know what to do if . . .'

Mamo shook his head as if he didn't understand what Dani was saying.

'We couldn't have left him there,' he said at last.

'It was all right,' said Dani. 'Hospitals are always like that. At least they look after you.'

'They weren't looking after him. He was all alone. He'd never slept on his own before. I'd be scared too, in a big soft bed like that.'

A gulf of incomprehension was opening up between them. Mamo seemed to sense it.

'It's not – I mean, when you're really sick, when you think you're going to die, even if you don't in the end, you need friends.' He was struggling to find the right words. 'People you belong to. That's more important than the stuff they give you.' He hesitated. 'If his soul goes out, it's not so bad for him. It's like he'll be going into the light. And we'd be there with him so he wouldn't be lonely.' He frowned and shook his head. 'But he won't die. He'll be all right now. Didn't you hear what Getachew said? He was worse than this before and he got better. He just needed to be with us again.'

Dani wasn't listening any more. He'd been jolted by a sudden image of Mamma, alone in a hospital in London. What if she was feeling like Karate had felt, lost and frightened in a strange place? What if she died there, without anyone from home being near her? Why hadn't he thought before about what it might be like for her?

He remembered with a blush of shame how he'd barely said goodbye the morning she'd left. He'd actually been angry with her for deserting him and leaving him to face his father on his own.

Did she know he'd run away? Had Father told her? Suppose she found out that he'd gone and was fretting about him? Would that stop her getting better?

He gripped Mamo's arm.

'Will you do something for me? Please?'

'What?'

'I've got to know what's happened to my mother. It's been ages now.'

'I thought you said she was away somewhere, in another country.'

'In England, yes, but my father will have news of her by this time.'

'You want me to find out?'

'Yes.'

'How?'

'Go to my house. Ask Negussie. He's the old guy who opens and shuts the gates.'

'What? I just go up to your house, knock on the gate, and say "Dani wants to know about his mum," then wait while they jump all over me and make me tell them where you've gone? No, thank you very much.'

Dani shook his head.

'Not like that, no.'

'How then?'

'Let me think.'

He tried to picture the house and the street.

'There's a little shop just near my house,' he said at last, 'and this really nice woman who knows my family. Negussie and Zeni talk to her all the time. Catch her on her own and ask her. She'll know. Please, Mamo, please go and ask her. I'll do something for you, I promise.'

'All right. I'll go tomorrow.' Mamo was secretly pleased. He liked the idea of seeing Dani's house. He'd often tried to imagine Dani in it.

That evening, fortune seemed to reward the group for rescuing Karate and returning to their old haunts. A particularly successful begging session at the traffic lights yielded enough for a good supper, and to cap it all, Buffalo, who had slipped off for a solitary scavenge at the dump, returned with a couple of old tyres and half a packing case. Million lit a fire with these, when darkness fell, and the boys crouched around it, licking the last of their supper off their fingers.

Only Karate ate nothing.

'I'm not hungry,' he croaked. 'They kept giving me stuff to eat at the hospital. I just want some water.'

He sat propped up between Million and Dani, swathed in the grey blanket. Looking down at him in the leaping firelight, Dani saw that he was breathing fast, with his mouth open, and that the dark corkscrews of hair were damp against his coppery forehead.

'You said you knew stories, Dani,' Getachew said. 'Go on, then. Tell us one.'

The others turned to him. Dani felt a twinge of anxiety. He'd forgotten about the stories.

'All right,' he said slowly. 'Wait a minute.'

He shut his eyes. There was one about a bird and an elephant, but it was too short and, anyway, he'd never liked the ending. And that one about the king and the flute – no, he couldn't remember the middle bit. But there was a good one about a brother and a sister that Zeni had often told to Meseret. He could probably remember most of it, and it was one she liked hearing again and again.

He opened his eyes. The boys were sitting in expectant silence, looking at him.

'OK,' said Dani. 'This one's about a brother and sister.'

He heard Karate beside him sigh with satisfaction.

'Once upon a time,' he began, 'there was a boy and a girl, and their mum and dad died and they were all on their own. They still lived in their parents' house, though.'

'Was it in Addis?' asked Mamo.

'I don't know. No, in the country. Anyway, this hyena came and cooked food for them and left it out for them to eat, but they never saw it.'

'A hyena?' said Getachew. 'Even if it was a hyena, it was still being kind giving them food.'

'No, it wasn't, because it just wanted to trick them and eat them.'

'How did they know?' said Shoes.

Buffalo pushed at him, making him almost topple over.

'Shut up and let him tell the story.'

'The kids wanted to know who was feeding them,' Dani went on, 'so one day the girl took the cattle down to the river instead of the boy, while the boy hid and watched. The hyena came and started to cook. She kept using magic, like if she wanted a spoon she just called out, "Spoon! Come to me!" and the spoon flew through the air right into her hand so the boy knew she was a magic hyena, like a witch.'

He looked round at the ring of faces. They were listening to him with rapt attention.

'The hyena saw him and made him come out of his hiding place. He was really scared but she was nice to him and said she wanted to marry him and told him to tell his sister. So when his sister came home he told her about the hyena and said he was going to marry her but not to worry, because she was nice and would feed them and look after them.'

Beside him, Karate had stiffened with excitement.

'His sister said, was he crazy? You can't trust a witch! And she made him agree to run away. So they did. They ran off into the forest with all their cattle. And there were other kids in the forest like them and they all got to be friends.'

'Like us,' murmured Karate.

'But the hyena was furious, and she hunted them out and found them, and turned herself into a really beautiful woman. The boy didn't know it was the hyena, and he fell in love with her and married her and he and his sister went home with her.

'But one night the girl went to stay at a friend's house, and the hyena woman saw that she'd got the boy alone at last and it was her chance to eat him. So she killed him and hid him in the field outside ready to eat the next day.'

Karate coughed. He lifted his head away from Million's arm and began to lean against Dani's shoulder. One thumb was in his mouth and his other hand was clutching a corner of the elephant shirt, holding it to his lower lip.

'When the girl came home,' Dani went on, 'she couldn't find her brother and she guessed what had happened.' He stopped. 'I can't remember the next bit very well, but anyway, she ran outside and met a rat and a monkey, and they couldn't help her, and then she got really upset and began to pray. And God came down and she told him what had happened and took him to where her brother was. And God stuck all his bones together and made him come alive again.'

'He can do that?' Karate said, looking surprised.

'And then the hyena chased them both and fell into a gorge and died.'

'Is that the end?' said Million, who had been trying not to look as interested as the others.

'Yes,' said Dani, 'except that the boy and girl went home and lived happily ever after. I didn't tell it very well. I haven't told it before and I missed out lots of bits. I can remember it better now.'

'I think it was lovely.' Karate said. 'Tell it again. Put in all the other bits this time.'

Dani looked round, expecting that the others would be bored, but they were watching him, their mouths slightly open, like an audience at the cinema.

So he began again, and as he told the story, something happened to him that had never happened before. His voice deepened, his imagination took fire, words rolled out of him, and the brother and sister, the hyena witch, the band of boys in the forest, seemed to leap into the circle of firelight, drawn there by the magic of his telling.

It was warmer than it had been for the last few nights, when the chill had been so severe that Dani had shivered on the ground until his teeth chattered. The cracked concrete paving stones on their old pitch still held some of the sun's heat, and they were dry, unlike the bare earth on which they'd had to sleep down the hill. Then, too, the last embers of the fire glowed red, warming the boys' minds as much as their bodies.

Yawning, they were shaking out their *shammas* and blankets ready to settle down and sleep. Karate lay with his eyes shut as if he had dozed off already, but as Dani went to lie down he turned his head and said, 'Sleep beside me, Dani. I want to ask you something.'

Dani sat down beside him. He was getting used to sleeping on the hard ground but he still delayed lying down as long as he could.

'I think that boy in the story was silly,' said Karate. His voice was weak and thick with phlegm. 'Why did he marry the hyena woman? He should have run away with his sister. I would have.'

'Yes, but he thought she was nice. She tricked him,' Dani said, smiling. Karate was like Meseret. The story was obviously as real to him as everyday life.

'Do you think it hurt when he got killed?'

'Maybe, but not for long. She must have done it quickly because he'd have started fighting back.'

'When he actually died it must have hurt.'

'No,' said Mamo, from a little way away. 'It doesn't hurt. It's nice. Your soul just floats away and goes to God.'

'I know what God looks like,' said Karate. 'I looked in through the church door. There's a picture on the wall there and it's an old man with a white beard.'

Dani said nothing.

'God's your father,' said Mamo. 'He looks after you.'

'Like Million,' Karate said, and closed his eyes again.

Dani lay down. He had a sudden urge to pick Karate up and cradle him in his arms but he didn't want to disturb him or offend Million, who was lying on the little boy's other side. Instead he reached for Karate's hand and squeezed it.

'Goodnight,' he said. 'Sleep well. You'll feel better in the morning.'

Karate must have died just before dawn because when the other boys got up his body was still warm, although his hands were quite cold.

Dani had woken with a start at first light. Million was sitting up, holding Karate's hands in his and crying. Dani stared down at the small still face. Karate looked peaceful, happy almost, but smaller somehow, as if death had shrunk him down. Dani's throat started to feel tight. He thought he might choke.

'It's not right! He was only a baby! No one should have to die like that!'

Million gently unwrapped Karate from the grey blanket and began to take off the hospital pyjamas. Dani stared at him, appalled.

'What are you doing?'

Million prised the elephant shirt off Karate's tight fist, eased it over his head and pulled it down to cover the still, thin chest.

'He wouldn't want to go in that thing,' he said, throwing the pyjama jacket aside.

He laid Karate down again on the pavement. The shirt, far too big, engulfed the little body. The sight of it was too much for Million. He picked Karate up and held him against his chest, and a high wail began to come from deep inside his throat. The others squatted round him, crying too.

'But it's all wrong!' Dani cried. 'We should have done something! I didn't realise!'

'What! What should we have done?' said Mamo, turning on him. 'His soul flew away. It's free. You couldn't stop it.'

Dani's anger died away. The others were right. There was nothing they could have done. Karate's soul had flown. That was all there was to it.

Like them, he began to cry.

None of them heard the two policemen approach. Million was the first to look up. He flinched at the sight of the khaki uniforms and black peaked caps.

Dani shrank into himself, his heart suddenly pounding, but the policemen had no eyes for him. They were looking only at the body of the little boy in Million's arms.

'He passed away in the night,' Million said. 'He's been very sick, for a long time. He was in hospital but he didn't like it there and he ran away.'

The older policeman bent down to look more closely, and clicked his tongue sympathetically.

'I know him. He's been hanging around here with you lot for ages.'

'He was our brother,' Buffalo burst out.

The man straightened up.

'Better send for the municipal,' he said to the younger policeman. He turned back to Million. 'What was his name? Who was he?'

'He was just Karate,' muttered Getachew.

'His mothers called him Wondemu,' Million said. He didn't have a family. He's lived with us for years. We looked after him. He didn't know anyone else.'

'Father's name?'

The boys looked round at each other.

'Million,' Dani said loudly, looking up. In spite of the risk of being seen, he couldn't stay silent. 'His father's name was Million.'

Chapter 14

Tiggist had never known anything like this new feeling that had possessed her. It had taken hold the very next day after she'd first seen Salma's brother, Yacob, at the gate. He'd come back while she was giving Yasmin her lunch and she'd met him properly, shaking hands with him and everything.

It had started right away, a sort of warm happiness, making her feel as if she was expanding inside. A smile was growing, spreading across her whole face without her even realising it. Then she'd seen the same sort of smile on Yacob's face, and had suddenly felt dreadfully shy. She'd dropped her eyes and covered her mouth with her hand, and had turned back to Yasmin who was waiting for her next mouthful like a baby bird in a nest with its beak wide open.

It was lucky that Salma was out, running an errand for Mrs Faridah. She'd have laughed and teased Tiggist, and then Tiggist would have clammed up completely and been unable to say a word. As it was, she found she could answer Yacob's questions quite easily, if she kept her eyes on Yasmin and didn't actually look at him.

His voice was low and gentle. You couldn't imagine it ever sounding angry. He asked her about her parents. She told him that her father had died in the northern campaign. It was what Ma had said sometimes, and it might have been true, though she'd wondered sometimes if Ma had been quite sure who her father was.

She couldn't help feeling just a little bit relieved that Ma had died. She wasn't the sort of person Yacob would have liked. She couldn't imagine him hanging round bars and drinking all the time, like all Ma's old men friends, and if he'd seen Ma drunk, and in one of her rages, she would have died of shame.

Yacob didn't seem to mind that she didn't have a family, except for Mamo, and she explained that she'd lost touch with him. He only seemed to be interested in her. Did she like being in Awassa? Was it nicer than Addis? Had she ever walked along by the lake in the evening, when the birds were flying in to roost, or been up to the top of the hill to watch the sun set over the water?

His questions opened up vistas in front of her. She'd seen nothing of Awassa. She'd never had the time, and even if Mrs Faridah had let her go out, she wouldn't have known where to go. She hardly knew how to answer him. She'd have liked to ask him questions too, but she didn't dare.

Salma came back just as her brother was going. She began laughing loudly, seeing the two of them together, just as Tiggist had feared she would, but then she looked from Yacob's face to Tiggist's and back again, stopped laughing and shook her head.

'Wow,' was all she said.

Yacob came every day after that. Tiggist was afraid that Mrs Faridah would notice and forbid him to come, but Yacob kept himself tactfully out of sight. Anyway, Mrs Faridah was completely occupied with her husband, who was sicker than ever.

Mr Hamid died a couple of weeks later. Tiggist had hardly ever seen him, except for occasional small glimpses through a half-open door, and she couldn't pretend to be sad, though she felt a bit sorry for Yasmin and Mrs Faridah. Instead she was worried. What if Mrs Faridah decided to go back to Addis and take Tiggist with her? She might never see Yacob again!

Mrs Faridah was upset at the funeral, of course, crying a lot and accepting everyone's sympathy with heavy sighs and shakes of the head, but Tiggist could see that she was relieved too. Mr Hamid had been sick for such a long time, and even before he fell ill he hadn't been much of a husband, by all accounts. It was Mrs Faridah who'd kept everything together, running the shop in Addis and bringing Yasmin up single-handed.

The blow fell a week after Mr Hamid's body had been laid to rest in the cemetery up the hill.

'We're going back to Addis, Tiggist,' Mrs Faridah said, tying back her hair in a black headscarf, and looking energetic and determined.

'When?' asked Tiggist. Her heart was sinking down and down, as if it was tied to a lead weight.

'As soon as possible.' Mrs Faridah was smiling at her in the old friendly way. 'Aren't you pleased? You must have missed it, being stuck down here in this sleepy hollow.'

'Oh no,' Tiggist said, biting her lip. 'I like it here.' Mrs Faridah pinched her chin.

'Well, you'd better start liking Addis again. Get Yasmin's clothes washed this morning. We'll be off the day after tomorrow.'

For the first time since she'd met him, Yacob failed to come that day. Tiggist was on tenterhooks, hovering in sight of the compound gates and looking up at every footstep.

Salma rolled her eyes at her.

'You've got it really bad, haven't you? I can't believe anyone could get so soft over poor old Yacob. He's so boring! He's not even handsome!'

'Not handsome?' said Tiggist, firing up at once. 'How can you say that? He's – he's got the most beautiful eyes.'

She stopped. Salma had let out a shout of laughter.

'Yacob! Beautiful eyes! I don't believe I'm hearing this!'

Reluctantly, Tiggist smiled too.

'Yes, but what's the use?' she said, her smile fading at once. 'I'm going back to Addis. I might never see him again.'

'Oh, you will,' Salma said comfortably. 'He may be a bit of a slowcoach, our Yacob, but he's persistent. I think he's really gone on you. He won't give up easily.'

That was the only comfort Tiggist had that day, and she nursed Salma's words as she went about her work. She'd begun to allow herself to paint rosy pictures of her future, of the shop Yacob would one day have, and the sort of house they might live in. She'd even dared to imagine what their children might look like, and what names they'd give them.

I must have been mad, she kept telling herself. He'll forget all about me once I've gone. Why would he want to marry me – a man like him? I'm from nowhere.

The house was in turmoil now. The funeral visits were over, but Mrs Faridah was sorting and packing, washing and organising, giving orders and countermanding them, watched listlessly by Mr Hamid's old mother, who had come in from the country, and who sat hour after hour in a corner of the compound, the only person, it seemed to Tiggist, who really mourned Mr Hamid's death.

Yacob came earlier than usual the next day. His slightly pockmarked forehead was furrowed.

'You're going back to Addis, then?' he said to Tiggist. 'I heard from the egg seller. I expect you're pleased.'

'Oh no! No! I love it here. I don't want to go at all!'

His frown cleared.

'I wanted to ask you –' he began.

Her heart started to pound.

'What?'

'I can't. I'm not ready yet. I still don't earn much money. Not enough, anyway. We couldn't – you know – until I've got my shop.'

'Oh, but I'll wait,' she said, daring to read his meaning. 'For as long as you like.'

'Will you?'

He took hold of her hand and she was amazed to feel that his was trembling. She felt calmer and more confident, almost powerful.

'Yes,' she said.

'Tiggist!' Mrs Faridah was calling urgently from inside the house. 'What are you doing? Come here and take Yasmin outside. She's been under my feet all morning.'

Yacob and Tiggist jumped apart.

'I've got to go,' Tiggist said. She wasn't too shy now to look into his eyes. She was gazing into them in fact, unable to drag her own away.

He fumbled in his pocket and pulled out a scrap of paper.

'Our neighbour's got a telephone,' he said. 'If you need me, call this number and leave a message. I'll come and see you, anyway, as soon as I can raise the money for the bus fare.'

She took the paper and folded it as carefully as if it was a 100-birr note.

'Tiggist!' Mrs Faridah shouted again.

'I've got to go,' she said, and ran into the house.

It was several days before Mamo could think about carrying out his promise to go to Dani's house. After the black mini van had come from the municipality, and the men had wrapped Karate in a white blanket and taken him away, the boys had felt the need to stick together.

'What'll they do with him?' Mamo asked Million. He was thinking of the cemetery where he and Dani had met. It wouldn't be a bad place to go. If Karate was buried there, they could even go and visit his grave.

But Million jerked his head towards the hill behind the city.

'There's a graveyard over there somewhere, a long way out. They put you there if they don't know who you are and there's no one else to bury you.'

'But is it a proper place? Near a church and everything?' Mamo said. He wanted to hold on to the picture of the cemetery.

Shoes lifted his head from a bag of strong-smelling stuff that he'd been holding to his nose. Even a whiff of it made Mamo's eyes water.

'Been there. Church. They wrap you in a mat,' he said jerkily.

Maybe it's where they put Karate's real mother, Mamo thought.

He felt a little better. It had been horrible seeing Karate disappear with strangers, like rubbish to be disposed of, but if he was in a churchyard, somewhere near his mother, he'd be all right.

Million was in an unpredictable mood after that. He and Buffalo got hold of some arak and drank themselves silly. Buffalo's eyes stared red and angry out of a thunderous face, but the drink made him clumsy and it was easy, if you kept quiet, to stay out of way. But Million was more dangerous. The more he drank the more his mood veered, affectionate and confiding one moment, resentful and hostile the next.

None of the group talked about Karate, but his passing had left a jagged hole, and it would be a while before it could close over.

On the third day the effects of the arak seemed to have worn off and Million and Buffalo were themselves again. Dani and Mamo, who had taken it upon themselves to forage for food during the last few turbulent days, had gone out early, before the sun had risen, and had come back with a good haul from the bins behind a new restaurant that had recently opened close by.

This was the best time of day, Mamo decided, as they sat eating together, letting the warmth of the day's new sun chase the chill of night from their thinly clad bodies. Now, with full stomachs and the day before them, with Million and Buffalo restored to normality and the balance of the gang familiar again, life didn't seem so bad.

Dani, waiting till the food had all gone and Million was sitting comfortably with his legs stretched out in front of him, asked the question that was in Mamo's mind.

'Million,' he said, 'is it OK if Mamo goes down to my house at Bole today? I want to know if – what's happened to my mother.'

He was tense as he waited for the answer, and breathed out with relief when Million merely nodded.

'I'll go with you to show you the way, till we're nearly there,' he said to Mamo and jumped to his feet.

Mamo, excited by the thought of doing something different, grinned at him.

'You could go all the way yourself, and knock on your own door,' he said. 'I don't think even your ma would recognise you now.'

·Dani looked down at himself, and Mamo saw that he'd made him anxious.

'Don't be daft,' he said roughly. 'It's just that you've got thinner, that's all, and your clothes don't look new any more.'

But it was more than that, he thought, as the two of them set off along the pavement, skirting the potholes and navigating round the street sellers, who were setting out their wares on cloths on the ground. Dani moved differently now. He was less shambling, more alert, his muscles becoming taut. Though he was constantly on the lookout for danger, he no longer skulked all the time in the shadows of walls, where he had been at greater risk of giving himself away with his hangdog air.

Mamo pulled down the brim of the cap Dani had given him, which he still wore night and day. It was good going off like this, to a new part of town, though he was a little worried about Suri. The puppy was too small as yet for an expedition this long, but was becoming more difficult to carry. He'd had to leave her in Million's care.

It was a long walk. They were soon out of the centre of town, but the road that led down to the suburb of rich people's houses seemed endless. They stopped at a petrol station and took a drink of water from a tap at the back, keeping an eye out for the pump attendants working round at the front who would chase them away the minute they were free.

'I'm not going any further than this,' Dani said, as they slipped out of the side of the garage on to the main road. He had found a piece of black-and-white checked cloth on the last visit to the dump, and in spite of the heat he now wrapped it round his head and shoulders. 'There's loads of people around here who could recognise me.'

He gave Mamo instructions. He had to turn left at the next fruit stall, go up the narrow tarmac road and right down the unmade-up lane where there was a sign pointing to the Sinbad restaurant. The kiosk was a little way along, on the right, no more than a window with a counter set in the mud wall. Dani's house was a bit beyond that, on the left. It was white, though you couldn't see it behind the high wall, and the metal gates were painted pale green.

Mamo was eager to go, but Dani seemed suddenly reluctant and held him back.

'Don't give me away. Don't say anything that'll give me away. Promise.'

'Of course I won't. I promise.'

'If you see a little girl with a nanny, it's probably my sister.'

'OK.'

'She might have pink bobbles in her hair.'

'I'll look.'

'No! Don't look as if you're interested in anyone there, or look at the house as if it was anything special.' Dani was becoming agitated. 'They'll suspect something. Negussie's always on the lookout for strangers hanging about.'

Mamo got away at last, glad to escape from Dani's fussing. He looked round curiously. He'd never been in an area like this before. Apart from a knot of shoe-shine boys on the corner by the fruit stall, no one else seemed to be around. They stared at him as he went past and one of them called out mockingly, 'Give us a birr and I'll polish your shoes, barefoot boy!'

'Give us a birr and I'll polish your face for you,' he shot back at them, then had to duck as a banana skin whistled past his ear.

Their laughter was good-humoured, though. He could tell they wouldn't bother him. He walked on up the road, squaring his shoulders, trying to look confident in this unfamiliar place.

Here it was. This was the corner with the pink and blue sign that Dani had described and there, a little way further up, was the kiosk.

Mamo hesitated. He hadn't thought out what he was going to say. How could he just walk up and ask the person behind the counter to tell him about the sick lady in the house up the road? What reason would he give?

To give himself time to think, he sauntered past the kiosk towards the long whitewashed wall and the big green gates further down the lane. That must be it. That must be Dani's house.

One of the gates was slightly ajar. Mamo slowed down, trying to see as much as he could. His jaw fell open. The place was a palace! Broad steps edged with flowerpots led up between pillars to a glass front door, and windows stretched away on either side. There were trees and a gravel drive, and grass, and bright flowers under the windows.

I didn't know it would be like this, Mamo thought.

He was filled with a mixture of awe and astonishment. Why on earth had Dani run away from all this? He must have been out of his mind.

An old man dressed in a khaki drill suit suddenly appeared at the open gate, startling Mamo.

'What do you want? What are you staring at?'

'Nothing,' stammered Mamo, stepping back. 'I just . . .'

'Get out of it,' the old man shouted shrilly, banging the gate shut.

Mamo walked back slowly towards the kiosk. A kind-looking woman was standing framed in the little window, leaning over to arrange some packets of sweets on the counter. Her eyes hardened when they took in Mamo's barefoot shabbiness, but he stopped and smiled at her ingratiatingly.

'What?' she barked.

'Could you let me have a glass of water?' Mamo said politely, and he added the beggar's formula, 'for the sake of Jesus.'

Her glance softened. Mamo stood respectfully away from the window as she bent down and poured out a drink from a container under the counter. She handed it to him and he drank it all down, though he was no longer thirsty, and gave the glass back to her with a murmur of thanks.

'What are you doing round here?' she asked. 'I haven't seen you before.'

A plan was beginning to form in Mamo's head.

'I'm looking for the church of St Raphael,' he said. 'It's round here somewhere, isn't it?'

'St Raphael? No. St Gabriel's is not far. You have to go out of this lane and turn up at the end. It's a good walk up the hill.'

'Perhaps that was it. St Gabriel.' Mamo nodded. 'I thought the lady said St Raphael but I probably got it wrong.'

'What lady?' The woman was leaning forward. Gossip was probably everything to her, Mamo thought. It was hardly surprising, in a quiet place like this.

'She lives near here,' Mamo said, thrilled with his own cleverness. 'She was in her car a while ago and she gave me some money for my sick mother. She was really kind. I could tell she was ill, though. I asked her if she was all right and she said she was going abroad for an operation, so I promised to pray for her at any church she liked. I thought she said St Raphael, but it must have been Gabriel, after all.'

The woman was clearly charmed. She heaved a sentimental sigh.

'Ah, that would be Woizero Ruth, poor lady.'

'Woizero Ruth! Yes, that was her name.' Mamo was trying not to sound too eager.

'She's beyond the help of prayers.' The woman was shaking her head. 'In this life, anyway.'

'Oh,' said Mamo, aware for the first time of the importance of his mission. Until that moment, Dani's mother had seemed imaginary, but she was becoming real now. 'Has she passed away, then?'

The woman hesitated, torn between a desire to be sensational but unsure of the exact state of affairs.

'I'm sure she has,' she said at last. 'There's trouble in that house. Something's happened. Woizero Zeni, she's the maid, and a good friend of mine, says she's on oath not to say a word, but the master, Ato Paulos, goes out every day looking like a thunder cloud. It's something to do with the boy. I know that much. I haven't seen him for a long time. Everything's been all upset there since Woizero Ruth went off for her operation, poor lady, but something else happened yesterday. Visitors were coming and going all day, wearing mourning clothes most of them. The whole place is in an uproar. It can only mean one thing, can't it?'

'I suppose so,' Mamo said. He heard a metallic clang and looked round. The pale green gates had swung open and a big black car, polished to a high sheen, was turning out of them, coming down towards him. He stepped back and watched as it went past. A man was sitting in the back behind the driver. Immaculately dressed in a dark suit, with a white shirt and black tie, he stared coldly for a moment or two into Mamo's eyes before the car swept past him in a flurry of dust and scattering of stones.

Ato Paulos had moved through every stage of anger, from his first irritation to all-consuming fury, but as time passed and he could find no trace of Dani anywhere, he started to feel afraid.

He'd felt the normal kinds of fear often in his life. He'd been scared as a child of his own stern father, often frightened in his youth during the years of revolution and war that had gripped Ethiopia, and while he was a soldier there had been moments of sheer gut-wrenching terror, when he'd seen his men blown to pieces all around him and had expected in the next instant to die too.

This fear was different, and much worse. Ato Paulos was afraid of his wife.

He wasn't afraid that she would die. Her operation seemed to have succeeded perfectly. But he was desperately frightened that when she found out that Dani had disappeared, she would be so angry with him that she would stop loving him.

Everyone believed, he knew, that he was the master in his house, and that Ruth was completely under his thumb, but in fact she'd always had her own way in the things that mattered, especially when it came to Dani. Ato Paulos had seen that she was spoiling him, but somehow he hadn't been able to put things right, and when he'd tried it had always gone wrong. He'd only made Dani scared of him and driven him back to his mother.

'You're so hard on Dani,' Ruth often said to him, her big eyes filling with reproachful tears.

If she came home and found that her darling son was missing, that he'd disappeared, vanished into thin air – he shut his eyes and swallowed. He couldn't bear to think of it. If only he'd known! If only he'd realised what the little fool would do!

Yes, but what had he done? That was the problem. Where could he possibly have gone?

Discreetly at first, but more and more desperately, Ato Paulos had checked on every person he could think of, telephoning some and calling in person on others. He knew people were beginning to wonder and talk. They'd started to call him back, wanting to know if everything was all right. He'd managed so far to put them off, but weeks had gone by now, and there was still no sign of Dani.

Surely, he said to himself again and again, he must be staying with someone. He can't be out there on the streets. He wouldn't last five minutes. He'd have come home if things were that bad. But the thought wouldn't go away.

Ato Paulos felt as if he was living in a nightmare.

Chapter 15

Dani stood quite still when Mamo told him, as gently as he could, that people were making funeral visits to the house. He felt stunned.

After a moment or two he turned round and began to walk quickly away. Mamo ran to catch up with him.

'But it mightn't have been her, your ma.' he said. 'That woman didn't really know. It could have been anyone.'

Dani didn't answer. He didn't want Mamo's opinion. He was sure that what he'd feared all along, what he'd known in his heart of hearts, was true. Mamma was dead. There was no hope for him at all now, no one there at home for him. He could never go back. He was doomed to live on the streets for the rest of his life.

'Listen,' Mamo panted, struggling to keep up with him. 'I'll go back again. I'll ask someone else. You can't be sure.'

Dani turned on him.

'I just want to be on my own,' he said. 'I'll see you later,' and he hunched his shoulders and veered off across the mass of crawling traffic to the other side of the road, leaving Mamo on the pavement, standing helplessly and watching him go.

Dani didn't look back. He was hardly aware of the road, the slow-moving cars, or the people walking past him. He wanted to find a place where he could be alone, a crack in a wall or a hole in the ground where he could hide, shut out the world and block his thoughts out too.

He found a place quite soon. It was a shady corner under a tree, just outside the wall of the church. He sat there, hardly moving, his arms round his knees, for hours.

It was late afternoon when he got back to the pitch. Mamo had told the others what had happened. They were sympathetic, clicked their tongues, shook their heads and offered him pieces of fruit they'd salvaged from behind the store, but they didn't really understand, and soon moved on to other topics. None of them had known what it was like to have a devoted, adoring mother, or if they had, they'd lost her so long ago the memory of her had gone.

Mamo sat close to him that evening, as they settled back down on their pitch after an expedition to a charity clinic to get some medicine for a sore on Shoes' face. Dani was still numb, unable to take in the disaster that had overtaken him. He was hardly aware of anything around him.

'Look,' Mamo said, touching his arm. 'Why don't you go and see your pa? Just try. He's probably all sad and he'll be really nice to you. You're his son, aren't you? Well, then.'

A scene immediately began to unroll like a film in front of Dani's eyes – the pale green metal gates swinging open, the beautiful house floating serenely in front of him, Meseret running away from Zeni to fling her arms round his knees, his father coming out of the front door and walking down the steps towards him.

I could, he thought. Why don't I? I will!

But then behind his father, in the still unfurling scene, he saw another figure. Feisal was standing behind his father's shoulder. Whatever else had happened, Feisal would still be there, waiting to carry him off to Jigjiga. And now he could see more clearly the expression on his father's face. It was a snarl of rage, his eyes blazing, his mouth contorted with fury. Anything would be better than facing his anger. Anything. Even this.

The vision had disappeared now.

So what if I'm his son? he thought bitterly. What does he care about that? I'm nobody to him. He despises me.

The sun had set a while ago and the chill of night was taking hold. Dani was shivering with cold now, as well as misery.

'Here, hold Suri for a moment,' Mamo said, dumping the puppy into Dani's arms. 'I'm going to get a drink of water.'

The puppy whined and licked Dani's hand. Absently, Dani stroked the rough yellow fur. He'd try to stop thinking about it all, for tonight, anyway. Maybe he was just living through a nightmare that would go away. Perhaps it would all look different in the morning.

During the next few days, Dani, sunk in gloom though he was, couldn't help noticing that something had changed in the gang. Everyone had been considerate at first, not pestering him with questions, even giving him more than his share of food, but their tolerance was beginning to wear thin.

Buffalo muttered now when Dani, who had stayed behind at the pitch all afternoon while the others went off and begged, was given a share of the food, and several times Getachew made a sharp comment under his breath. He caught Million looking at him too, with a considering frown. Only Shoes, lost in his own dream world, didn't seem to care.

Mamo was doing his best for him, Dani could see, shielding him from the group's growing irritation and standing up for him whenever an argument broke out. But there was no doubt about it. Dani could tell he was a burden. He wasn't pulling his weight. The clothes he'd brought into the group at the beginning had been paid for long ago, by weeks of food and protection. He'd have to start begging soon, and make his contribution, or he'd be out.

But I can't beg, thought Dani. I'd see someone who knows me. I'd get caught. And I'm still too fat, a bit. Anyway, I could never do it. I just couldn't.

Like he always did with worries, he tried to push the thought aside.

He was sitting as usual one morning, slumped against the wall while the others were out begging, idly watching Suri who had been left once more in his care. The puppy, who was growing almost visibly now, was tussling with an old root which was sticking up out of a rough patch of ground beyond the pitch, no doubt under the impression that it was a bone.

Her vigorous scrabblings were dislodging bits of earth and small sharp stones, but as Dani watched, something else, something long and thin with a blue end caught the sunlight.

He stood up and went across to look. Suri had dug up a biro. Dani picked it up. It was dusty, but still full of ink.

I wonder if it works, he thought.

He was still carrying the notebook he'd found at the dump. It was in the inner pocket of his now filthy bomber jacket. He wasn't sure why he'd kept it. The pages were bent and crumpled, with dog-eared corners, but he'd never quite wanted to throw it away.

He took it out, rubbed the dust off the pen, and tried it out. It didn't work at first but he scribbled hard for a moment or two and suddenly there they were, circles of blue scrawled across the page.

Dani sat down again. It had been so long since he'd written anything, he almost wondered if he'd forgotten how to shape the letters, but he balanced the book on his knee, smoothed out the cover and wrote *Daniel Paulos* across it in his best handwriting. Then, almost without realising what he was doing, he opened it to the first blank page and wrote, '*The Wicked Hyena*'. He underlined it.

He could remember exactly how it had been the evening before Karate had died, when he'd told the story for the second time. He'd had the group right there, in the palm of his hand. They'd hung on every word. He'd told it right. Brilliantly, in fact.

He shut his eyes for a moment, blocking out the sounds of the street all around him. Then he began to write.

He wrote for hours, covering page after page with his large untidy handwriting. It felt wonderful! He was doing something he could do, and doing it well.

He'd almost finished when the others came back. They looked tired and irritable.

'Where's Suri?' asked Mamo.

Dani looked round vaguely.

'She was here a minute ago.'

He realised guiltily that he hadn't seen Suri for hours. Mamo looked anxious and went off to hunt for her. Million gave Buffalo a small handful of coins.

'Get some bread,' he said. 'That's all we've got. It won't buy much.'

Buffalo came back after a few minutes with three small rolls. Million broke them in pieces and gave some to Getachew, then to Buffalo and Shoes, keeping one back. Dani closed his notebook and went to squat with the others but they took no notice of him. Dani held out his hand to Million. Buffalo nudged him sharply, making him almost fall over.

'Why should you have any?' he said.

Dani bit his lip and edged backwards.

Mamo came back looking hot and annoyed.

'She was miles away, right down near the butcher's,' he said accusingly to Dani. 'She might have got hurt.'

'Sorry,' mumbled Dani.

'You've got nothing else to do all day. You could at least have looked after her.'

'Nothing else?' said Getachew jeeringly. 'He's been hard at work, our little prince, writing in that notebook of his.' He leaned over and snatched it out of Dani's hand, opened the book and frowned down at the writing. 'What's all this rubbish, then?'

He put his finger under the title Dani had written and pointed to the letters one by one, slowly spelling out, *The Wicked Hyena*'.

'It was good, that story,' Shoes said dreamily. 'I liked it.'

'What's the use of this?' Million said, taking the book out of Getachew's hand. 'We don't run around all day getting money to feed you, just so you can sit and write stories.'

He held the book up, about to tear it in half.

'No! Stop!' cried Dani. An idea had come to him, a stupid one probably, but it was all he could think of to save his story. 'You could tear out the pages and sell them. Sell the story, I mean.'

Million was gripping the book tightly, his hands already poised to rip it, but he stopped.

'No one would buy a thing like that.'

'You could try.' Dani's toes were curling with tension inside his shoes. 'Please, Million, why not just try?'

Million stared at him, then he laughed shortly and flung the book back to Dani. Carefully, Dani tore out the written pages.

'Buffalo can do it,' Million said.

Buffalo scowled. Dani closed his eyes. Buffalo would mess it up, he knew that. He'd deliberately fail to sell it, and then sneer at Dani, and things would be worse than ever.

'Give it to me,' Mamo said. 'I'll give it a go.'

He was still annoyed with Dani, and didn't look at him, but he took the pages out of Dani's hands and disappeared once more into the darkness.

Dani moved away from the others. He was taut with nerves. He realised that a crisis had suddenly come. Make or break. In the gang or out of it. He was sweating. He wanted to stand up and walk about but he made himself sit still, holding on to Suri, determined this time not to let Mamo down.

Mamo came back after only twenty minutes. He thrust some money into Million's hands and grinned across at Dani.

'Two birr,' he said. 'Look at that, Million. Two whole birr.'

Tiggist hated being back in Addis Ababa. All day long, as she went about her duties in the shop, or kept Yasmin happy and out of mischief, she thought about Awassa. In Awassa, everything was lovely. People went about smiling there. The flowers on the trees were brighter, the streets were cleaner, the air fresher. Even the food tasted better. In her memory the town was bathed in a permanent golden light, as if the sun was perpetually rising.

But what was there for her here in Addis? Only a mat to sleep on at the back of the shop. Only a small shelf to put her things on, in a place where anyone could interfere with them. Only work, work, work, from morning till night.

There was no snug little room to share with Salma. There was no Salma, either, no friend, no one to talk to and laugh with, no one who knew about Yacob.

Things were different in the shop now. Mrs Faridah's brother-in-law, who had been left to run the business while Mrs Faridah was away in Awassa, was still trying to be in charge, keeping a sharp eye on everyone and finding fault all the time.

In spite of it all, though, Tiggist couldn't be unhappy. She was warmed all day and every night, when she lay on her mat and stared up into the darkness, by the thought of Yacob. She replayed in her mind again and again their last conversation, trying to conjure up exactly how she'd felt when they'd exchanged those long passionate looks.

'I wanted to ask you,' he'd said. 'We couldn't – you know – until I've got my shop.'

He'd never actually said they'd get married, but she'd known what he meant. She was quite, quite sure about it.

The scrap of paper with his neighbour's phone number on it was almost illegible now, she'd handled it so much. It didn't matter. She'd read it again and again until she knew it off by heart. She chanted it to herself whenever she felt the slightest bit anxious or lonely. It was like a charm. It lifted her spirits as if by magic.

She tried not to daydream too realistically about what might happen in the future in case it never did. It might even be unlucky to make too many plans. But she couldn't stop herself. Rosy visions kept popping into her head: being with Yacob; being looked after by someone kind and strong; being in her own little house, with her own nice things.

She was too busy for the first few days, back in Addis Ababa, to think about looking for Mamo, but as soon as she could get permission for a few hours off she slipped away to visit Mrs Hannah.

'No, dear, I haven't seen sight nor sound of him,' Mrs Hannah said. 'Now why don't you come in for a bit, and tell me all your news?'

Tiggist had spent a lovely afternoon with Mrs Hannah, and while she'd talked on about Awassa, and hinted blushingly at the existence of Yacob, she'd forgotten all about Mamo. But on the way back to the shop she thought about him again.

Where could he have got to? It was so strange, the way he'd disappeared, on the very day she'd gone to work with Mrs Faridah, without leaving the slightest trace behind.

She was passing the street corner where he used to hang out with a crowd of boys. A new bunch of kids was hanging around there now. She didn't know any of them except for one, an undersized boy with sawdust in his tufty hair. He was standing outside a paint supplier's shop, waiting for a group of people to come out so that he could go in.

She went up to him.

'Hello,' she said. 'It's Worku, isn't it?'

He looked at her blankly.

'I'm Mamo's sister.'

'Oh.'

'I've been down in Awassa.' She'd picked up the flicker of disdain in his eyes at the mention of Mamo's name, and was alarmed. 'I've lost touch with him. Do you know where he is?'

'Mamo?' He shrugged. 'He was away for ages, but he's back now. He's on the street. I don't see him and his lot much. I've got a job. In a furniture place with my dad.' He waited, as if he expected her to congratulate him. 'My dad says I've got to stop going around with people like that. Mamo hangs out down there.' He pointed down the hill with his chin. 'He's in Million's gang.'

In a gang! Tiggist's eyes flew open. Surely Mamo hadn't become a criminal?

The boy was looking into the shop, eager to get away.

'If you see Mamo,' Tiggist said quickly, 'can you tell him that his sister's back in Addis? Tell him it's Tiggist. I'm at Mrs Faridah's.'

'OK,' the boy said. 'If I see him.'

He saw his chance, darted into the crowded shop, and began to worm his way up to the counter.

Slowly, Tiggist walked back to Mrs Faridah's. So Mamo was on the street! A *godana*! The lowest of the low!

She felt guilty, although she hardly knew why. There was nothing she could have done for him. If he'd wanted her to help him he shouldn't have run away.

Mohammed, Mrs Faridah's brother-in-law, was standing at the door of the shop when she got back.

'Where have you been all this time?' he said.

'To visit my old neighbour,' Tiggist said meekly, not wanting to get into trouble. 'Mrs Faridah said I could.'

'Got on inside,' he said. 'The floor needs sweeping.'

He didn't move out of the doorway and Tiggist had to squeeze past him to get inside. She shrank away, trying not to touch him. Even though he spoke to her roughly he'd been giving her funny looks since she'd come back. He kept following her with his eyes. She'd have to watch her step.

She sighed as she fetched the broom and started sweeping the floor. Everything was so complicated here in Addis. If only she was back in Awassa.

Getachew, who had bumped into Worku on one of his forays into the centre of town, gave Mamo his message as they went off together to a church where a forty days ceremony was rumoured to be taking place.

'I nearly forgot,' he said. 'I saw Worku yesterday. He says your sister's around again. She's been down in Awassa.'

'Tiggist? In Awassa?' Mamo stared at him, astonished. 'What's she been doing down there?'

'How should I know? She's back, anyway, working in someone's shop. He didn't say which one.'

'She'll be at Mrs Faridah's, I bet,' said Mamo.

He'd almost forgotten about Tiggist. He'd felt, in an illogical kind of way, that she'd let him down, going off like that, and he'd put her out of his mind. But suddenly here she was again, real and close by. His head buzzed with excitement at the thought.

'You go on alone,' he said. 'I'll see you later.'

It was a long way to Mrs Faridah's. Mamo started off fast, running along the edge of the road, darting between people and donkeys and bicycles. But as he came nearer to the shop, he began to slow down, and when he came round the last corner and saw it there, with its smart green awning pulled down over the front, and the lame boy in his starched overall leaning against the fruit stand outside the door, he stopped altogether.

What would it be like, seeing Tiggist again, after all this time had passed, and everything that had happened? She'd made a success of herself, with her job and everything. But he was nothing but a ragged, dirty beggar boy.

She'll think I'm scum, he thought.

He nearly turned round and walked away, but then he remembered that last morning, when they'd been together in the old shack, and she'd got up and had given him some breakfast.

'She's still my big sister,' he thought. 'She always did look after me.'

Slowly, his heart beating fast, he crossed the road and covered the last two hundred yards to the shop.

The boy in the overall was still leaning against the fruit stand.

'Yes? What?' he said, jerking his chin up as Mamo approached.

'Is Tiggist here? Someone told me she's come back.'

Mamo spoke quietly, afraid that the angry man who'd sent him packing last time would come out and shout at him again.

'In there,' the boy said, pointing into the shop.

Mamo didn't move. He didn't have the courage to go inside. The shop was too smart and clean.

The boy seemed to understand. He levered himself away from the stand and hauled himself up the steps.

'Tiggist!' he called out. 'Someone here for you.'

Tiggist came flying out of the shop, her face alight with joyous expectation. When she saw Mamo, she looked disappointed for a moment, and then, as she recognised her brother in the tall, ragged boy in front of her, she gasped with astonishment.

'Mamo!'

She looked quickly over her shoulder, then grabbed his arm and pulled him round the side of the building. They stood staring at each other.

'What's the matter? What is it? Where have you been all this time?' said Tiggist.

Her voice was full of the rough love he'd known so well. It cut into him. He'd relied on it once but it had let him down.

'Where have I been?' he said bitterly. 'I'll tell you where I've been.'

He told her some of it, in fits and starts. It was harder telling Tiggist. He kept wanting to cry, and he had to break off from time to time to pinch the tears out of his eyes and wipe his nose on his sleeve. She listened, horrified, asking questions and shaking her head, but Mamo knew she'd never understand even half of the loneliness and terror and misery he had suffered.

'I couldn't have known where you'd got to, could I?' she said defensively, when he'd finished. 'And I couldn't have done anything about it, anyway.'

They stared at each other, both feeling helpless and miles apart.

'Worku said you were in a gang now,' Tiggist said at last, and Mamo bristled at the disapproval in her voice.

'Not like that. It's just some friends. We look out for each other.'

'You've got a place, then? Where you sleep.'

He hesitated. He couldn't bear to tell her the truth.

'Yes.'

'But you haven't got a job or anything. How do you manage?'

'We get by.'

She didn't seem to have heard.

'Look at the state you're in!' she said, touching his dirty sleeve.

'I'll clean myself up.'

He looked down, as if noticing the wreckage of his clothes for the first time.

'I've got some money,' she said. 'Savings. From my wages. I could give you some if you're desperate.'

He felt prickly with pride and shame.

'I told you. I do all right.'

The vegetable boy's head suddenly appeared round the corner of the house.

'She's looking for you,' he said. 'Mrs Faridah is.'

'I've got to go,' said Tiggist. She leaned forward and gave Mamo a quick hug.

'Mamo, it's amazing, seeing you. I'm so glad. I've been really, really worried. Don't disappear again. Where can I get hold of you?'

'You can't. Not easily,' he said awkwardly. 'I'm round and about. You don't have to worry about me any more. I'm doing fine. And I'll come again soon. I promise.'

Chapter 16

Dani's position in the gang had changed since Mamo had sold his story. Million had grasped the potential of the new idea at once. When the others had set out the next morning on their usual round of scavenging and begging, Million had stayed behind. He had hovered round Dani, watching as he settled himself down with the remains of the notebook on his knee and the biro in his hand, poised to begin writing another story. Then he'd stood guard over him, looking after Suri, peering over Dani's shoulder from time to time to see how much he'd written, and asking him encouragingly how he was getting on.

Dani was too polite to tell his *joviro* to be quiet and go away, although Million's attentions were distracting.

Mamo had been almost as pleased as Dani at the success of the story idea. He felt like a parent whose late-developing child had suddenly learned to walk. The odd friendship between the two boys took a new and deeper twist. Neither said anything about it, but they both felt even more bound to each other, their mutual trust stronger than ever.

Selling Dani's stories, which he was now writing busily every day, was the only bright point in Mamo's life after his visit to Tiggist. Seeing her again had cast him down into a horrible pit of despair. Somewhere, at the back of his mind, there'd always been the idea that if he could only find her again they would go back to their old life. She'd make a home for him and look after him. But everything had changed between them, he could see that now. Tiggist had her own life now. There was no room in it for him.

So what? he thought to himself angrily. What do I care? I don't need her. I'm doing all right.

But he felt miserably ashamed. He hated the memory of the way she'd looked at him, seeing all the dirt on him, smelling on him the aura of the beggar.

I'll keep away from her, he told himself, until I've got myself out of all this.

It was selling Dani's stories that cheered him up. The others were no good at it at all. They waved the stories uselessly under the wrong people's noses, and soon gave up in disgust. But Mamo was beginning to discover that he had the talents of a salesman. Only certain people, he reasoned, would want to buy what he had to sell. He would have to seek them out.

It didn't take him long to realise that he should try the university. The people there did a lot of reading. Dani's stories might appeal to them.

It worked. It took a while, sometimes, but nearly every day he made at least a couple of good sales. Every morning he set off up the hill, a sheaf of Dani's written pages in his hand, towards the university at Siddist Kilo.

He would target people carefully. There was no point in trying to sell to foreigners, who couldn't read Amharic, or to students, who were too hard up themselves to part with any money and were anyway only interested in each other. The best chance was with the middle-aged, bespectacled teachers and professors, who came and went through the magnificent stone gateway to the huge university compound, their books and files clutched under their arms.

They sometimes stopped for him as he hovered outside. They'd read a few lines, smile and reach into their pockets for a couple of dog-eared birr notes, then they'd walk on under the carved archway into the tranquil gardens, reading what Dani had written and chuckling to themselves, and he'd watch them with satisfaction, till they disappeared down one of the little pathways between the big old trees and grey stone walls.

Every time Mamo made a sale, his self-esteem rose a notch. Perhaps, he allowed himself to dream, he could be a peddler one day, one of those boys who sold chewing gum and paper tissues and cigarettes from neat little boxes. Then, if he saved a bit, he could work his way up, and . . .

But the dream dissolved every time he returned to the pitch and put the money into Million's outstretched hand. He was only one of the gang. How could he possibly branch out on his own? He needed them too much.

He had worked the university gates for several days, selling the stories well, when the guards, who vetted everyone coming in and going out, ran out of patience with him, and yelled at him to clear off, waving their fists at him. He wasn't particularly bothered. They were only making a show of it, he could tell. If he stayed away for a few days, then slipped back again, they'd probably leave him alone. In any case, he'd sold stories to everyone round here who was likely to buy them. It would be a while before they'd want to come back for more.

He decided to try somewhere else.

He walked slowly away from the university gates. It wasn't the only place in town, after all, where people liked to read. There were the big schools where rich children went. The teachers there might be poorer than the university teachers, but it would be worth giving them a try.

And yes, now he came to think of it, there was a big school between here and the pitch. It was now mid-afternoon, and the timing would be good. When he got there the boys and their teachers would be pouring out through the school gates at the end of the working day.

He trotted off down the road and arrived outside the school just as the boys were starting to come out through the gates in a steady stream of royal blue uniforms. They were cheerful and laughing, pushing at each other, some jumping into waiting cars, others striding off down the hill.

Look at them, Mamo thought enviously.

He shook his head. Dani had been one of those boys, but he'd given it all up. Things must have been really awful at home to make him do it.

OK, thought Mamo, so it was daft of him, but at least he's not soft, like they are. He's all right, Dani is.

Almost too late, he remembered the unsold story in his hand. There was a bunch of teachers coming out now, a group of them together. He ran up to them, his salesman's patter ready.

'A story, look, a wonderful one. The king and the beggar woman. It's got a really exciting ending. Please, look at it. Very interesting. To help me, for the sake of Mary. No food today. No mother, father dead, for the sake of Jesus . . .'

That wouldn't do. His sales talk had wound down into the usual beggar's plea. That wouldn't impress anyone. It certainly hadn't impressed the teachers, who were walking past him, ignoring him completely.

Two more brushed him aside too. The flood of pupils and teachers had slowed to a trickle now. Mamo redoubled his efforts, darting from one adult to the next, thrusting Dani's stories under unresponsive noses.

The school guards were about to swing the heavy gates shut, and Mamo was about to give up and turn away, when one last man came out. He was short and unkempt. His tie was coming adrift from his collar and the shirt buttons strained across his large stomach. He went to stand at the side of the road, and put up his arm to flag down a taxi.

'An original story, look,' began Mamo, running up to him.

The man waved him away, but Mamo persisted.

'It's a wonderful one. The king and the beggar woman. Really exciting. Only three birr.'

The man smiled.

'Three birr? Are you crazy? What do you take me for?'

'OK, two birr,' said Mamo eagerly, scenting a sale.

A taxi had responded to the man's wave and was pulling into the kerb.

'One fifty,' said Mamo desperately.

The man put his hand into his pocket and pulled out a one-birr note and a few loose coins. He put them into Mamo's hand.

'An entrepreneurial approach to literary endeavour ought, I suppose, to be encouraged,' he said, took the story and jumped into the taxi.

Mamo counted the money. It came to one birr eighty cents. Delighted, he pocketed the money and set off down the hill. There was no need to go back to the pitch just yet. He'd stop near the music shop and listen to whatever they were playing there. It was ages since he'd heard any music.

His skin tingled with pleasure as he approached the tiny shop. It was no more than a corrugated-iron booth with a lopsided painted sign over the door, and a loudspeaker fixed to the roof, but the tinny music crackling out from it sounded wonderful.

Bob Marley! They were playing Bob Marley, his favourite! The familiar voice, full of magic, drowned out for him the din of the heavy trucks and buses which were wheezing up the slope out of the dip at the bend of the road.

Mamo almost laughed aloud. He loved these songs. And now that Dani had told him what some of the words meant, he loved them even more.

He mouthed the lines under his breath, trying to imitate the unfamiliar English words, but when it came to his favourite chorus, he shut his eyes, threw his head back and sang properly, just as he'd done all those months ago for Hailu and Yohannes, out in the open fields.

'We are the survivors! The black survivors!'

The chorus ended. He opened his eyes. The shopkeeper was standing in the doorway of the booth, grinning at him.

'I wondered who it was. You've got a nice voice. Very nice,' he said. 'You don't often hear one like that.'

Mamo walked off, glowing, a smile spreading over his face. He cleared his throat and began to sing again, softly now that he was away from the masking support of the canned music.

Would that be something he could do? Sing? Would anyone ever pay him to do that?

With his head full of daydreams and the money for Dani's story in his pocket, he was happier than he'd been for a long time.

Ato Mesfin, Dani's old Amharic teacher, sat in the back of his taxi, staring down at the closely written sheets of paper in his hand.

'But I know this handwriting,' he was muttering to himself. 'It's Daniel Paulos's. Now how on earth did it get into the hands of that street urchin?'

He looked unseeingly out of the window as the taxi hooted its way across a busy intersection.

I never quite believed that story the boy's father told the headmaster, he thought, about taking Daniel out of school in Addis Ababa to send him off to Jigjiga. Jigjiga! Who in their right mind would send a child down there?

He shifted himself, easing his bulk into a more comfortable position on the cracked brown leather that covered the sagging springs of the taxi's back seat. He'd missed Dani in his classes since the boy had left school. It wasn't often that he came across the real thing, a real talent, waiting to be nurtured. He'd found just that in young Daniel Paulos.

I'd better go and see the father, he thought. There's something odd about all this. Something that's not quite right.

It took Ato Mesfin several hours to summon his courage before he felt brave enough to call on Ato Paulos. The man was a tartar, everyone knew that. He was famous in Addis for the ruthless way in which he'd built up his business, and his temper was legendary. He wasn't likely to welcome the visit of a shabby old school teacher.

'Not one to suffer fools gladly,' Ato Mesfin murmured to himself as he waited for the bus that would take him down to Bole. 'But then neither am I.'

It was already dark, and the crowds on the streets were beginning to thin out when the bus dropped him off at the garage on the Bole Road. Some shoeshine boys were perched like a row of hopeful young storks along the wall on the corner. Ato Mesfin beckoned to them.

'A birr for whoever takes me to Ato Paulos's house,' he said.

They leaped off the wall and crowded round him.

'Me! Me! Please!'

He picked one of them. The chosen boy began to scamper off, beckoning Ato Mesfin to follow him.

'Good. Go on with you now,' he said, when they reached the big green gates, giving the boy a crumpled green note. 'No, don't wait. Shoo!'

The boy ran off. Ato Mesfin waited a moment until he was out of sight. He didn't want anyone to witness the humiliation he was expecting.

Taking a deep breath, he rapped on the gate. It opened almost at once. The old watchman, his blind eye half covered by the thick *shamma* swathing his head and shoulders against the cold night air, stared out at him suspiciously.

'Yes? What do you want?'

'I've come to see Ato Paulos,' said Ato Mesfin, trying to look dignified.

'Does he know you? Is he expecting you?'

'No, but . . .'

'Then he won't see you,' Negussie said. 'No one comes calling at this time of night,' and he began to shut the gate.

'Wait!' said Ato Mesfin, though he was talking now only to the gate. 'Tell him it's about his son.'

The gate opened a crack. Old Negussie was looking round it, staring at him.

'Stay here,' he said at last, and he hobbled off towards the brightly lit porch of the house.

A few seconds later, the front door burst open and Ato Paulos came running down the steps.

'Don't go!' he called out. 'Who are you! Come in. Negussie says you have news of Daniel?'

Ato Mesfin stared at him. He would hardly have recognised the man. His face was haggard and his eyes, which had always been so sharp and haughty, looked almost imploring. Ato Mesfin forgot the speech he'd prepared. His suspicions had been right, then. There was a mystery here. Something terrible must have happened. Ato Paulos looked like a man on the rack.

'Well,' he said, 'I'm not sure if I've got news of him or not. It's this story, you see. I was very surprised when I recognised his handwriting. I thought you ought to see it.'

'What story? Daniel's handwriting? My dear fellow, please, come inside and tell me.'

Ato Mesfin followed Ato Paulos into the house's big sitting room and sat down on one of the elaborate gilded chairs that lined the walls.

'Please,' said Ato Paulos, putting out his hand. 'Show me.'

Ato Mesfin pulled out the story he'd bought from Mamo and passed it to him. Ato Paulos stared down at it and his hands began to shake.

'Where did you get this?' he whispered.

'I bought it from a street urchin outside the school. I'm Daniel's Amharic teacher. Mesfin.'

'I know. I remember you.'

Ato Paulos was still staring down at the pages in his hand.

'What's happened?' Ato Mesfin said gently, amazed to find that the terrifying Ato Paulos was filling him with pity. 'Daniel's disappeared, is that it? Has he run away?'

'Yes. Weeks and weeks ago. I've searched everywhere. I'm at my wits' end.'

'So you didn't send him to Jigjiga?'

Ato Paulos shuddered.

'No. Look, it's a long story. Let me get you a drink.'

Ato Paulos talked for a long time. He wouldn't have believed, a couple of months ago, that he would ever have given more than a curt greeting to this crumpled old school teacher, but he found himself pouring out everything, his past irritation with Daniel, his efforts to undo his wife's spoiling, Feisal and the Jigjiga scheme, the awful realisation that he'd scared his son into running away, and his desperate fears for Daniel's safety.

The relief of telling someone at last was wonderful.

Ato Mesfin listened without interrupting, his head on one side, drawing his breath in from time to time sympathetically.

'So you think Daniel might be living on the street?' he said, when at last Ato Paulos fell silent.

Ato Paulos held up the story.

'I didn't know what to think! But now, with this – well, it's a clue, isn't it? The first sign I've had that he's still alive. I'm – well, I'm extremely grateful to you for bringing it to me. The question is, what do I do now?'

Ato Mesfin was already standing up.

'You look for him, of course.'

'Look where? How?'

Ato Paulos looked strangely helpless.

'I'll show you.' Mesfin was already walking towards the door. 'You have a car, don't you? It'll be easier if we drive.'

Ato Paulos had often driven through Addis Ababa at night on his way to or from dinners and receptions. The city streets emptied rapidly after nightfall, and only a few figures, muffled against the cold, flitted along the empty pavements. Ato Paulos had never really noticed the still, huddled shapes wrapped in dingy blankets that lay against the walls of the city's buildings. Tonight, though, as he cruised the streets with Ato Mesfin beside him, he craned forward, trying to spot where the *godana* lay.

Before they'd reached the centre of town, Mesfin had made him stop at a cheap restaurant and they'd bought rolls of *injera* and some fruit.

'You can't wake people up and ask them questions if you don't offer them something in return,' he'd said awkwardly, afraid that his alarming companion would march up to the first sleeping forms he saw, shake them awake and demand news of his son.

Astonishingly, Ato Paulos took his instructions humbly and let Ato Mesfin take the lead. The two men would stop the car and approach a sleeping group quietly. Ato Mesfin would cough gently to waken them and hand the sleepy people a gift of food. Sometimes they recognised him and greeted him by name. Only when they had exchanged courtesies did he let Ato Paulos ask them any questions.

As they moved from group to group, Ato Paulos became more and more silent.

'You've done this before, haven't you?' he said, after they'd visited their seventh group of sleepers. 'You know some of these people.'

Ato Mesfin grunted in agreement.

'After my wife died, I felt – I don't know – that God had blessed me all my life. That but for his grace I could be in their place myself.'

He shot a curious look at Ato Paulos, who said nothing.

They were about to get back into the car when one of the men they'd been questioning called out, 'Ato Mesfin!'

Ato Mesfin went over to him. Ato Paulos watched while he squatted down and talked to him.

'What did he say?' he asked Ato Mesfin eagerly, when the teacher came back to the car.

Ato Mesfin was frowning.

'He wanted to know who was asking for Daniel and what it was you wanted from him.'

'He knows something!'

Ato Paulos was already starting back towards the sleepers.

'No!' Ato Mesfin caught his sleeve. 'They won't tell you anything, even if they know. They'll protect him, if he doesn't want to be caught.'

'Protect? Huh!' Ato Paulos seemed to have momentarily recovered his old manner. 'No one protects anyone if you offer them money. Go back and tell them I'll pay.'

'I could,' Ato Mesfin said uneasily, 'but . . .'

'But what?' barked Ato Paulos.

'Is that how you want to find Daniel?' Ato Mesfin said diffidently. 'By making someone betray him? Will that make him want to come back to you?'

'Of course he wants to come back! Who would choose to live like this? Once I've explained that – that I forgive him, that he can have another chance, sit his exams again, that I won't send him down to Jigjiga . . .'

He stopped, his shoulders sagging as if he no longer believed in what he was saying.

'I'm not sure if it's as simple as that,' Ato Mesfin said quietly. 'I don't know if you'll be able to start where you left off. I'm beginning to think that Daniel is a rather remarkable boy, and that there's more to him than either of us ever guessed.'

Chapter 17

Tiggist was getting worried. She'd been back in Addis Ababa for weeks now and there had been no word from Yacob. She hadn't expected a letter or anything (he probably realised that she couldn't really read) but she'd thought there might have been a message of some kind, through a friend maybe, someone coming up from Awassa, who could have called on her and said – well, just said hello from him.

I didn't imagine it all, she told herself anxiously. He loves me, I know he does. We'll get married one day, like he said.

But she kept wondering if he was forgetting her, meeting other girls perhaps, who were prettier or cleverer.

They'll all be after him, she thought, a man like that. I suppose I shouldn't count on him. I'll probably just have to manage on my own.

Managing was getting harder. Mrs Faridah was leaving the shop more and more to her brother-in-law and taking more interest in Yasmin.

'She's all I've got left of my dear, dear husband,' she'd say, showing Yasmin off in her new dress to her friends. 'He absolutely doted on her.'

No, he didn't, Tiggist thought, biting her lip. She'd never seen Mr Hamid show the slightest interest in his daughter. A couple of times he'd even called out to Tiggist, in his weak voice, to take Yasmin and her noise off to the other side of the courtyard so that he wouldn't be disturbed.

She'd learned ages ago that she couldn't rely on Mrs Faridah. When she was being nice she was lovely, but when she'd got an idea into her head she was really tricky.

In the last week or two, ever since Mamo had shown up that day, Mrs Faridah had started to be unfriendly again. She'd heard all about Mamo's visit from her brother-in-law, who'd seen Tiggist slip off round the corner to talk to him, and watched Mamo walk off again afterwards.

'We don't want people like that hanging round the shop,' she'd said to Tiggist. 'It puts the customers off.'

'But he's my brother!' Tiggist had burst out, feeling suddenly furious. 'It's not his fault if he . . .'

'Are you answering me back?' Mrs Faridah said coldly. 'Let me tell you, my girl, that there are plenty of others who'd like your job if you've decided to get above yourself.'

'Yes, Madam. Sorry, Madam,' Tiggist said humbly.

She'd noticed that when Mrs Faridah was in one of her moods it helped if you called her madam.

The real problem, she knew quite well, wasn't Mrs Faridah at all. It was her horrible brother-in-law. He was making Mrs Faridah feel nervous, taking control of the shop all the time and pushing her aside.

Tiggist hated him. She tried to stay out of his way as much as she could but he kept coming after her. Sometimes he'd find fault with her over silly little things and be bullying and unreasonable, but then he'd come sidling round her when she was alone and try to kiss her.

Mrs Faridah had caught him at it once or twice but by the look on her face Tiggist could see that Mrs Faridah thought she was to blame. She'd tried to explain that she hadn't been leading the man on, and she just wanted to be left alone, but Mrs Faridah had looked at a point on the wall behind her and said, 'It's up to you, Tiggist, the way you want to live your life, but I'm telling you now that your mother's example is not one I'd advise you to follow.'

'It's so *unfair*,' Tiggist muttered to herself that night as she tossed and turned on her hard little mat. 'Oh Yacob, why don't you come like you said you would? When am I going to see you again?'

In the darkness, somewhere nearby, a scuffling noise made the hairs on her arms and legs stand up with fright. He wasn't coming now, was he, that horrible brother-in-law, creeping up on her in the darkness when no one was around?

The scuffling stopped, then started again. Tiggist breathed a sigh of relief. It was only a mouse, after all.

But he will come, one of these nights, she thought. I won't be able to escape. And after that Yacob mightn't want me any more.

The idea was so terrifying that it gave her courage.

I'll do it. I'll phone Yacob in the morning. He said to, if I needed him. And now I really, really do.

She began chanting the magic telephone number in her head, until the rhythm of it rocked her to sleep.

She woke with a sense of purpose. She got up, tidied away her sleeping mat, combed out her hair and washed her face. The she pulled out from its hiding place the box where she kept her savings, took out some coins and, looking over her shoulder to make sure she hadn't been seen or followed, she slipped out of the shop and hurried down the road to the public telephone round the corner.

She'd only ever used a telephone once or twice before and it took a while for her to remember how to make it work. At last, though, her trembling fingers had pressed the numbers down and she was holding the receiver to her ear, listening to the long beeps as it rang, miles away, in Awassa.

'*Abet?*'

A strange voice answered. She couldn't even tell if it belonged to a man or a woman.

'Yacob,' she said quietly. 'Is Yacob there?'

'*Abet?*' the voice said again.

'Yacob!' Tiggist said loudly. 'I want to speak to Yacob.'

'Yacob is not here,' the voice said.

'No, next door. He lives next door to you,' Tiggist said, speaking slowly and clearly, sure that the person hadn't understood.

'I told you.' The voice was getting impatient. 'Yacob's not here any more. He's not in Awassa. He's gone away.'

A stone seemed to have lodged itself in Tiggist's stomach, and it was becoming heavier and heavier.

'Where is he?' she shouted.

'In Addis. He went to Addis last week. Hello?'

Tiggist couldn't think. She stood clutching the receiver, no longer hearing the voice at the other end. Yacob wasn't there! He'd come to Addis a week ago and he hadn't even bothered to come and see her!

He's forgotten me, she thought. It was all rubbish, what he said. He didn't mean it at all.

She replaced the receiver and began walking slowly back towards the shop, stumbling over the uneven paving stones, not seeing where she was going. The world seemed suddenly to have come to an end.

What am I going to do? she thought. If I stay in the shop I'll have to do what that awful man wants, in the end. But if I walk out I won't have anywhere else to go. I'll end up on the street, like Mamo, or – or do the things Ma did.

Without realising it she'd stopped walking and was standing still in the middle of the pavement, with the people hurrying on their way to work streaming past her.

'Tiggist! I've found you! At last!'

She looked up. He was there! Yacob was there! He was standing right in front of her, looking down at her, his hands held out awkwardly as if he wasn't sure whether she was pleased to see him or not.

For a moment she thought she must be dreaming, but no, he was solid. Real. She could smell the faint tang of soap on his hands and feel the warmth radiating from him.

'Oh, oh,' was all she could say, before she burst into tears.

She felt him take her by the elbow and lead her along the pavement, and a moment later they were sitting in a corner of a bar and he was calling for tea.

'I'll be late for work,' she said, though she didn't care, at that moment, if she never went to work again.

'Did you miss me?' was all he said. 'Did you think about me?'

'All the time. Every day.'

'Me too. I waited but you didn't call me.'

'I did! Just now. I was coming back from the telephone. Your neighbour said you'd been in Addis since last week.'

She couldn't help sounding a little accusing.

He laughed.

'I wanted to make sure if it would be all right,' he said, 'the new plan I'm going to tell you about, and then I couldn't find your shop. I've been going from one place to the other looking for you. No one seemed to know where Mrs Faridah's was. Oh my little Tiggist, it's so good to see you again!'

She was so charmed at being called 'my little Tiggist' that she could barely take in what he was saying.

'I've been with my cousin,' he went on. 'He's got a shop here in Addis. Down the Debre Zeit road. Builders' suppliers. Taps, plumbing materials, everything you want to build modern kinds of houses. He wants to take me on to build up the electrical side. He's a really nice man. You'll like him. He called me up last week in Awassa and said he was looking to expand and that he'd thought of me because I know about electrics and anyway he'd rather have a member of the family. So I came up to Addis to see how it would be and talk things over with him, and it's brilliant. The whole set-up. I'm starting at once! Do you see what this means? In a year or two, if all goes well and I save enough, and you put by what you get from Mrs

Faridah, we'll be able to get married! Have a place of our own! Why, sweetheart, don't start crying again. What is it? You haven't changed your mind, have you? Don't you still want to marry me?'

'Yes, yes I do!' She clutched her glass of tea, hardly noticing her burning fingers. 'I've needed you so much. Oh, you've no idea.'

She started trying to tell him about her life at the shop, and Mrs Faridah's brother-in-law.

'And my brother,' she said. 'I've seen him again, but he's a – he's . . .'

She couldn't bring herself to go on. If Yacob knew that her brother was a street boy, in a gang, he might be so disgusted he'd turn against her.

Yacob wasn't interested in Mamo.

'That man, in the shop, he's touched you?' he said. The muscles were standing out along his jaw as he angrily clenched his teeth.

'No. Not like that.' Tiggist didn't dare tell Yacob about the way the man had tried to kiss her. 'But he keeps, you know, bumping into me, and trying to get me alone, and the way he looks at me . . .'

'If he tries any of that again I'll ram his teeth down his throat.'

Tiggist had no idea that her gentle Yacob could look so fierce. He was squaring his shoulders now.

'Thought you were all alone, did he, without anyone to protect you? He'll soon find out.'

Tiggist took her hand away from the tea glass, tucked it under her armpit and wriggled with pleasure.

Yacob was frowning down at the flowery plastic tablecloth.

'We'll have to see how it goes with my cousin,' he said. 'If I thought you were OK at Mrs Faridah's I wouldn't mind you staying there, for the time being at any rate. But if it's like that . . .'

'It'll be all right now you're here,' Tiggist said, who couldn't believe that anything horrible would ever happen again. Daringly she put out her hand and laid it on his arm. He put his own large hand over hers and she felt a warm feeling course all the way up to her shoulder.

'We'll have to see,' Yacob said again. 'If the business expands the way my cousin thinks it will, we're going to need more help in the shop. There are meals to think of too. A couple of bachelors like us – we need a bit of looking after. Maybe you and I shouldn't wait too long after all.'

He smiled at her. Here in Addis Ababa he seemed more confident than he'd been in Awassa. His shyness and awkwardness had gone.

'I'd marry you tomorrow if I could,' he said, pinching her chin.

'And I'd marry you right now, today,' she cried, her heart bursting with happiness.

Chapter 18

Mamo had noticed, without quite putting it into a thought, that Dani's position in the gang had changed. From being the outsider, increasingly despised, he'd become a kind of treasure, his skills and knowledge fully respected at last.

It had become a habit now for the gang to gather round him in the evening for a story or two. Million would drag a crate forward for Dani to perch on, and the group would sit hunched in their *shammas* round his feet.

Mamo liked the way Dani changed when he was telling his wonderful tales. His voice would rise and fall as he acted out the characters, while his hands flew about in descriptive gestures. There wasn't a spare ounce on him now. He was as lean and hard as the rest of them.

Almost the best moment was when the story was finished, and everyone talked about it, going over the bits they hadn't understood the first time, and telling Dani which stories they thought would be good to write down and sell. Million and Getachew argued about it sometimes, and even Buffalo threw in his opinion. Shoes was unpredictable. Sometimes he followed the stories with breathless excitement, laughing riotously at the funny parts, and sometimes he hardly seemed to listen, sitting morose and withdrawn on the edge of the group.

Every evening, as Dani talked and the others listened, Mamo thought with a pang of Karate.

One morning, after a marathon story session the night before, Million led the group towards a new restaurant that had opened nearby. It was a Saturday and as usual at the weekend the pickings around town were likely to be scanty. The lunch-goers, enjoying their day off work, offered the best chance of the day.

Dani, tired of writing, had given himself a day off and had gone with the others. He still couldn't bring himself to beg, and he hung back, out of the line of sight of anyone who might still recognise him, but he enjoyed watching the others as they worked, noticing with amusement how the rich people responded to them.

Mamo was the last to leave the pitch. He was trying to train Suri to stay with the group's bundle of blankets and plastic sheets, which they stowed every morning in a discreet pile in an angle of the wall. The puppy had grown enormously in the last few weeks and her teeth, always sharp, were becoming a formidable weapon. She needed a good deal of persuasion, every time, to stay behind on guard, and whined piteously until Mamo was out of sight, but she was beginning to settle down to her role and Mamo was very proud of her.

Suri flopped down at last on top of the blankets, put her nose down on her paws and accepted Mamo's command with a reluctant thump or two of her feathery tail. Satisfied, he left her to it, and hurried after the others.

A car was pulling up to park on the rough patch of ground outside the restaurant. The others were already moving in on it, ready to accost the driver as he got out. The man was quite tall. He wore a jacket slung casually over his shoulders and as he bent down to lock the car door, a watch on a loose strap flopped down over his wrist.

A memory stirred in Mamo. He stared at the back of the stranger's head, then, as the man turned and he saw the faint scar running down his cheek and recognised the thin face, a shudder of loathing and fear shook him from head to foot.

The man bent to brush a speck of dust off his trousers and walked into the restaurant.

'It's him! That was him!' croaked Mamo, grabbing the arm nearest to him in a painful grip. He was almost too choked to speak.

'Hey, Garbage King, stop that,' said Million irritably, pulling his arm away.

'But it was Merga. The man who stole me and sold me.' Mamo shook his head, as if trying to clear it. 'It was him,' he said again.

Half of him wanted to run away. The other half wanted to burst into the restaurant and kill Merga with his bare hands.

'That man who went in just now?' Million said. 'Are you sure? He catches boys and sells them? He really is the one who did it to you?'

'Yes, yes!' Mamo was dancing up and down. 'I know him, I told you. And look, he's even got his own car. He's got rich! From selling people! I'm going to kill him. When he comes out of there, I'm going to murder him.'

Million was looking thoughtfully towards the car. Dani, watching him, saw an impish flame light up his eyes, before they narrowed to purposeful slits.

'You, you and you,' he rapped out, pointing to Getachew, Buffalo and Shoes. 'Go and beg for a birr, anywhere, anyhow. Be quick.'

'It's Saturday, Million,' objected Buffalo. 'Where are we going to—'

'Get it,' Million said, cutting him off.

The three dashed off obediently.

'Come on,' Million barked out to Mamo and Shoes, as another car pulled up in front of the restaurant. 'We need two birr at least. We've got to get some money from here.'

He put on his most soulful expression and sidled up to the woman stepping out of the car.

'Sister, very hungry,' he murmured, his hand out.

Half an hour later, the other three came back and Buffalo dropped a few coins into Million's hand.

'Ninety cents,' he said, 'and that's a miracle.'

Million counted up the coins in his own hand.

'It's enough. Getachew, go as fast as you can to the hardware store. Buy a bag of nails.'

'Nails?' Getachew frowned at him, puzzled.

'You heard me. Run!'

Five minutes later, Getachew was back. He handed the bag to Million and bent over, panting, trying to get his breath back.

'Mamo, keep out of sight in case he comes out,' Million ordered. 'He mustn't see you. Dani, come and help me. The rest of you, keep watch. If anyone comes near or seems interested in what we're doing, start singing to warn us.'

'Yes, but Million, what are we doing?' Mamo said. He felt dissatisfied. He wanted Million to make a battle plan, or prepare an ambush, he didn't quite know how.

Million didn't answer. He was already behind Merga's car, looking down at the ground. He glanced round quickly, saw that no one was looking, then bent down and began to arrange nails around the back offside wheel, digging the heads into the ground so that the points stood up in wicked spikes exactly where the tyres would roll over them.

Mamo gave a crow of laughter as Million's plan suddenly became beautifully clear. Million took more nails from the bag and began to work round the two front wheels. Five minutes later, they strolled away from the car, Million stowing the empty bag in his pocket as he went.

An agonising hour passed. Mamo's hands were clammy and his skin prickled with anticipation. Every time the door of the restaurant swung open, his heart lurched.

'Keep out of sight,' Million kept hissing at him. 'He mustn't see you.'

Merga came out of the restaurant at last. He was smiling and relaxed, as if he'd had a bit too much to drink and eaten very well.

He stood by the car for a moment, fumbling for his keys, not noticing the boys who were standing nearby watching him, and over whom a strange stillness had fallen.

Finally Merga opened the car door and started the engine. He put the car into gear and let out the brake. As he drove off, Mamo watched with glory in his heart as the nails, biting into the rubber, did their work and a sweet, soft, hissing noise came from the collapsing tyres, all four of them together. The car stopped before it had even reached the road.

The driver's door opened and Merga got out. He looked down at the front nearside wheel, muttered angrily, then walked unsteadily towards the back of the car. He was lifting the lid of the boot in search of his spare tyre when he noticed the back nearside wheel. He cursed aloud, walked round to look at the far side, and saw that both offside wheels were flat too.

Furiously, he kicked out at the nearest tyre, then began hammering his fists furiously on the roof, his face suffused with anger.

Mamo, who had been watching from behind a nearby Land Cruiser, felt such rage he could hold himself back no longer. He darted under Million's restraining arm, ran up to Merga and came to a halt right in front of him. Then, saying nothing, he stood still, crossed his arms, drew himself up to his full height and tried to stare into Merga's eyes, waiting for the man to recognise him.

Merga didn't look at him. He didn't even seem to notice him. He pushed past Mamo, working his way round the car, checking on one wheel after another as if he couldn't believe what had happened.

Mamo put out his hand towards the nearest object within reach, which happened to be the car's wing mirror, and began to tug at it.

'Hey! What do you think you're doing?' Merga yelled, noticing him at last.

Mamo didn't answer. Using both hands now, he wrenched at the mirror with all his strength, twisted it right off and dangled it in front of Merga's outraged face.

Merga took a step towards him, his arm raised as if he was about to strike, but suddenly he seemed to recognise Mamo, and he faltered and stepped back.

'You,' he said. 'What are you doing here? You . . .'

Before Mamo could answer, he was shouldered aside. Million and the gang were all around him, edging Mamo back away from Merga and the car.

'Oh sir,' Million was saying to Merga in a honeyed voice. 'Whatever's happened? Is this guy giving you grief? Don't worry about him. He's a proper little troublemaker. We'll deal with him for you. What's happened to your car? Won't it go?'

Merga, shaken, pointed down to the nearest wheel.

'You've got a puncture?' Million said, his voice dripping with sympathy. 'Where's your spare wheel? We'll help you to fix it, if you like.'

The others were circling round the car.

'Hey!' said Getachew, trying to sound concerned, though Dani could hear that he could hardly stop himself laughing. 'This tyre's down too, and the other front one.'

'Oh dear.' Million was bending down, looking solicitously at a wheel. 'What was it? Broken glass? No, look, there's a nail in this tyre. And another. Look at this one. How careless of somebody. I tell you what, sir, there's a tyre place just round the corner from here. Come with us. We'll help you bring back some new ones.' He dragged Dani forwards. 'Just give my friend here a birr, to guard the car, and the rest of us will go to the tyre place with you. I know the owner. He'll give you a good price. You can trust me.'

Merga shook himself, trying to object and assert his authority, but it seemed to Mamo, watching from a distance, as if Million was weaving some kind of spell around him. Half fuddled as he was, and feeling vaguely intimidated, Merga obediently pulled a birr out of his pocket, gave it to Dani, then stumbled off down the road with Million, Buffalo, Getachew and Shoes circling round him like malevolent young sprites.

Mamo, who was still trembling with the shock of being face to face with the man, turned to look at Dani, who was staring down at the birr in his hand, a grin breaking out across his face.

'I'll be back in a minute,' he said, and he darted across the road and disappeared into a shop on the other side.

Seconds later he returned with a thick stubby pen in his hand.

'A magic marker,' he said to Mamo, unscrewing the top. 'Very difficult to wash it off.'

He stood back for a moment, studying the car with his head on one side, like an artist surveying an empty canvas, then he began to scrawl words across the hood in big sprawling letters.

A deep, pure joy was welling up in Mamo's chest.

'What are you writing? What does it say?'

'This – man – is – a – slaver,' Dani said, enunciating each word as he wrote it. 'He – steals – boys – and – sells – them.'

He finished, stood back, and looked at his work with satisfaction.

'Write something else,' Mamo said. 'Here, on the side. Write, "God will punish this man. He will run but he will never escape from justice."'

Dani bent down and wrote again. By the time he'd finished, the car doors on both sides, the roof, the back and the windscreen were covered with thick, black, accusing words.

'Quick, they're coming,' Mamo said, as he put the finishing touches to the back window.

They scampered off and hid behind the nearby Land Cruiser again, peeping out round the side to watch.

The boys, each one carrying a tyre, were walking too close to Merga, crowding him. He was smiling uneasily and even from a distance Mamo could see that beads of sweat had broken out on his forehead.

They reached the car. Merga saw the scribbles all over his car, broke free of the others and gave a howl of outrage. Dani could see that Million and the others were hesitating, unable to read the words, and, afraid that the momentum would be lost, he came out from the shelter of the Land Cruiser and sauntered, as casually as he could, across the car park towards them.

'Look at that!' he said, affecting the light, ironic voice that Million had used. 'I only turned my back for a second. Someone must have slipped in here and written – well I never. Look at what it says! *This man is a slaver. He steals boys and sells them.*"'

The others were drawing in their breath and staring at Merga accusingly. The man had turned a strange grey, dusty colour. He was trying to edge away from the car but the boys, obeying a signal from Million's lifted eyebrows, were closing in on him in an ever tighter circle.

'Now what does it say here?' Dani said, who had discovered that he was hugely enjoying himself. He walked slowly round the car, reciting the words with his eyes on Merga's face. '*God will punish this man. He will run but he will never escape from justice.*'

A strangled sound came from Merga's throat as he tried to break away but he was brought up again and again by Buffalo's massive chest, as the boy dodged in front of him.

'You haven't paid us,' Million said, his voice suddenly flinty hard. 'We took you to the garage. We carried the tyres back for you. Pay us.'

Merga fumbled in his pocket and pulled out a handful of notes. Without looking at them he pushed them into Million's hand. Then he broke free at last and began to run, looking back over his shoulder with fear and fury in his eyes.

Million looked down at the money in his hand. The others crowded forward to watch as he counted it.

'Twenty-three birr!' whistled Getachew. 'What are we going to do with it?'

Million looked round at them and opened his crooked mouth in a grin, showing his broken front teeth.

'We're going to have a party,' he said.

It was, thought Dani, hours later, as he sat with the others round the embers of the fire they'd lit, the best party he'd ever been to. In fact, now he came to think of it, it was the only party he'd ever really enjoyed.

The euphoria that had swept them all up in an huge happy wave when Merga had run away had made them want to shout and dance about, right there and then, but Million, with an eye on the restaurant, where the doorman in his long khaki greatcoat was already beginning to look too closely towards them, had herded them quickly away, and they'd flitted off, stopping at their pitch only to collect Suri and their blankets before heading down the hill through the back lanes to the open ground where they always took refuge when danger seemed to threaten them in the streets above.

The money had all gone in a glorious burst of extravagance. They'd lashed out on a feast of *injera* and spicy meat, bottles of heady *tej* and a packet of cigarettes. Million had sent them off to scour the ground for twigs, sticks and discarded rubber tyres and when night fell they'd lit a bonfire and danced round it, singing and whooping with triumph.

They'd subsided at last, replete, and in varying degrees of intoxication. Dani, unused to alcohol, had sipped at the *tej* when it was passed to him but had stopped when his head started feeling muzzy. Mamo, who seemed to have grown a whole metre taller since the afternoon, had swigged at the stuff more carelessly. He sat against Dani now, one arm flung affectionately round Dani's shoulders, crooning his favourite songs, oozing a dreamy contentment that lapped round Dani too.

He looked across the fire at the others. The tyres were still burning, though less fiercely now, and the light flickered on the boys' coppery faces, casting shadows on their features which seemed tonight as familiar to Dani as his own.

They're my brothers, he thought, surprising himself. They're more my family than my real one ever was.

The depression that had numbed him since he'd heard that his mother had died had lifted tonight.

We did something today, he thought. It was fantastic.

Million and Buffalo had drunk more than the others. Million had become livelier while Buffalo was sinking further and further into a sullen silence.

'Did you see him? His face?' Million said, reliving for the tenth time the events of the afternoon. He was letting out gasps of laughter, rocking from side to side and slapping Buffalo on the shoulder as he spoke. 'And then he . . . you . . .' He pointed the nearly empty bottle of *tej* across the fire at Dani. 'You got that pen and wrote all that stuff. What was it again? What did you write? Tell us.'

Enjoying the admiration, Dani recited the words he'd written on the car again.

'It was Mamo who thought of some of it,' he said, 'the bit about God and justice.'

'He will never escape from justice!' crowed Million, tipping his head back as he drained the bottle. He straightened himself and wiped his mouth. 'Eh, I wish I could write like you. An educated man, that's something, isn't it, Buffalo? Takes an education to think of a thing like that.'

He pounded Buffalo on the back harder than he'd intended, knocking him forward. Buffalo lifted his head again and stared at Dani. His eyes were hot and red.

Dani's heart jumped. Suddenly, he knew what was going to happen next. He shook Mamo's arm off his shoulders and tensed himself, ready to leap to his feet.

The mood of the group shifted. The exhilaration of triumph had evaporated, and so too had the relaxed comradeship that had followed it. Now the boys were watchful and excited.

'No, Dani,' Mamo said quietly. 'You can't. I'll take him. Leave him to me.'

But Dani was already on his feet, watching Buffalo, who had stood up first and was glaring at him, fists bunched. Dani took a deep shuddering breath. He'd always known, since that very first day, that sooner or later it would come to this. In the past he'd ducked away from Buffalo every time a fight seemed to be brewing, slipping expertly sideways, effacing himself, taking refuge behind Mamo, or manoeuvring Million into intervening.

Tonight, though, he wouldn't run away. At last he'd stand his ground and fight.

The alcohol he'd drunk made Buffalo stagger a little as he circled round the fire to where Dani was waiting for him.

Mamo had jumped up too.

'Leave it,' Dani said to him. 'Just give me some space.'

Mamo looked across at Million, expecting him to say something, but Million, seemingly unaware of what was going on, was staring dreamily into the fire, a smile hovering round his mouth.

'Give me *space*,' Dani said again, shoving Mamo with his elbow.

Reluctantly, Mamo stepped aside and went to stand behind Getachew and Shoes, who were watching with wary eagerness as Buffalo and Dani squared up to each other.

Buffalo came in first, his head low, his powerful arms punching forward. Dani, who had never fought anyone before in his life, instinctively dodged aside, then swung his own right arm inexpertly round, giving Buffalo, more by luck than by design, a buffet on the jaw. Buffalo rocked sideways, roared and came in again, trying to grab Dani round the waist and pull him off his feet, but Dani, whose every muscle was powered with an uprush of energy that he had never felt before, twisted sideways and caught Buffalo's flailing arm in both hands, wrenching it painfully round.

The watching boys were silent, except for Mamo, who was muttering encouragement to Dani under his breath, and the only other sound was the shifting of their feet on the dusty ground and their grunts as they wrestled backwards and forwards.

It was luck that finished it. Dani hooked his foot round Buffalo's knee at the very moment that Buffalo, turning in an effort to pin Dani's head in an armlock, had half lost his balance. Buffalo's grip loosened and he began to fall slowly over on to his side. Horrified, Dani realised that he was going straight down into the fire.

'Watch out!' he shouted, and lunging forwards he yanked with all his might at Buffalo's shoulders, twisting him round at the last so that he would fall away from the smouldering tyres.

Buffalo crashed heavily on to the ground. He lay as if stunned for a moment, then looked up at Dani, who was swaying on his feet, weak with exhaustion and astonishment.

The hot redness had left Buffalo's eyes.

'Yeah,' he said, as if nothing had happened since Million had last spoken. 'It was good, thinking of writing on the car like that.'

Dani laughed shakily, put down his hand and hauled Buffalo to his feet. They stood awkwardly for a moment, then Buffalo patted Dani on the shoulder and went back to his place beside Million, who had barely seemed to notice that he had moved at all.

A strong, beautiful peace entered Dani's soul as he stood, gazing down into the glowing heart of the fire. All his life he'd imagined moments like these, casting himself in impossible roles as the victor, the champion, the hero. How sad all those fantasies seemed, set against the glorious reality of the way he felt right now!

He lifted his eyes from the fire and turned to move back toward Mamo, who had sat down again in his old place, but then he saw, at the edge of the circle of light, that two people were walking towards him.

'Look out,' he said warningly to the others. 'Someone's coming.'

The boys, afraid as always of the police, gathered themselves, poised for rapid flight, but the two men who stepped out of the shadows weren't wearing uniforms. The sight of the first one, a short, stout, crumpled figure with a bush of greying hair round his shiny bald head, made Dani yelp with surprise as he recognised Ato Mesfin. But now he was looking beyond him. Behind the old schoolteacher was someone else, someone rigid and sombre, with a face almost unrecognisably haggard with anxiety and sleeplessness.

'Father,' whispered Dani.

For a long moment Ato Paulos and Dani stared at each other, both too shocked to move. Dani saw a man who had inexplicably shrunk and aged and in whose face, instead of the fury he had dreaded, was a painful uncertainty. Ato Paulos saw a thin, taut, wild-eyed boy dressed in stained worn clothes, about whom clung an air of reckless triumph. He strained forward, screwing up his eyes, barely able to recognise his son.

'Daniel, is it really you?' he said, breaking the silence first.

Dani took a step backwards. He felt almost breathless.

'I'm not going to Jigjiga,' was all he could think of saying, and then he stopped. All that business seemed

256

absurd now, as if it had happened a long, long time ago, in an inconceivably distant past.

Ato Paulos didn't seem to have heard him.

'Where have you been all this time? Why did you do this? Don't you realise how anxious I've been? What on earth have you been getting up to?'

The moment of weakness that Dani had sensed in his father seemed to have passed and the old anger was creeping back into Ato Paulos's voice. It sent a thrill of remembered terror through Dani. He took another step backwards. He'd always been paralysed in the presence of his father, and he was beginning to feel numb again now. In a minute he'd be meekly saying, 'Yes, Father. I'm sorry, Father. I don't know, Father,' like he always had done.

Then he sensed a movement behind him. Million and Buffalo, miraculously sobered, were moving up to stand beside him.

'Is this your father, then?' Million said to Dani.

Dani nodded once.

Million lifted his chin questioningly towards Ato Mesfin.

'Who's that?'

'My old Amharic teacher.'

'Guy who taught you to write stories?'

'Yes.'

Million smiled, leaned forward and put his hand out to Ato Mesfin. Gravely, Ato Mesfin bent over from the hips and shook it.

Mamo was standing alongside Dani now, with Getachew and Shoes close beside him. Dani, reading disdain in his father's eyes as they swept over his ragged band of friends, tried to shake off a creeping sense of shame. Then to his surprise he felt Buffalo's heavy arm encircle his shoulders, and Mamo's hand, on the other side, grasp his elbow. He felt strong again, and looked back at his father.

'No,' he said.

'What do you mean, no? What sort of answer is that?' said Ato Paulos, but Dani realised with a flash of new understanding that behind the anger his father was at a loss. He was blustering because he didn't know what to do.

'You know why I ran away, Father,' he said, managing to sound calm rather than defiant. 'You were sending me to Jigjiga and I wouldn't go.'

'Ridiculous,' scoffed Ato Paulos. 'You can't have chosen to live like this, just for that.'

Million, who had been watching closely, cleared his throat and spat expertly into the fire.

'You heard Dani,' he said. 'He's not going there, to that place.'

Ato Paulos rounded on him.

'Who are you? What's this got to do with you?'

'Who are *you*?' Million riposted.

'I'm Daniel's father, that's who I am.' The veins were standing out on Ato Paulos's neck. 'And I'll thank you to . . .'

'And I'm his *joviro*,' Million said, jauntily adjusting his woolly hat.

'His what?'

'His *joviro*. He does what I say.'

'No, he doesn't,' Mamo said unexpectedly. 'He does what he wants. He can, now.'

Dani felt like a bone being tugged at by fighting dogs and although his heart was pounding he almost smiled. His confidence was beginning to rise a little.

Ato Mesfin took off the hat he had been wearing and scratched his bald head.

'Why don't we sit down,' he said, moving towards an upturned crate abandoned nearby, 'and talk things over?'

Million grinned delightedly and swept his arm out towards a second crate with an exaggerated flourish.

'You are our guest,' he said to Ato Paulos.

'Preposterous,' muttered Ato Paulos, but he lowered himself gingerly on to the crate, gathering the skirt of his long coat round him.

Ato Mesfin leaned forward to warm his hands at the dying embers of the fire.

'Well, Daniel,' he said. 'You've certainly managed to surprise us. I'd just like to say, straight away, what an excellent story you wrote.' He took the story he'd bought out of his pocket and waved it towards Mamo. 'I believe it was your friend here who sold it to me. I was most impressed.'

All of a sudden Dani who was feeling odd, as though none of this was happening, could smell the classroom at school. He shuddered.

I can't go back there, he thought. What's the point? I'd only fail at everything all over again.

Ato Paulos started to say something but Ato Mesfin put out a hand to stop him.

'I've missed you in my class, Daniel,' he said gently. 'You are by far the most talented writer I've ever taught. I want to teach you again.'

Dani looked up at him.

'But I can't do all the other subjects,' he said. 'I'm no good.'

Ato Mesfin nodded.

'I've been thinking about that. There are things we can do to help out there. I'm not sure if the school's the best place for you right now. Not just yet, anyway.'

A snort came from Ato Paulos.

'What exactly do you—'

'Please,' said Ato Mesfin. He turned back to Dani. I've been talking to a couple of colleagues. No, not your old teachers. Friends of mine from outside the school. They've agreed to tutor you for a while to get you over the hump, to bring you up to scratch in your other subjects. It would take a term or two, probably. You could start back at school again when you're good and ready.'

The boys were squatting in a circle round the fire, listening hard and looking from one speaker to another. They reminded Ato Paulos of the council of elders in the village where he'd grown up. The old men had sat together, just like this, passing judgement on everything and everyone. The comparison was annoying and ridiculous, of course, but he couldn't get it out of his mind.

Now they were looking anxiously from Ato Mesfin to Dani, trying to understand the offer he was being made, envy and awe in their eyes.

Million laughed jerkily. His confidence was visibly ebbing away.

'An educated man,' he said.

Dani felt as if a path had appeared in front of him. It was temptingly lit, and offered a way out, up and away. But it was impossible to imagine taking the first step. It would mean leaping over a bottomless gulf out of which, once he'd fallen in, he'd never be able to climb again.

He shook his head. Mamo's hand had tightened on his arm, but now it relaxed again.

'You didn't tell me about this plan of yours,' Ato Paulos was saying irritably to Ato Mesfin.

'No. I thought it would be best for Daniel to decide for himself.' Ato Mesfin shot a nervous look at Ato Paulos, then turned back to Dani. 'If you prefer, Daniel, you could live with me while you get back on your feet. There's plenty of room in my house, since my wife – I would be glad to have you.'

'No!' The anguish in Ato Paulos's voice startled everyone and their heads whipped round towards him. A struggle seemed to be taking place inside Ato Paulos. Dani, who felt as if he'd never known his father before, watched as the mask of anger visibly dropped from his face and real feeling shone through.

Ato Paulos put his hand up to shade his eyes, as if he couldn't bear to be watched.

'Please, Daniel,' he said. 'Come home. I've missed you so much, you've no idea. Please come back with me now.'

Dani swallowed. He was feeling something new and peculiar. It was as if he was almost sorry for his father. It was almost as if he loved him.

The abyss between him and the lit path was still there, but it was starting to close.

'I don't know,' he said. 'I'd only disappoint you again. You'll only get furious with me and send for Feisal.'

Million flung his hands up into the air.

'Are you crazy, man? Give me a chance like that and look what I'd do! Ask any of us!'

The other boys, except for Mamo, nodded, muttering to each other in disbelief at Dani's reluctance.

'Your mother's coming home next week,' Ato Paulos went on. He was frankly pleading now. 'What's she going to feel if you're not there?'

'*Mamma?*'

Dani had been looking down into the fire, but his head shot up and his eyes seemed almost to start out of their sockets.

'Yes. She called today. She's arriving on—'

'Mamma's *alive?*'

'Of course she's alive. Why, you surely didn't think . . .'

'But the funeral at the house. Mamo saw the mourners. The woman at the kiosk said . . .'

'What funeral? Oh, you mean cousin Asselefech. How did you find out about that? No, there's nothing wrong with your mother now. The operation was a total success. She's feeling better than she has for years and years.'

'Oh, oh!'

Dani dropped his head down on to the dirt-stiffened knees of his trousers and began to shake with dry sobs. Ato Paulos stood up, hesitated for a moment, then went across to him. Awkwardly, he lifted Dani to his feet, and pulled him into a crushing hug.

Mamo watched unbelievingly as Dani walked away between his father and Ato Mesfin.

'Mamo's coming with us,' Dani had said, once he'd given in and agreed to go home, but Mamo had seen the look of horror on Ato Paulos's face and had shrunk away from Dani's outstretched hand.

Dani hadn't insisted. He was looking dazed and confused, obviously hardly able to take in what was happening to him.

When he'd gone, vanishing into the night like a disappearing dream, Mamo felt stunned. Everything had happened so quickly. One moment they'd all been having a terrific party, and he'd been relishing his triumph over Merga and Dani's victory over Buffalo, and the next minute everything had changed for ever. He couldn't take it in.

He squatted by the dying embers of the fire, rocking backwards and forwards, a horrible feeling of sadness and loneliness washing over him. The others were subdued too.

'Dani's dad,' Million said at last. He stopped. Mamo looked up at him. Million's mouth was twisted sideways and his face had the cunning expression it always wore when he started calculating possibilities.

'What about him?' said Getachew, stirring the fire with a charred stick.

'He's rich. He might do something for us. Get us a place to live even. He could afford anything.'

Buffalo spat, making the hot ashes sizzle.

'No chance. You saw the way he looked at us. He thinks we're scum.'

'Yeah, but Dani might . . .' began Getachew.

'Dani? We won't see him again,' Buffalo said sourly. 'He never was one of us anyway.'

'I wish he was here to tell us a story,' Shoes said wistfully, wrapping his arms round his chest as the cold wind attacked him.

'Well he isn't,' snapped Buffalo.

'Sing us a song then, Mamo,' Shoes said. 'Sing us that one about wake up and live, you know the one I mean.'

Mamo jumped to his feet.

'Why don't you all just shut up and leave me alone?' he burst out.

He couldn't bear to sit still any longer. He walked away from the dim firelight, stumbling over the stones that littered the ground, until he came to a high concrete wall that bordered the patch of rough ground. He crouched down, leaning his back against it, and felt tears trickling down his nose.

Everyone always goes away and leaves you, he thought. You can't trust anyone, not a single person in the whole world.

Something cold touched his hand. It was Suri's wet nose. He could make out her pale shape in the faint glare of light from a house some way away. She had rolled over on to her back and was waiting for him to tickle her tummy.

He picked her up and held her tight against his chest. She licked his nose.

Dogs are the only people who really love you, in the end, he thought.

Suri snuffled and settled herself more comfortably in his arms. The feel of her warm body made him think of Tiggist, of how she'd carried him around on her hip when he was little.

I'll go and see her again, he thought, his spirits lifting a little. I'll go tomorrow. She's my sister, after all.

He stayed by the wall for a long time. At last he stood up, stretched his cramped limbs, which the cold seemed to have penetrated, and went back to the others. The fire had gone out but there was still a little warmth radiating out from the ashes.

He pulled his blanket out of Dani's old bag, now stained and battered almost beyond recognition, which Million had kept beside him all evening, wrapped himself in it and lay looking up at the stars, unable to sleep.

The boy who sold fruit wasn't at his usual place outside Mrs Faridah's shop when he reached it early the next day. Mamo stood on the pavement, hesitating. There was no point in going inside to look for Tiggist. He'd only get sent away with a flea in his ear by that horrible man who'd shouted at him last time.

He crossed to the other side of the road and leaned against the wall in a patch of shade, waiting for the boy to reappear.

He came soon enough, limping round from the back. Mamo screwed up his eyes to try and see if anyone was hovering around inside the shop doorway, but he couldn't make anything out from this distance.

He darted across the road and stopped in front of the boy.

'Is Tiggist here?'

To his surprise, the boy gave him a friendly smile.

'No. She's gone off with her boyfriend.'

'Her what?'

Mamo's heart sank. If he'd lost Tiggist again, he'd lost everything.

'She said to tell you if you turned up. She's given up her job here. There was a real old carry-on, I can tell you. Him . . .' he jerked his head towards the shop and lowered his voice, 'the boss, he was making up to your sister, and she didn't like it. Then along comes this boyfriend of hers, and he makes a scene like nothing on earth. Quiet-looking guy he is too. You should have heard him! And he tells your sister to get her stuff, and off she goes with him just like that.'

'Who is he? She never had a boyfriend before.'

'Yacob, his name is. Met him in Awassa. She's been mooning around after him ever since she got back.'

'She's gone off to live with him?' Mamo was struggling to take it in.

'Yes, I told you. They're getting married and everything. That's what the guy told the boss, anyway. She's OK, your sister is. Before she left, you know what she did? Gave me five birr out of her savings. I couldn't believe it. They're living down the Debre Zeit road now. She said to tell you if you came by. You have to cross the railway line and go down as far as the Shell petrol station. It's a shop on the other side of the road. It sells taps and electrics and stuff like that.'

It was a long, long way to the Shell station on the Debre Zeit road, and by the time it came into view halfway down a long sloping hill Mamo was footsore, hungry and very thirsty. He was anxious too. What if the boy had told him wrong, said the wrong road maybe, or, even worse, sent him off on a wild goose chase for fun? If this all turned out to be another horrible disappointment he didn't know what he'd do.

Unable to bear the suspense, he ran the last long stretch down to the petrol station, in spite of his sore feet. He looked across the road and saw the shop at once, or at least, a shop that might be the one. It was quite new looking, with metal pipes and coils of wire and rubber tubing in the window.

Mamo hesitated. This place looked too new and smart, too sort of professional and business-like for the sort of boyfriend he'd expect Tiggist to have.

If that guy back there sent me all this way as some kind of joke, he thought, I'll murder him. I really will.

He crossed the road, dodging expertly through the lines of crawling, lumbering trucks and buses, then, plucking up his courage, he walked in through the shop's open door.

It was clean, bright and tidy inside. A big man with a pock-marked face was standing behind the counter. He was untangling a heaped-up pile of electrical flexes.

'Yes?' he said pleasantly.

Mamo swallowed.

'I'm looking for my sister. Someone told me she'd be here. She's Tiggist.'

The man's face opened out into a smile.

'You're Mamo, are you?'

Mamo's heart leaped with surprise and relief.

'Yes. Is she here?'

'Wait, I'll get her.'

Yacob went through a door behind the counter and Mamo heard the murmur of voices. Then, with a glad cry, Tiggist came running out.

'Oh Mamo, I didn't know where to find you!' she cried. 'I didn't know if you'd ever get my message.'

He straightened his back and smiled at her.

Tiggist lifted a flap in the counter and pulled Mamo through, then dragged him on into the room behind the shop.

'Look,' she said. 'I can't wait to show you everything. Isn't it lovely here? Yacob,' she shook her head with an embarrassed little laugh, 'he's my husband now. He and his cousin, this business belongs to them. I told them all about you. They couldn't believe that stuff about the man that sold you. Yacob says you can stay here now. You can help out selling things. Look at this, Mamo. This is where I do all the cooking. We'll make a place for you to sleep somewhere in here, or in the shop, maybe. You'll soon get used to selling things. I know you've never done it before, but Yacob'll tell you what to do. He's so great. He's . . .'

Mamo was no longer listening. He was standing in the middle of the room smelling the onions that Tiggist had been frying on top of a little gas burner. They smelled exactly like the onions that Ma used to cook, a long long time ago, in the old shack down the lane on the far side of town.

It's like being at home, he thought, with a shock of surprise. It's as if I was coming home.

Chapter 19

It was three months later. The Big Rains had come and gone, the air of Addis Ababa was sparkingly cool and the fringe of hills above the city was clothed in fresh new green.

'Darling, are you nearly ready?' said Ruth, putting her head round the door of Dani's room.

Dani was standing by his bed, packing something into a bag.

'Ready?' he said, looking up in surprise. 'What for?'

'We're going to the pool, of course,' said Ruth. 'It's Sunday, or have you forgotten?'

'Sorry, Mamma,' said Dani, 'but I'm not coming. I'm useless at swimming, and anyway, nobody I like ever goes there.'

Ato Paulos appeared behind Ruth's shoulder.

'So how do you propose to spend the afternoon?' he said.

'I'm going out,' said Dani shortly.

'Out?'

'Yes. I'm seeing a friend.'

'And who, may I ask . . .'

'No one you know, Father.' Dani looked up and met Ato Paulos's eyes.

'You'll have to see your friend another time,' Ato Paulos said impatiently. 'I need you to make up a four at tennis. Not that you're much of an asset on the court. Your back hand . . .'

'I can't,' said Dani. A familiar tightness was closing round his throat, but he held his father's eyes all the same. 'I told you, I've arranged to meet someone. I promised.'

'Call them then. Put them off.'

'No,' said Dani.

Ato Paulos seemed about to explode into speech when his eye fell on the bag that Dani was packing. A look of alarm crossed his face.

'Daniel, what on earth . . .'

Dani crossed over to the door.

'I'm going out for the afternoon,' he said patiently. 'There's someone I've arranged to meet. I'll be home before it gets dark. I'll see you later.'

Gently, he shut the door in his parents' faces.

Mamo was waiting for him outside the pastry shop where, months earlier, they had glimpsed each other for the first time. He was wearing a nearly-new sweatshirt and there were shoes on his feet. He smiled almost shyly as Dani came up to him.

'What's in that?' he said, looking at the bag that Dani was carrying over his shoulder. 'Not running away again, are you?'

'Course not.' Dani led the way into the shop. 'Come on. I'll tell you later.'

They spent a long time choosing cakes at the counter, hovering luxuriously between the brightly coloured confections, and when Dani had paid they sat down at a table in the corner with a bottle of Coke and a plateful of cakes in front of each of them.

Mamo sat on the edge of his chair, looking round at the noisy Sunday afternoon customers.

'I never thought I'd actually come in here,' he said.

Dani felt self-conscious. He could see that Mamo was uneasy. Perhaps the pastry shop hadn't been such a good idea after all.

They were both relieved when they stepped outside again into the hot sunshine.

'Are you getting on all right, then?' Mamo said, 'at your school and everything?'

Dani grimaced.

'It's OK. I'm doing the year over again. I get by.'

'Your pa going on at you still?'

'When he does,' Dani said, laughing, 'all I've got to do is say I'll run away again and he lays off me. It works every time.'

'You wouldn't though, would you, run off again, I mean?

'No.' Dani shuddered. 'He doesn't know that, though.'

They walked on without speaking, their feet taking them by silent agreement towards their old pitch.

'How about you?' said Dani. 'Are you OK? I haven't seen you for weeks. I thought your sister sounded a bit edgy when I called into the shop.'

'She is. She's going to have a baby. Keeps going off to be sick. Yacob's making such a fuss about it you'd have thought he was having the baby himself.'

'Wow,' Dani said, impressed. 'You're going to be an uncle.'

'Not for ages. Not till after Easter. I'll have learned to read by then. Yacob's started paying for me to go to night school.'

He looked sideways at Dani, hoping to impress him.

'Do you like it? Night school?'

'Not much. It's really hard work.'

'Don't I know it,' said Dani with feeling.

The pitch was ahead of them now. There was the old street corner, the patch of ground behind the pavement, the wall against which they had so often slept. It was achingly familiar and yet strange to both of them, as if it belonged to another life.

'They're not here,' Dani said, not sure if he was relieved or disappointed.

'They don't sleep here all the time now,' said Mamo. 'Million's being working on getting a better pitch, down

270

near the station. They might be back later. Let's see if their stuff's here.'

They walked over to the cleft in the wall where the gang had always hidden their bedding during the day. Some ancient blankets and Dani's old bag, battered now beyond recognition, were piled up neatly, and lying on top of them, her nose twitching as she slept, was a little yellow dog.

'Suri!' Mamo cried.

Suri woke at once, leaped up and launched herself at Mamo, whining and barking in ecstasy.

Mamo crouched down to pet her.

'Oh Suri, I miss you, all the time,' he murmured.

'I thought you'd taken her with you to your sister's place,' Dani said, surprised.

'Tiggist wouldn't have her.' Mamo was scratching Suri's favourite place under her chin. 'She's scared of dogs. I had to bring her back and leave her with Million. He looks after her all right, though. It's why I visit him, really, to check on Suri and make sure she's OK.'

Dani put his bag down, squatted down beside Mamo and pulled one of Suri's ears. She gave his fingers a swift lick and turned her adoring attention back to Mamo.

'You didn't tell me,' Mamo said at last, 'what's in the bag?'

Dani unzipped it.

'It's just some more stuff for them,' he said, 'a few clothes, and a new pair of shoes for Shoes. There's a bit of money too. It's not much. My father won't give me any more. I suppose I'll have to take it all home again, since they're not here.'

'No you won't,' said Mamo. 'Leave it with the blankets. Suri'll guard it. It's getting late, anyway. They'll be back soon.'

Dani pushed his presents out of sight between the blankets. Mamo gave Suri one last pat and stood up.

'Stay, Suri. On guard,' he said.

Whining, Suri climbed reluctantly back on to the pile and lay down, her head cocked, watching Mamo's every move.

Behind the boys, the cars were slowing down for the traffic lights. Two ragged children had appeared as if from nowhere. They were darting from car to car, their small hands tapping on the closed windows.

'No father, no mother,' they were chorusing. 'Very hungry. Stomach zero.'

They caught sight of Dani, and seeing his expensive clothes and the flash of a watch on his wrist, scampered across to him.

'No fa—' one of them began, tugging at Dani's sleeve.

'Who's your *joviro*?' Mamo said, interrupting him.

The boy's eyes widened.

'What's that to you?'

'It's Million,' the little one said proudly, pushing himself forward. 'We're with Million.'

'Look after your stuff,' Mamo said. 'We've left some things for Million. Suri's guarding it.'

'Who are you?' the older boy said, frowning at him suspiciously.

'Million will know,' said Mamo. 'Say hi to him from us.'

He smiled awkwardly at Dani.

'I suppose I'd better go home,' he said.

'Me too,' said Dani.

They shook hands with a kind of formality. Dani punched Mamo lightly on the shoulder, and Mamo buffeted Dani back.

'I'll see you around,' said Dani.

'Yes,' said Mamo, and he turned and walked quickly away, whistling between his teeth as he went.

Afterword

I have known many boys (and some girls) who have lived on the streets of Addis Ababa. One in particular helped me to write this story. He gave me a message for you, the reader, and here it is:

What I want to say (because I think many people might read this book) is to the children who want to run away, because you might think that life on the street is easy and sort of exciting. But I'm telling you, it isn't. It isn't. And before you run away, think about your life, and be happy with it.

And if you're out there already, living out in the city, you've got to be brave. I know you're hungry and cold, but one day God will give you a chance, and until he does, you've got to be patient. It's so hard to live on the street. You'll get really sad, but you can be happy too sometimes, and what I want to say to you is, don't be tempted to kill yourself. Don't try to die. The power of God will come some day to visit you.

With thanks I finish my story.

If you liked this, you'll love...

Jake's Tower
Elizabeth Laird

Jake's life is a misery. He lives in constant fear of his mother's violent boyfriend, dreading the moment when he walks through the door. It seems that happiness and safety is something that only exists in dreams.

0 435 13069 2

Hiding away in an imaginary tower is one form of escape, but as Jake begins to learn, it's only in reality that dreams can begin to come true…

www.newwindmills.co.uk

Heinemann
Inspiring generations

If you liked this, you'll love...

No Turning Back
Beverley Naidoo

When twelve-year-old Sipho runs away from his violent stepfather he heads for the bright lights of Johannesburg. Streetwise Jabu befriends him, and before long he learns the tricks of survival with a gang of black children who live on the streets.

Then a white family offer him a place in their home and Sipho accepts. But Sipho and the family soon find themselves in trouble and Sipho is once again on the run...

0 435 12481 1

www.newwindmills.co.uk

If you liked this, you'll love...

Red Sky in the Morning
Elizabeth Laird

'As long as I live, I shall never forget the night my brother was born.'

Anna adores her baby brother, but afraid of being teased by her friends, she hides from them the fact he is disabled. Only when Anna admits to herself that, although she loves Ben, she is ashamed of him, can she find the strength to face her friends and the crises that follow.

0 435 12355 6

www.newwindmills.co.uk

The best in classic and

Jane Austen

Elizabeth Laird

Beverley Naidoo   Roddy Doyle

Robert Swindells

George Orwell

Charles Dickens

Charlotte Brontë

Jan Mark

Anne Fine

Anthony Horowitz